Last Bus To Korat

Last Bus To Korat

Robert A. Johnson

iUniverse, Inc.
New York Bloomington

Last Bus To Korat

This is a work of fiction. All of the characters, names, incidents, organizations, and dialogue in this novel are either the products of the author's imagination or are used fictitiously.

iUniverse books may be ordered through booksellers or by contacting:

iUniverse
1663 Liberty Drive
Bloomington, IN 47403
www.iuniverse.com
1-800-Authors (1-800-288-4677)

ISBN: 978-1-4401-8804-6 (pbk)
ISBN: 978-1-4401-8805-3 (ebook)

Printed in the United States of America

iUniverse rev. date: 11/18/09

Chapter 1

So here I am, stuck all alone and sweating my balls off in the middle of the friggin' jungle in central Thailand, also known as the land of Rest and Relaxation to all you old Vietnam veterans like me.

I'm sitting three white-knuckled hours via a kamikaze taxi drive north of fabulous Bangkok, Party Central for Southeast Asia, and a million miles from anywhere else. I have no one to blame but myself. Back in the world, in a moment of desperate weakness, I had suggested the month long trip to my adorable wife's homeland.

That happens to me sometimes.

Being nice, I mean!

I thought it would be kind of fun trying to live the life of Riley, at least part-time, and sample a taste of early retirement where I can tell everyone else to go to hell. You men out there know what I'm talking about.

Pick up my tired feet in a final attempt to enjoy life. Have unlimited cold beers delivered to my hammock by beautiful foreign women wearing sleek colorful silk sarongs. Take long leisurely afternoon naps just swinging under the palm trees beneath a warm and soothing sun. Be gently summoned when an exotic buffet of gourmet food is perfectly prepared and properly served to the new king of the jungle.

Being here is sort of a trial run of kicking back in a fascinating country, attempting to live on my upcoming miserable pension—they can keep the fuckin' watch—and hoping my every personal need will be fulfilled without me lifting a single, lazy, stubby finger.

Just like weekends back home!

It's been too many years since my darling wife had returned to visit her family. All two hundred and fifty of them! Well, maybe not that many, but it sure seems like it whenever my refrigerator is full of beer and the cupboards are loaded with salted snacks and dried squid jerky. They are good people, though, and I've learned to like them a lot. But to be honest we haven't been that close, and I can't pronounce most of their names. Hell, many of them even look alike.

Some of the guys remind me of my own brothers with whom I get along quite well, especially since we live three thousand miles from each other. Ah, mom and dad, god rest their souls, would be so proud at how tight we are. I haven't seen the brothers since the last funeral and probably won't see them again until I get another call for the next planting.

For me it's been thirty-five years since I've been back here in the land of my youthful, wartime innocence. That's when I turned in my two Air Force stripes and once again became a genuine, non-saluting, independent, kiss-my-ass civilian.

I had gladly cashed in my military chips. I refused to live out my energetic and productive youth as a loser lifer wasting my life in the NCO Club, walking around in a daze all day with a coffee cup glued to my hand, and wondering what the hell happened to me some twenty years later.

Life in a uniform just didn't fit my image, so I decided to retire after only four years of refusing to kiss butt and barely surviving without being court-martialed for my few, though quite innocent, indiscretions frowned on by military justice. Who knew that selling your monthly ration card could get you in so much damn trouble?

I was much happier being Mr. Swift of Boston, Massachusetts, home of my beloved Red Sox, rather than being Airman First Class Swift of the 601st Photo Flight, First Squadron, Barracks B, bed number twelve. I was stuck in a sort of identity crisis and wanted to be known simply as Bob to all my friends.

Or as most of them called me, B.S.

To tell you the truth I think the American government was just as happy to see me leave as I was about to say so long. Although, I must admit, there are times I do look back and think about the possibility of having retired at a ridiculously early age of thirty-eight, collecting a government check every month for doing absolutely nothing, and working part-time for extra beer money as a friendly people greeter at the local Wal-Mart.

That would have suited my character just fine, me being a people person and all.

"How the hell are you folks?" Wearing my pretty blue vest and large name tag I could welcome the shoppers as they entered the store dragging their ugly, unruly kids with them. "You need a friggin' basket, or what?"

On second thought, perhaps I'm not cut out for that sort of work either. I have this thing about shopping. I also tend to call it like it is, which, not surprisingly, a lot of people can't handle.

Well, fuck 'em!

Somehow I knew over here in Thailand I was going to get myself into big trouble without really trying. Trouble just seems to follow me like a big dark thundercloud always ready to rain on my parade. My problem is I never carry an umbrella, and bad weather, in a metaphoric sense, has a knack of hanging over my head. No matter where the hell I go, other people always seem to get me in a jam.

What the hell's with that?

While growing up in dismal inner city three-family tenements my mother tried to teach me the straight and narrow path to righteousness. She encouraged me to be happy, to be content, to get along with people, not to cause problems, to avoid confrontations, to respect people's differences, and not to lie.

"You're a good boy Bobby. Be nice to people Bobby," my sweet mother told me everyday up until I moved out. In other words, she wanted me to do the impossible, to look at the good side of life, to be friggin' grateful, almost cheerful.

What a nice, but stupid, way of viewing things!

On the other hand, my dad, who worked in the Charlestown shipyards for forty-something years, warned me about the crooked and devious ways of the world, about the schemes, and scams, and cons, and in-laws.

"Trust no one and verify everything," he hammered his sage advice into my thick, young skull. "Life is tough and unfair, and a man must be ready to fight for what he wants. Take no shit from nobody," he told me in no uncertain words, his Boston accent as thick as native clam chowder.

What a cynical but realistic way to live.

Maybe that's why I'm so fucked up!

It ain't easy being me!

Before I go any further I think it's only prudent to warn those of you who may be seeeensitive to what I consider normal daily colorful, and in my opinion, essential can't-confuse-straight-forward language. Caution goes out to those who have an aveeeersion to cuss words, or heaven forbid, are religious zealots who out right condeeeemn people when we feel like cursing or talking about sexual tendencies.

You know, normal shit.

Hey! That's what I do, so deal with it!

Okay, by now you probably already don't like me—the prudes in the audience anyway—but that doesn't bother me a damn bit, and to tell you the truth I really don't give a shit what you think.

So there!

Well my holier-than-thou friends, now is the time for you to put this book down before I get into my story sprinkled with offensive commentary, a few tales of sexual fantasy and deviancy, and graphic views of downright moral turpitude perpetrated by members of the human race.

All fact, no fiction.

And then I'll tell you some bad things!

Go find something safe and proper to read, like a Martha Stewart cookbook, or better yet, a pop-up book about rainbows where your senses won't be offeeeended. Because, my puritan readers, there are occasions, though rare, that I tend to swear a bit…

God-damn it!

I just stubbed my friggin' big toe for the second time against the son-of-a-bitching fucking piece of shit dresser…hurts like a motherfucker… oh you friggin' no good cock sucking bitch!

Ah…sorry! But I did forewarn you.

Anyway…

Oh, fuck it! Too late now.

Chapter 2

Man, time certainly does mess with a guy's memory. Yep, the last time I was in this beautiful country was a lifetime ago as a nineteen-year old punk-ass kid with a freshly skinned head, chin pimples, a wicked bad attitude, and a boner harder than a steel pillar that wouldn't quit. All compliments of good old Uncle Sam and my friendly local military recruiter.

He was truly a lying son-of-a-bitch!

My recruiter, I mean.

"See the world on two hundred and forty dollars a month, three square meals a day included," the recruiter told my impressionable pals and me. We were contemplating either running away to Canada and learn French or staying put in the depressed blue collar neighborhoods of Somerville, just outside of Boston, and taking our chances with the armed forces lottery, also known as the military draft.

It's the one lottery you don't ever want to win.

"Put in your twenty and earn a great pension," the recruiter added, trying to earn his monthly quota and signing bonus. "You'll receive free education, a lifetime of medical care, commissary and PX privileges, cheap movies, free clothing, and guaranteed job placement," he kept piling on the lies to buy our miserable souls.

Me and my dumb friends were all ears.

Cheap movies sounded pretty damn good!

Yeah right, and save the planet in three hundred sixty five days while in a combat zone, a scenic group tour to end all tours.

Join the war and enjoy the squalor and unabashed poverty of a war torn country. Live face to face with the open competitiveness of opposing political views where everyone carries a weapon and is ready to shoot your ass. Be consumed by the sweetly seductive abundant drugs bundled and sold in handy bushel bags for less than the cost of a Happy Meal, complete with twigs and branches.

Embrace the friggin' constant humidity that clings to your sweating body like an incurable rash. Discover the unbridled nightly hot spots in the dark and dingy alleys of GI infested red light districts ripe with incurable venereal diseases, carried by some of the most beautiful women in the world. A moment that stays with you for a lifetime.

Ah…those were the good old days!

I ask you. How can an eighteen-year old choose his journey in life at such an innocent, inexperienced age? How can he know which way to turn with such life and death choices hovering above him? How can he decide what is right for him and his future?

Answer me this. How much is a young man's soul worth?

Well, apparently about two hundred and forty-dollar's worth, along with a bunch of hollow promises. So me and my best friend Ralphy, along with Billy and Johnny from the projects, still recovering from our high school graduation hangovers, signed up on the spot, mostly because it was too fucking cold in Canada and the foreign travel plans sounded pretty damn exciting.

If I ever see that bastard recruiter again, I'll…

The slick government brochures were blatantly deceptive, but me and the guys were itching for some action and hero worshipping. The traveling and excitement were guaranteed a hundred-proof if we were lucky enough to survive the excursion.

Some of us weren't so lucky.

Johnny got capped by mortar fire his first week in Nam while he was taking a shit in one of those plastic portable toilets. Billy came back mentally fucked up after living nearly a year in the boonies sleeping in mud holes and eating bugs. Lots of my other buddies never turned in their round trip ticket either. They were teenagers just out of school dying for their country and the fucked up, lying, son-of-a-bitching politically incompetent bureaucrats running it.

They were my friends.

Fortunately, I got out of there still completely normal.

I thought it would be safe being on an Air Force base, a huge fenced-in compound far from the real battle, fighter-jet miles away from the real fighting. But there was a real war going on at the time and young troops were getting killed in every corner of Southeast Asia. Excuse me. It wasn't officially a war, but only a friggin'conflict. Sounds better that way. You may have read about it in the history books, if the fuckin' pansy-ass liberals still teach it. It was in all the newspapers too if you don't believe me.

The Asian morning sun rose like a simmering orange ball of fire, perfectly round and contained in the early horizon, promising yet another oppressively hot day. Steamy wisps of jungle vapor hung over the large glassy lake behind our modest home as I took my usual early morning walk down the narrow streets lined with new houses.

I carried a long stick to stave off the packs of marauding dogs from the hood and uncharacteristically wore a straw hat to ward off the sun from my balding head. I looked like a lost refugee searching for aluminum cans on the side of the road or a deadpan city employee cleaning up his section of the highway.

Hot and sticky!

That was the typical weather over here most of the time. That was one thing I did not forget. The fucking heat and humidity. Jungle rot heat. Sweat city. Change your shirt three times a day, unbearably wet climate. It was so damn hot the chickens next door were laying hard-boiled eggs. It was so friggin' humid the fish in the lakes and canals were sweating their gills off.

"How's the weather over there?" my friends asked me via e-mail every time they sent me the latest porn photos of Jennifer Lopez and gossip about who's doing who in the office. Some things never change. I always suspected Buffy was spending too much time "straightening out the boss's files."

"Damn hot and unbearably sticky," I wrote them back, my fresh tee shirt already drenched with dripping perspiration just thinking of the intense heat. It was nothing like the comfortable heat I was used to back home in the high mountain deserts of Arizona where we had moved to some twenty-eight years earlier.

Ah, but that's a dry heat.

Yeah, like a blast furnace!

Anyway, the mid-summer sun was gradually burning away the morning mist, though the thick air still felt like a cheap Turkish sauna fed with a handful of quarters. At this rate I had no doubt I would sweat off some poundage, which wouldn't be such a bad thing if you could see me in profile.

Visit equatorial Thailand in the middle of August, you dumb shit. Great move. That fucking travel agent! Lose your fat the easy way, sweat it off faster than six weeks with Jennie Craig.

The extra tire around my gut had actually become a full set of new radials. I was beginning to look like the junior Goodyear blimp or the Michelin tire guy with my abundant love handles. I chalked it up to nearly sixty years of good but rather dormant living. You know how it is. Being a dedicated pencil pushing, paper shuffling desk jockey whose only form of exercise, besides taking out the trash, was jumping up and down and screaming at the no good blind umpires favoring the opposing team.

I admit it. I'm a consummate couch potato with all the fixins. I also happen to be a connoisseur of great food. Overall, I'd have to say I'm probably your typical pampered American male. Guess I could blame it on my fabulous wife, who happens to take very good care of me and is a terrific cook. No, make that a fantastic cook. Chef Emeril Lagasse would be proud of her. I swear, she watches a thick pork chop being grilled on the TV and the next day I'm in hog heaven.

Pork rules!

"Yeah, that's it. I might be a little thick around the middle but I can't help it Doc," I told him as he 'tsked, tsked' me while looking over my records and shaking his own fat head. "I know I'm overweight, but it's not my fault. It's my wife's fault. She cooks too much."

Determined to stay hydrated during my past week as a recent visitor to this diversely enchanting and uniquely third world country, I discovered the local varieties of beer, admittedly one of the few vices I've successfully struggled to retain. Searching for different and exotic brews is almost like a hobby of mine. I can't build birdhouses and I don't crochet. Besides, those are too much like exercise.

I love beer so much I'll even go to the store with my delightful wife if I hear there's a new brew on the market. My stocked sports bar back home on the patio is lined with hundreds of beer bottles from all over the world as my personal tribute to the global ales. They're all empty of course.

It seems I've given up just about everything else I love. The married years have taken their toll. Oh, have they ever. I'm a changed man. Or I should say, a remolded one. That's what marriage does to us guys. We allow ourselves to be reshaped by the women we love.

The smokes are gone, no good for the constricted heart and congested lungs. The rugged Marlboro man is now the Juicy Fruit guy. It's truly a sad sight. I don't go to the track anymore. I used to enjoy betting on the dogs, but I had to make lame excuses to sneak out of the house or take extra long lunch breaks to lay down my two-bucks. Besides, I almost always lost.

It's okay though, the kids still went to community college.

Even the romps in the sack are getting fewer and fewer, as, I hate to admit it, I look forward to sleeping more often then a call to arms. But you can bet your sweet ass I would never openly admit such a thing to my good buddies. I still have a reputation to uphold. I'm sure they'd lie about it too.

Hell, I'm even a card-carrying member of AARP. How fucking pathetic is that? Shit, my dad was a part of that discount, handi-capped, onery old, looking-for-a-senior-coffee crowd. What the hell are they doing sending me coupons for cheap term life insurance and adult diapers? I'm way too young for this crap and refuse to participate in the pot-bellied club until it's absolutely necessary.

Good thing I don't own a friggin' gun. I just might do something stupid and dangerous like a freaked out postal worker at the end of his Christmas shift. God bless your soul Fitz. You were the best damn mailman around.

I wouldn't shoot myself, but maybe someone else. Like the fucking old blue-haired bag trying to see her way through the steering wheel while driving on the wrong side of the friggin' road on her way to

Walgreens to save ten cents on a bag full of high blood pressure medication and denture cream.

Hey, a man my age still needs a few harmless pleasures to keep him from going over the edge. He stills needs to have something to look forward to every day.

So beer is my thing.

And then you die!

Chapter 3

Funny how every place in the world has its own versions of fermented beverages, from the watered down wimpish light brewskies back in the States, to the stout heavy ales from the continent, to the formaldehyde-tainted beers in Southeast Asia.

Home grown beer is a universally welcomed elixir, the organic juice of life, nectar of the drunken gods and mortal men like me. But when it comes right down to it, on a friggin' scorching hot day like today most of them taste about the same and go down as smooth as mother's milk, although I have to say I do feel a bit more preserved over here.

My limited selection of cold alcoholic drinks includes Singha, a national favorite carried in just about every corner grocery shack or roadside vendor. Roadside beer stands! They're everywhere around here, from little rickety pushcarts to dilapidated tin roofed shacks next to the bus stops.

Now that's fucking ingenious! It's something you think Texans would have invented a long time ago.

Hell, I was even served generous portions of frosty cold ones while my terrific wife and I were browsing around a furniture store looking for things we didn't need. I was drunk with their hospitality while we spent hours admiring hutches, table lamps, throw pillows, and other unnecessary household items. People over here know how to make shopping fun.

"These would go well in the living room, don't you think honey?" my house decorating wife asked me about the ugliest pair of curtains I ever saw.

"Yes dear, they're very nice," I said, just to answer her. I learned a long time ago in Marriage 101 to simply say 'yes' to everything she asked, even if I didn't hear her question or didn't know what the hell she was talking about. Most of the time it's the right answer, and by following that basic rule of thumb the odds of getting into trouble are slim to none.

Besides, she was going to buy the puke green drapes no matter what I actually thought. I really don't know why she bothers to even ask my opinion since she typically complains that I don't listen to her anyway.

Or something like that!

Then there's Chung Beer with a picture of an elephant on the label that initially made me a little suspicious about its origin, if you know what I mean. They also have Leo the Lion beer and Tiger beer to make you strong and manly. Then there's Sexy Beer (yeah, I'm not making it up) to help with the you-know-what. I happened to run through a case of that shit right quick and ended up with nothing but a false sense of virility and a fucking wicked headache that wouldn't quit.

Think I'll stick to my little blue buddy pills when my manhood needs some help.

But I couldn't find any American beers. No Miller, no Bud Lite, no Schlitz. There wasn't even a Red Dog anywhere to be found. Now that's really sad. Apparently they couldn't make the cut, so I generally hit the Singha Lite.

Tastes great, less filling!

Which reminds me. Our miniature five cubic foot frig was completely empty of any of these delights, and the first order of business today was to restock if I could get enough cash from the wife. I'm told drinking plenty of fluids in this heat is essential for good health so who am I to question medical research?

Before my morning walk my women had already gone to the local village ten klicks away, which is about six miles in the civilized world.

That's what I call them. My women. It's great for my over-inflated male ego. Also adds a sense of mystery and jealousy to the guys watching us walking to the stores. "Lucky bastard," they must think. My adorable and very beautiful wife, who I love dearly, and her two sisters who live here year round, went everywhere together.

The village they were headed to is only ten minutes away by the local slow poke bus, a little less than that by motor bike— a minimum of three people per cycle, or nearly a full day by ox drawn wagon. No shit! They still do that here. The diehard traditionalists who can't afford the gas, anyway.

It was part of the ladies' daily ritual. Shopping, that is. A renown institution religiously adhered to by the female of the species, even in this neck of the world, to honor thy merchants. At the markets they would undoubtedly gather large sacks of strange weedy greens, exoticly shaped and colored fruits, and some gross smelling fish-like things. Most likely they would pick up some very bizarre edibles that you can bet your sweet ass would never find a place on my plate.

I'm funny like that. Peculiar, some would say. Particular about my meals. A fussy eater some might agree. I refuse to eat anything that still moves, or looks back at me, or tastes like it came from the tail end of an animal. Except for eggs of course.

Like most women my lovable wife loves to shop. Being the man and chief bread winner of the family I obviously hate shopping. The only stores I frequent are the convenient mart down the street from our home in the States or the package store for a case of beer or two, and some Powerball tickets. Potato chips too.

One time I was tricked into stopping by the grocery store for my ill wife who was bedridden with the flu. I had filled her shopping list and at the check-out counter a nagging question kept popping into my often inquisitive mind.

So I asked the pretty little clerk, "I never get out and I'm stuck shopping for my sick wife. Do you know if this four-pack of toilet paper is enough for all this food I'm buying? You know, just to be safe."

She looked at me as if I were an imbecile, or someone not very smart, and refused to answer what I thought was a very legitimate inquiry. Needless to say, my embarrassed wife won't let me go shopping anymore. At least not by myself. Or at that store.

Too bad!

My most caring wife assured me that she and her sisters would be back late in the afternoon after their foraging was complete. They were also going to visit their extended family, all of whom lived in the ancient ancestral village of Chok Chai, a gathering of shanties wedged between acres and acres of rice paddies and farm lands painstakingly worked over the centuries.

Her family is a terrific group of people. In-laws are always great when you live twelve thousand miles apart, see each other once every thirty-five years, and don't speak their language.

I love mine!

Several brothers, more sisters, various in-laws, uncles, aunts, grand parents, nieces and nephews, and a strange assortment of unclaimed odd balls. I truly think the whole damn village is one gigantic happy rice eating family.

"Sure my love," I silently said to my fabulous absent wife. "Leave me alone again in this foreign land. An unsullied, unprotected babe in the woods. The only white boy for hundreds of miles around unable to intelligently converse with the locals except through woeful hand signals and gibberish misunderstandings that can only get me in trouble. Give me up to the savage natives while you go eat your weeds and have fun.

"I might not be here when you come home. Maybe I'll be sacrificed to the mysterious forces of the jungle, or be eaten alive by massive flocks of murderous blood sucking mosquitoes in search of deliciously rare sweet white meat. You know how bright and attractive my white-boy legs are. Or I could fall prey to a nest of slithering rice field snakes, king cobras perhaps.

"It's possible I could be trampled by wandering herds of water buffalo, notoriously mean son-of-bitches with their bullish horns and snaring snouts. I might even be overcome by dark menacing natives faithfully guarding their tribal lands from a big, clumsy outsider trying to mind his own damn business.

"But don't worry about me, dear. You girls go enjoy your day and say 'hi' to the fam. Buy me some goodies if you remember. I'm a survivor. I'll be just fine," I lied to them from my walking path well out of hearing distance as they disappeared down the narrow dirt trail thickly lined with banana trees heavy with pods of fruit.

"Good bye honey. I love you."

I was left semi-prepared for my home-alone experience. I had a handful of odd-looking green and red Thai bills and some loose change with undecipherable squiggly markings. I felt like a school kid with a limited allowance to scratch out a living and hoped I had enough to get more than a bowl of Mac 'N Cheese.

I figured it was plenty to buy lunch at the primitive lean-to food stand out front near the highway. The open shack had become my favorite haunt where I could comfortably order a dish of my favorite spicy fried rice and a cold beer for under a buck whenever the women went food harvesting, which was just about every single day. Thank god for nasty, dirty little food shanties catering to those of us left behind.

It was my McDonald's of the Far East, and to tell you the truth I kind of enjoyed the quiet time without the women around me all the time. Hopefully I had enough money left over to buy a few extra cans of Singha for later in the day when I had absolutely nothing to do but drink.

Hell, maybe my busy wife messed up and gave me enough cash to get a plane ticket out of here. I couldn't tell. Wouldn't do me any good, though. The nearest airport was two countries away and I had a hard enough time just finding the bus stop. Money with a bunch of zeros usually excites me, like a fistful of beautiful green Ben Franklins, my dear and loyal friends back home. The true gods from which I hail. But in this case, in my ignorance I contained my foolish enthusiasm.

I might need it later on!

I had the entire day ahead of me and I wasn't going to stay in our neat little bungalow with not a damn constructive thing to do. Hell, I was on vacation, a trial run for when I retired. I wanted to go someplace exciting. I wanted to see people. I wanted to do something adventurous, even if it was wrong. I needed some action. I was getting restless.

The hell with my afternoon nap, I thought. Screw the dangers. Throw caution to the wind. Carpe diem. Seize the fucking day and all that crap. Join the world pal.

After an over complicated conversion of Thai baht to dollars I figured I held about fifteen bucks worth of local currency in my hands. Enough to buy this boy a little excitement but not nearly enough to get me into too much deep shit.

Fuck it!

I was going to downtown Korat.

Chapter 4

First I wanted to clean up and get presentable for my day trip.

I shaved with a miniature disposable plastic razor, brushed my teeth with a bottle of purified water, and took a quick shower. A very quick one since we only had cold water. No hot water heater here. Where did I think I was? America?

Well, actually, the first person in the house to shower had the luxury of bathing in warm water stored in the sun-baked pipes running along the outside wall. Solar energy in its most basic form. But it was fine.

Who the hell needs hot water? I'm a tough guy and can handle a little chill, though it does tend to cause a bit of shrinkage. Male raisins. The old frightened turtle syndrome. You men who have gone swimming in the freezing Atlantic Ocean up New England way know what I'm talking about.

We lived in a truly Thai-style house. The shower was an extension of the small bathroom and it was roofless. Yep, through the glass sliding door you stood there naked as a jay bird, wide open to the peeping eyes of nature, as if it really wanted to spy on a rugged stud like me.

It gave me the feeling of being in the glorious outdoors. Every private part of the old body exposed to the clear blue sky, completely nude in the light jungle breeze, the rustling sounds of palm trees beyond the fence, the birds passing over head taking precise aim at the big white hairy target. It was a cool sensation, and I must admit, almost a naughty experience.

The devil in me loved it!

After my shower I began preparing for my excursion. It would be unwise to travel without the necessary tools of survival in such a hostile environment. I was headed to the big and dangerous city and had to be ready for the unknown. A prepared traveler is a smart traveler. I gathered everything I thought I might need, and a few extra items.

Just in case!

First I checked my wallet, which carried my official American ID just in case I was unexpectedly detained for questioning, or worse yet, if it was needed for forensic purposes. My driver's license, whose crinkled photo showed a much younger man, had an old address from ten years ago, but nobody over here knew that, so it really didn't matter.

Inside my wallet there were two credit cards, which if ever stolen, would fool the unlucky thieving bastard since they were both way over their limits. Ha! Let him pay the extra charges. That will teach any fucking thief to steal from a law abiding, over drawn, close to retired, all-American Republican capitalist.

I also had my high school library card that expired in 1968, a dollar off coupon for a Burger King Double Whopper, and a faded picture of a buddy and me falling down drunk at a chili eating contest back in Tucson. I swear, I don't know who the naked babe passed out on top of me was. I hope my loving wife never rifles through my billfold. I'm not certain but I think I won that contest.

The chili part, anyway!

In my billfold I also had a picture of my dear bride when she was a young girl and said 'yes' to a dreamer's offer of marriage. That was the happiest day of my life, accept for when the Red Sox beat the fucking Yankees in the World Series back in '04. I carry that beautiful photograph with me everyday as a reminder of our glorious thirty-seven years together.

She was about seventeen years old when that picture was taken. In some countries I would have been tossed into prison for what I was thinking, and castrated for what I had done. But fuck it, I was in a friggin' war zone at the time and anything goes.

Even to this day, whenever I get the chance I show off my young sweetie to some of the old bastards at work who think I'm the luckiest son-of-a-bitch in the world. I have no idea why they think she's my current teenage mistress.

By the way, speaking of carrying stuff, one of my ex-friends back home gave me a fanny pack so I could tote all my crap while traveling. Can you believe that shit? A fucking fanny pack! Like I was really going to strap on one of those faggy things around my waist so everyone in the world would know I left my balls at the boarding gate.

"Look at that big guy over there with that sissy fanny pack hanging from his stomach," they would snicker behind my back. "Must be another pussy American who left his balls at home. Maybe his beautiful wife is carrying them for him in her purse. Ha ha ha!"

Never happen pal!

By the way old friend, any day now you'll be receiving a package from UPS. Happy fucking birthday you ball-less wonder. Ah…just joking boss! Hope you enjoy your man-purse gift. I just cherish mine.

And finally there were twenty-seven dollars in large bills, U.S, slipped into a secret zippered hiding place in my beat up K-Mart wallet. It was my mad money, which admittedly wouldn't allow me to get too crazy at all.

Always planning way ahead, my wonderfully thoughtful wife held onto my passport and return airline ticket for safe keeping and to make sure I couldn't get very far.

I love that woman.

So much for my identification and important papers. I secured my new Sony digital camera in a buttoned down pocket on the leg of my Safari cargo shorts. I love these pants. I could carry everything I ever needed in dozens of pockets and still have my hands free should I step into a problem situation, like running for my life or chasing bad guys. There's enough room in these pockets to carry supplies to live on for a month.

Although, there have been occasions when I've actually lost things in undiscovered side pocket compartments. Once I found a half-eaten hot dog from a baseball game we went to a few years back when the Red Sox lost to the fucking Yankees. There was also an unwrapped, but still perfectly good, purple **'HOT LOVE'** condom that must have belonged to someone else.

Of course, when I'm fully loaded down sometimes I tend to rattle a bit while walking along the street. My pants legs were bulging with all sorts of gadgets. I would never make it pass airport security but I still think these pants are friggin' cool. I need to find a matching shirt with secret pockets. Maybe a vest and a jungle hat.

The camera was cool too. It was small enough to carry everywhere and allowed me the advantage to blend in with the locals without looking like a geeky tourist with one of those huge 35 mm Minoltas strapped around their necks. My stealth camera, I called it, gave me the benefit of taking snap shots of unsuspecting characters without being accused of stalking.

From my previous trip with the wife and entourage to the great city I had snapped quite a few shots of the local markets and colorful landmarks. Touristy pics. The foods were fantastic, the sights astonishing, the people interesting. I even ran into a full-sized elephant being led through the market by its trainer trying to make a few baht selling posed photos with the smelly peanut-eating pet. The beer company should plaster a sign on this roaming pachyderm on their trucks.

There're a lot of new and exciting things to see in this country and I had taken tons of pictures for the folks back home to prove that we were really living here. The majority of the pixels, however, were devoted to the most beautiful, eye appealing, god-given resources of Thailand.

Their women!

I'm talking drop dead gorgeous!

The young ladies are indeed the most delightfully attractive females on earth with their naturally beautiful Asian features, long black silken hair, demure mysterious smiles, petite and sleek figures. Whoa! Maybe that's why I married one. I took another look at my wife's picture in my wallet.

Yep. What a lucky bastard I was!

I told my incredible wife I wanted to take lots of photos for my friends back home so they could see how lovely the people really were. That's what one of my buddies convinced me to say. At first I thought he was trying to set me up, you know, fucking with me to get this old boy in trouble with my fun-loving wife. But to my surprise she fell for it and actually encouraged my enthusiastic hobby.

So I kept taking pictures of the Thai ladies.

Have I told you how much I love that woman?

I also stashed my sleek cell phone in a zip-locked pouch. Yes, I am proud to say that I have my very own Thai cell phone with three hundred pre-paid minutes of talking time. Like I have anyone to call. The first day we arrived in country my caring wife bought the phone in the unlikely case I got separated from her in the crowded streets of Bangkok. Like just in case I got detoured into one of the gazillion bars along the fun and sleazy alleys, or maybe if I fell victim to the calls of the sweet, scantily clad women of the night flashing some skin and promising a "Good joy time."

Hell, I didn't want to leave my caring wife's side. I was scared to death of losing sight of her. She was the only person I knew in the entire country who could speak English, though apparently at some places it really wasn't a prerequisite. Based on that fact alone I was extra nice to her.

Wasn't I, darling?

But she was concerned that I might somehow get misplaced and thought it was a good idea to carry a phone. And it would be too, except I can't read the damn thing. The Thai numbers don't correspond to real numbers. Squigglies mean nothing to me. What the hell number does X?&S mean in English?

Heaven help me if I actually had to use the phone. Hope to god no one calls me either. "Hello? This is Uncle Bob." That's what the family members and Thai friends calls me, 'Uncle Bob,' in deference to my sage wisdom and old age, and partly, I suspect, due to my secure financial status. 'Click.' But having a phone does give me a strange comforting sense of security. I could never get lost ever again.

At least not by accident!

I wonder if 911 is the same here?

Finally, still getting ready for my trip, I scooped up the foreign bills and change along with the keys to the house, and stuffed them in my front pocket. I calculated that I had just enough money to pay for the bus both ways, maybe do a little bit of freelance shopping on the cheap, get something familiar to eat, and still splurge on a few Singhas.

Sounded like a plan. That is if I didn't get mugged, ripped off, or heaven forbid, violated.

What more does a guy need?

Chapter 5

So I **WAS PACKED**, geared up, and ready to go.

I slipped a paperback book into a large side pocket should I find myself with some free reading time on my hands. Like that was going to really happen. I thought about leaving a note for the wife, just in case she got home before me and became worried sick about my surprised absence. But then I thought it best not to. It might sound like a suicide note in the wrong hands, and besides, I knew I would be home before too late.

No problem!

I jammed a few pieces of tamarind candies into one of my pockets and padded myself down checking to make sure I hadn't forgotten anything. I was loaded for bear. Then I remembered there was one very special thing I was intentionally not taking with me.

My undies!

Yep, you heard me correctly. My under draws, the old Hanes sack protectors.

Only a few days earlier I had decided to uncage the boys. The constant humidity and stifling heat had begun to chafe my delicate creamy white bottom and surrounding private areas from the restraining briefs I was so used to wearing.

The rash was becoming extremely uncomfortable, and frankly, quite embarrassing. I itched like a son-of-a-bitch in places I wasn't allowed to scratch in public unless I was a professional ball player. It was like I had poison ivy on the old Johnson or had somehow caught the crabs and they were nibbling away at my manhood.

Not the seafood type either!

I had dumped the Fruit of the Looms and switched to loose fitting boxers. They offered only limited relief and threatened to further irritate the family jewels. Although the boys weren't the sparkling polished gems of yesteryear, they still had a few good shots left in them and I wanted to make sure they were ready whenever they were called up to bat.

So, without telling anyone, especially my traditional underwear-wearing wife, in my new daring and adventurous way, the rebel that I am, I decided to go completely unrestricted.

My unsecured twins and their big brother Slick were free to roam their limited boundaries. There was lots of flipping and flopping going on which constantly reminded me of my traveling companions, but I have to admit it felt great. It was like unleashing the puppy dogs while taking a leisurely walk through the park. The fresh air and exercise were most exhilarating.

To hell with jungle rot. To hell with old dress rules. To hell with conventional standards. I had become a new man who had seen the light and refused to be put into traction ever again. I am an American, damnit, and I can do whatever pleases me.

Let freedom ring!

The only concern I had was that my terrific wife might notice none of my skivvies in the laundry. I'm sure it would take a while for her to discover my mutinous behavior, if ever she did. But for now it was still my devilish little secret. Mum's the word, I promised myself. I wanted to push the envelope, to stretch my rebellious streak, to press my luck until I got busted.

Ready to go I checked the house one last time, made sure the doors were locked, and then sat down on the front steps to put on my traveling sneakers.

I have to admit it was a pretty little house, a two bedroom, one bath, single story bungalow just under a thousand square feet. It was enough room for us as our proposed yearly vacation to the motherland, just as I had promised my dear wife.

The entire house was built out of concrete and steel. There wasn't a stick of wood in it, which was probably a good idea considering the excessively humid climate and abundance of hungry insects. Even the picket fence was made out of concrete and the interior walls too, which made it damn near impossible to hang a picture, or twenty.

The floor was a highly polished tile with the look of expensive marble. The tiny kitchen was typical for this Thai-style structure with a small sink, very little counter space, and no upper cabinets. On the ceramic counter sat a two-burner propane stove with a gas tank sitting right next to the dinky fridge, just like we have connected to our back yard grill at home. Can you believe that? A large propane tank resting in the kitchen. Safety isn't much of a factor over here.

Apparently OSHA hasn't expanded this far.

Construction on the little dollhouse was completed just as we arrived. We were pleasantly surprised at its exotic design and the neutral color schemes my wife had selected long distance, having only seen the house in photos sent by my sister-in-law.

Just to show you how fun-loving and spontaneous we are, as our taxi entered the city before we even saw the house we had stopped at a large furniture store nearby and purchased everything to furnish the place.

We bought two complete bedroom sets with armoires, a four-seat dinette set for us Americans who don't eat off a rolled-out floor mat in the middle of the kitchen, a small kitchen hutch, and a comfortable living room combo with floor lamps, throw pillows and area rugs. I've learned over the years you can never have enough throw pillows and area rugs.

Isn't that right, honey?

We bought so much furniture, to our delight the gracious owner of the establishment threw in a plastic wall clock and a two-slice Chinese toaster, just like you get when you open up a savings account with Cochise Savings and Loan.

We were thrilled!

Of course I had to have a color television with remote and DVD/CD player. Hey, I still wanted some of the comforts of home. I had packed half a suitcase with DVD movies, making certain to bring my classic *Three Stooges* episodes, some Steven Segal action flicks—the ones before he got fat—and the 2004 taped World Series games when the Sox whipped the Yankees' ass to everyone's surprise, laying to rest the 'Curse of the Bambino.'

I also brought a bunch of my music from home. Willy Nelson, Toby Keith, and Faith Hill, who I fell in love with after seeing her in concert. Too bad she's married to that cowboy dude. There were some Oldies but Goodies too, but of course that's to be expected.

After the first hot and stuffy sleepless night in our new house early the next morning I ordered two air conditioners to make life tolerable. When the units were installed that same day the house was like an ice cream parlor, but they were the best damn investment we ever made.

Then, while the women were in their spin of setting up nest with their plastic ware and linens and flowers I had the pleasure of nailing up curtain rods and hanging thirty-six fucking double sets of drapes throughout the small house.

I've come to learn that completing such a task without killing someone is truly a remarkable test of a strong marriage.

Don't you agree, dear?

On the outside front patio I still marveled at the overall cuteness of our quaint Thai home. The lush landscaping was a testament to the diverse array of tropical floral arrangement. The crew that had planted the bushes, trees, flowers, and grass on the day we moved in apparently knew what the hell they were doing. They had instantly transformed the barren corner lot into a paradise of color and comfort.

I swear, the property could be featured on the front of Thai House and Garden magazine.

There were lotus trees in full fragrant blossom, delicate white flowers dangling from the tips of their rubbery branches. Multi-colored bougainvillea bushes brightly displayed their vibrant petals of reds and oranges and yellows in the morning sun. Giant sunflower plants stretched ten feet and higher, their full faces smiling at the rising glow. Mango trees draped low with ripe green fruit ready for the picking. Long chunky papayas hung from stalky trees with thin umbrella ferns offering welcoming shade.

I was getting to like it here!

Banana trees and palm trees bordered the concrete wall surrounding the entire residential complex. Tall and short coconut trees lived beyond the walking paths, their massive clusters of greenish-yellow husky pods huddled in clumps like giant grapes just beneath the waving fronds of the glorious plants.

During my morning walks I was known to knock down a few coconuts, smuggle them home, and present the gifts to the women as an offering to keep me in good standings.

I considered it cheap insurance.

Hey guys! Go fuck yourself. I have a sensitive side too.

Hardy orchids of varied hues tilted in the breeze, growing solid in their potted earth of smooth stones and moist coconut mesh. A low fish pond stocked with miniature swimmers sat next to our porch, white and pink water lilies anchored in the wide pot to offer the fish protection from birds stopping for a drink or a quick snack.

Small statues of elephants and lions and dragons adorned the front steps and narrow perimeter walls to ward off evil spirits and to welcome well-wishers. Assorted tiny concrete figurines of various other domestic and wild animals rested among the flowers like happy knick-knacks content to be outside.

It was truly home away from home.

A wide, barely flowing murky canal meandered behind the back porch, just feet from our short wall, making it a convenient place to toss a line in search of some kind of red fish for dinner. The 'No Fishing' sign, written in Thai, hardly a deterrent, was probably meant for year round residents.

The canal cut through the neighborhood separating manicured back yards, connected beneath roadways and bridges, and nourished the thick vegetation and private gardens along its steep muddy banks. A small white paddle swan boat floated lazily, tethered to a narrow wooden platform.

Two large lakes, probably forty acres around, fed the snake-like klongs at either end of the community giving it a resort-like ambience. Short wooden piers with covered gazebos at the ends extended into the man-made lakes.

It was indeed a nice home, although for only a brief stay. A month of vacation, a sampling of retirement, a test to determine if this was a place we would like to live. It offered a sense of solitude and a quiet place without stress, the great Western man-killer. No clocks, no watches, no schedules, no pressing issues.

Just casual, no-hassle living.

I had to smile as I took in the scene that surrounded me. Pretty damn relaxing, I thought. Boring too.

But right now I was looking for some action. I closed the front wrought iron gate and walked down the side path. I couldn't help but turn one last time and admire the little house on its perfect little corner lot.

Me and my boys were headed to town!

Chapter 6

I TOOK LONG, LIVELY, unencumbered, easy flowing, rash-free steps toward the bus stop at the front of our gated community.

It was a leisurely half-mile walk that I had made at least twice a day since my arrival. Once in the early morning as my daily exercise while strolling the grounds just as the sun was rising, and again in the afternoon to get a cup of coffee from the small store near the entranceway.

It was actually my daily beer run but sometimes I did buy an iced coffee from one of the cute little girls who worked in the shop. They always smiled and looked quite happy to see me every time I stopped by. They also liked when I spoke Thai to them and generally laughed at my jokes which none of them understood. I think the little one with the long black hair and nice teeth wanted me, but I had to let her live in her frustrated fantasy world. I'm a happily married man.

Aren't I, honey?

But I did take her picture!

My journey took me past rows of newly built houses, all of them strangely designed to my Western senses, though uniquely attractive with their peaked tile roofs and gingerbread appearance. Several were under different stages of construction and were swarming with laborers.

Women workers, who seemed to have the harder jobs, were mixing concrete with hand tools in big dented metal tubs. They were hauling the heavy wet mixture in tightly knit straw baskets to spots where the guys were simply pointing at the holes to be filled. Men workers were cutting and piecing together long steel rods, welded on site as part of the framing and roof trusses.

On two of the structures stucco and brick walls were being built with the simplest of hand tools. Child-like play bricks were stacked in neat piles for the front of the houses. I didn't even see a wheelbarrow or tractor or power tool in sight and judged that human labor here was much cheaper than buying machinery or power equipment.

Six bucks a day can buy lots of manpower.

Rickety stick scaffolding secured with rusty bent over nails leaned against tall concrete pillars while bricklayers and metal workers casually perched themselves on the precarious framing. There seemed to be not an ounce of urgency in their work efforts as every one of them methodically tended to their jobs. None of the workers appeared to be more than ninety pounds and most looked like they were kids. And in the hot wet sun they worked all day at a slow and steady pace that would drive most high-strung type-A people insane.

Continuing my walk I carried a cane as my ultimate dog stick in a lame attempt to protect myself against the packs of patrolling canine totally disregarding the leash laws, if there were any. The hungry, chops-licking bastards knew my route as I quietly moved over to the far side of the sidewalk. I was familiar with the ones to steer clear of. "Nice doggies," I said in my most dog-friendly voice.

But them being Thai dogs they couldn't understand a fucking cowering word I was saying.

I lifted my cane, held it against my outstretched left arm pretending to aim the bogus weapon at the miserable beasts. Pulling the imaginary trigger I kept shooting the little fuckers that insisted on yapping and nipping at my feet while I walked through their territory. Not a one went down, but to my surprise most of them scattered from the sound of the blasts coming from my mouth.

Bunch of dumb shits!

"Hey, I live here too you little bastards," I let them know in no unmistakable terms.

As a precaution I made certain to avoid the bigger dogs that had larger teeth and failed to fall for my trick rifle and blank shots. I made a mental note to engineer some 'hot' hotdogs and one pleasant morning feed them to my furry, teeth bearing friends.

Two mixed mutts a safe distance away stared me down with evil intent. The mangy mongrels reminded me of the time, when as kids, my friend Billy and me tossed a few loaded wieners at a couple of mean feral bastards who always chased us innocent children down the road snapping at our skinny legs.

We had slipped several doses of Exlax borrowed from Mom's medicine cabinet into a bunch of Oscar Mayers and let them rip. Those mean son-of-a-bitches gobbled up the meaty time bombs like there was no tomorrow. Later that day we saw the flea bags doing the doggy butt walk that lasted for a week. After that they never bothered us kids again and instinctively refused our stuffed treats. It was so funny the dogs would actually veer away from us harmless youngsters.

And people say old dogs can't learn new tricks.

Along the way I met several of the groundskeepers who had the unfortunate job of working all day in the oppressive jungle heat. The kid who cuts my grass back home has it easy compared to these folks. I only walked a short distance and was already sweating my balls off, even though they, as you recall, were somewhat ventilated.

The landscapers were covered in several layers of clothing to protect themselves from the beating sun. I, on the other hand, proudly strutted my snow-white legs and blond arms in defiance against the rays. I had my wraparound sunglasses on too, an American movie star on site.

I looked damn cool!

Seeing the workers everyday and being the outgoing, friendly foreigner that I am, I would always nod their way and say hello the best I could in their language.

"Sawadee," I said to each one of them, which in Thai had many meanings. It typically meant hello...how are you doing?...what's happening?...how's you're day going?... how's it hanging?... and a variety of yet unlearned greetings.

'Sawadee' also had the flip side covered. It could mean goodbye... so long...see you later...arivederci...hasta los wages...bonjour...and nice to see you, why don't you stop by again when you can't stay so long.

I had the coming and going down pretty well, but had no clue on the in between stuff.

I knew the Thai people liked foreigners attempting to speak Thai. Though I must admit it is a difficult language to speak and absolutely impossible to read.

It was particularly tough for me since I had grown up in Boston proper where our language upbringing was not very flexible. We were steadfast in our vernacular and extremely xenophobic, which means we really didn't like any one from outside our neighborhood, especially if they talked funny or had a weird accent. We insisted on "pawking the caw in the yawd" or where ever the hell we wanted and took no shit from nobody.

Anyway, Thai writing actually looks like a combination of hieroglyphics, ancient Sanskrit, and cryptographic chicken scratchings. If you look at it sideways and squint your eyes a bit the squiggly letters sort of resemble some of the street graffiti that low-life punks with red spiked hair and rings in their fucking noses spray paint on shopping mall buildings and the hood of your shiny new car if you park on the fucking street overnight.

But I would still join in trying to bridge the language barrier since I'm such an easy going and likeable guy. Just ask my PO. Well, when I had a parole officer. But that was a very long time ago when I was young and dumb and not as understanding as I am now in my more mellow years.

Don't you agree, darling?

I have since promised not to beat the shit out of the next fucking asshole who tries to steal my wife's purse while we're walking together in the city minding our own damn business. I also promised not to crush anyone's friggin' throat 'til he turns a pretty shade of blue-purple, gasping for his last miserable breath wishing he had never gotten out of bed that day.

To ensure my continued good behavior the state also made me promise not to break anymore kneecaps with my elbow while the asshole is pleading for mercy lying on the sidewalk attempting to voluntarily return the purse he had ripped off.

These things I promised, as a changed and reformed man. But if I remember correctly, I had my fingers crossed.

Just in case!

Some of the landscaping crew came up to me, admired my rifle-cane, and with huge grins on their faces asked me what my name was.

I guessed that's what they were asking, or else they wanted my sunglasses. I gave them my big I-want-to-be-your-friend smile and told them, very slowly so they could understand.

"My name is Bob. B-O-B."

Duh! As if they could spell it.

They proudly nodded their covered heads in unison, looked at each other, and repeated back to me, "Boob," with a strange accent, each one of them pleased with their new English word.

"Ha, ha! Very funny guys." I had a strange feeling they knew they were fucking with me and enjoying every minute of it.

In return I asked them their names by pointing my finger at them, which I later discovered was a no-no. It's something akin to calling them a no good son-of-a-bitch with a not too honorable reference to their mother. I tried to remember not to point at anyone else unless they really deserved it. But the grounds crew got the gist of the game and told me their full, completely incomprehensible who-in-the-hell-would-name-their-children names.

To make things easier I smiled again and said, "Yes." Then I quickly assigned them all more suitable and manageable nicknames that any foreigner could remember. It became a simple matter of expediency and diplomacy.

Chom Pon Na Korn, who looked like an old Air Force buddy of mine, though about a hundred pounds lighter, was newly named Chucky Baby. The Chucky I knew was actually a real butt wipe and just so happened to be my supervising sergeant while stationed at Korat. But my new Chucky seemed to be an okay guy.

The big guy, well over five feet tall and quite thick for a native, Phon Lo Pranee, was Jake the Snake, in honor of his wrestler's physique. He kind of reminded me of The Rock, only a little darker, and a lot smaller, and much less intimidating.

Thule Pron See assumed the name of Suzie Q because beneath all that clothing she had a very pretty round face and appeared to have a figure to die for. She reminded me of someone I had a relationship with a long time ago back when I was a young troop far from home. I'm ashamed to say that looking at Suzie brought about several wicked images through my perverted brain until I turned my thoughts to my other all time favorite sport, baseball.

Then there was my favorite landscaper in the whole third world. He was the always-laughing Lhon Kim Katook who was the life of the party. He immediately became Rodney, as in Dangerfield, whose bulging eyes and reddish nose were either from a permanent nasal infection or too much Singha. I respected that guy.

Lhom Kim I mean.

It seemed that every one of my new friends were pleased with their English handles by the way they smiled and laughed when I called out each one. I gave every one of my new buddies a slapping high-five, after several attempts at teaching them to hold their damn hands above their heads. We had lots of international fun with that one.

We all soon became one big happy family who could barely understand a single friggin' word amongst us.

Just like my family back home!

I waved good-bye to my buds, said my Sawadees, and continued toward the road. The massive residential complex had a terrific design. The wide paved sidewalks were bordered with blossoming flowers, exuding a thick sticky sweet fragrance as I trolled along. The perfumes in the air were smells of paradise.

A small, fenced putting green spread out to the right of the walkway, just behind the mini-mart. I really didn't think anyone around here knew anything about golf, but the manicured grass knoll looked inviting. Next time I'll have to remember to bring my putter if the manager of the municipal golf course I used to frequent would be kind enough to return it to me after that unfortunate incident.

The tiny store was no 7-11 like the ones run by the Arabs back home who we so dearly love, but it carried the absolute essentials. Beer, chips, wine coolies for the women, and coffee. Did I mention that some cute girls ran the shop?

It was my happy place!

Chapter 7

As I got closer to the highway just outside my gated community there stood a small block built security guard building in the middle of the grand entranceway.

The guard's one and only duty is to open and close the metal roll-away blockades to protect the residents paying his salary by keeping the riff-raff out of the neighborhood, except for the traveling ice cream man and some of my wife's relatives. Oh, and after hours the beer delivery guy too.

I still had a difficult time remembering that drivers here ride on the wrong side of the road. That's how they walk in the stores too, always bumping into me. Left side for northbound, right side for southerly traffic. Almost got myself blindsided one day by three bad dudes on a 125 CC rice burning hog going right on a left lane road. Good thing I don't have a left-handed driving car or else I'd have to teach these people a thing or two about driving safely.

I nodded to the guard who was closing the gate after a minivan school bus had passed through to pick up some of the children in the complex. He was checking out a small pick-up truck heaped with wooden crates of fruit before allowing the salesman into the compound. I swear he was on the take because once the truck had passed through

I saw the guard munching on a large ripe mango and pocketing a hand full of peanuts.

"Sawadee George," I said to the short man who stood guard for twelve-hour shifts. It was impossible for me to say his real name during our past encounters so he immediately became George, which, I thought, is a good hardy name for such a dedicated man. I later found out that the guards worked their long hours with only one day off per week, earning a paltry salary of 5200 baht per month, non-union, of course.

That's around one hundred fifty dollars, or about a month's beer tab.

I felt sorry for the guy sitting there all day at his post with no A/C and only a miniature fan in his cramped quarters. So every time I made a beer run…aah…I mean…went for a coffee, I would smuggle him a cold Pepsi to keep him on his toes. I figured if I gave him a beer he'd either book out early or doze off, leaving the gateway wide open to who knows what. So I took it upon myself to limit him to only soft drinks and water, like real prisoners get, to ensure the protection of the residents.

George said something about seeing my wife and her two sisters catching the Chok Chai bus earlier. I said something about the friggin' hot weather. Without animated hand signals we'd both be lost. Neither one of us understood more than a word or two between us, but we smiled at each other a lot and nodded in agreement. He really didn't say it, but I think George was impressed with my growing command of the Thai language.

I'm quite proficient that way.

In picking up languages I mean!

In high school I took six years of French class because a language was required to graduate and the French teacher was an absolute knock out. Of course there were mostly boys in her class. Even some of the… ah…shall I say, less academically inclined students from wood shop and auto repair enjoyed their French lessons.

Tres bien!

It was an adolescent boy's wet dream just watching Ms. Antoinee's lush full red lips mouthing phrases like, "Parlez vous Francais?" or, "Respondez vous, si vous plait." I've actually used that second one a few times since, when I sent out invitations to a back yard Fourth of July BBQ and to a rib cooking cook-off. Being bi-lingual comes in handy sometimes.

At least French uses the same alphabet as English. Some of the words are pretty damn close too, like café, l'hotel, and menage a trois. A variety of French words are commonplace in English also, used in everyday conversation, such as *femme fatale, soup d'jour,* or *sans.* It's a good language to know.

I see that last word all the time in things I read, and if it weren't for Ms. Antoinee's dedication to higher education I would never know what I was reading. Now, whenever I read a sentence like, "He went into McDonald's *sans* his wallet," I understand that he was *without* his wallet. Or to put it in more relevant and personal terms, "I was traveling down the road feeling loose as a goose *sans* my undies."

Now, I don't really care for the French all that much, them being communists and all, but they have a damn nice language. So, as you can see, since I learned to master French, I know in time with more one-on-one practice I can at least pick up the basics of the Thai language.

In front of the guard shack was a huge circular driveway anchored by a monstrously large fountain like the kind you would see at an expensive luxury resort hotel or in front of a defense attorney's house. The vast array of flowers and colorful bushes attracted attention to all passersby shouting, "This is the place!"

No doubt the entryway to the community was meticulously maintained in an attempt to attract potential well-to-do Thai and foreign house buyers to purchase the overpriced but safe and comfortable homes.

They weren't selling houses, they were selling a lifestyle.

Worked for me!

I had to cross a busy four lane highway to wait for the north bound bus going to Korat. The girls and I had gone that way a few days before to check out the sites and visit the busy open market places. We came back with ten kilos of greens and assorted fruits. I told you about all the pictures I took, though I never really showed all of them to my sometimes jealous wife.

I remembered I had to catch the blue and white bus, the one that said Korat on the front, though the writing was in Thai and did me no damn good. Chicken scratch. The road was a major highway leading from the south to the central plains of the country. There was a mix of travelers making their way to and from their destinations in all sorts of modes of transportation.

Commerce baby!

Large transport trucks, doubles and even triples, obviously overloaded, zoomed by me toward the city. Smaller trucks which appeared to be powered by open lawn mower engines, moved along at an excruciating slow pace, packed to the gills with freshly picked potatoes, or sacks of rice, or piles of tree limbs waiting to become charcoal bricks or fuel for the burning kilns.

There were hundreds of small pickups stacked with produce of all sorts and boxes loosely piled and tied ten feet higher than the truck beds. The roadway was an accident waiting to happen.

Motorcycles and the much smaller, more prominent motorbikes whizzed by on the shoulders of the road like swarms of mosquitoes heading for a feast. Some of them were driven by young kids, perhaps no older than thirteen or fourteen, going to school, or maybe even to work. Others carried entire families, their shopping goods loosely secured to the back.

I was amazed to see the tiniest of scooters carrying a full Thai family of four as if there was nothing unusual about it. A small child, knowing exactly how to hold on for dear life, sat in front of his dad who handled the controls. Another baby was squeezed between the father and its mother who wrapped herself around the back of the seat. Talk about carpooling. These people have it going on.

Some motorcycles drove in the wrong direction, riding the soft highway edge as they headed against the traffic flow, completely disregarding the north-south rules of travel, going a short distance to work or to the nearest market. It seemed everyone knew the manner of merging and yielding and I am glad to say, not a single wreck occurred on my shift.

I knew the bus came by about every half-hour or so, or whenever it damn well felt like it. Most people who had business in town would go early while the markets were still packed with fresh fruits, veggies, fish, and meats. It was nearing nine o'clock now, late for most travelers, and I was waiting for the last bus of the morning, the last bus to Korat, hoping I wouldn't be stuck too long frying my fair face in the sun while resting my fat ass at the makeshift bus stop.

With some time on my hands while waiting for my ride I went over a list of Thai numbers, some words, and new phrases I had been studying on my own. I am a big believer in self-study, especially after my dear wife refused to teach me any Thai, reminding me in her sweet way, "You'll never get it."

I love the support I get from my patient wife.

I feel it is important to show the people of this fine country that, as a visitor, I would make a serious attempt to assimilate into their culture by at least learning the fundamentals of their language. Street talk to all you ignorant foreigners.

After all, here I am the outsider, and it is up to me to try to fit in. It would be ludicrous for me to expect the wonderful Thai people to accommodate me, an English speaking American, in their country. Although it would certainly be a hell of a lot easier if some of them could speak more than a few words of broken English.

Come on guys. Get with the economic program. Back home we expect the same from our Mexican neighbors, except for the ones who sneak over our porous borders, hop the fences, dig the tunnels, run through the washes, and end up in line at our local food banks and DES centers waiting for free cheese.

In my mind, while the traffic was racing by, I reviewed some of the things I had learned which I would most likely need to know when in the city. I was pretty familiar with the Thai numbers one through ten. However, if anything cost more than ten baht I was fucked.

Some of the phrases that stood out in my brain were rather crucial.

When hiring a taxi to get around, I had to remember, in Thai, "Where the fuck are you taking me, friend?"

There have been stories of foreigners being over charged by the local hacks, a practice that probably originated in New York City and spread to the Far East. I've even heard of at least several westerners who had a reputation for being rude and obnoxious and arrogant never making it to their final destinations. A few local cab drivers now wear cowboy hats in their daily runs, apparently in honor of those poor lost tourists.

Where they got the hats I have no idea.

When ordering a bowl of rice soup or noodles, I'd remember to say, again in Thai, "What the fuck is in this?"

And I should point at the strange insect-like thing swimming in my food so the cook knew exactly what I was asking. Although the book suggests that one should never show any signs of anger or raise your voice in such a situation because you never know what's going to be in the next bowl you get.

Sound advice, sort of like never sending your undercooked hamburger back to the sleaze ball working in the kitchen at Denny's. There are some very strange Thai foods out there and I tend to stick to the ones that I've seen on Food Network, Bizarre Foods excluded.

Of course, if my day got really interesting and I met one of those beautiful young Thai women, I was ready with the ultimate piece of conversation to sort of break the ice. "How much baht for one hour?"

I should ask the innocent question by holding up one finger, remembering not to point, to clarify my inquiry and prevent any international misunderstanding. I didn't yet know how to say fifteen minutes, which in reality was about all the time I would really need, including the nap.

I'm actually joking, honey. I love you very much and would never do such a thing even if my buddies back home dared me.

So, with my gear all packed and my Thai phrases polished to perfection I was ready for my solo adventure.

I saw a dilapidated white and blue tin can bus chugging up the hill, smoking it's way toward me like a condemned prisoner. It had some squiggly writing on the front.

My ride was here!

Chapter 8

I TOOK MY LIFE in my hands and stepped into the busy street to flag down the bus.

With the noisy traffic going both ways it was a dangerous tactic, but I was ready for danger. I lived for it. Parts of the bus were blue and white so I figured it must be the right one. The bus came to a screeching stop, its worn out brakes sounding the driver's intention some one hundred yards before me.

With absolute precision he stopped forty feet beyond where I was standing. I had the feeling he did that on purpose to let me know who the boss was on this trip. I ran to the bus as the driver began grinding the gears, grabbed the railings and pulled myself up the steep stairs through the open front door. No sooner had I lifted my feet off the ground the bus was back in motion.

I nodded at the driver who looked like my fifteen-year old paperboy. Everyone looked young here, except for the really old ones. He smiled, a few of his front teeth were missing, and then he motioned to sit in the back. There was a ROCK STAR sticker on his beat up console and a tall stack of music CDs to make the ride more enjoyable. A faded cardboard Santa Claus was pasted on the side window for whatever reason, and a Chinese movie poster hung over the back of the driver's seat.

Home sweet home!

I stood in the center aisle of the bus, my neck turned at a sharp angle so my head wouldn't scrape the ceiling. I'm almost six foot tall, well…a tad over five feet eight and a half, but in this world of short natives I was a giant. Rows of black haired small people stared at the white monster working his way down the narrow aisle. I smiled at each one of them as if I had arrived at a private party, working my way toward the back, grinning and greeting my fellow travelers like a junior politician looking for easy votes.

With my shades on they must have thought they were in the presence of a famous American action movie star. The Thais are crazy about American movie actors, especially James Bond, Stallone, and Arnold Baby. I gave them my Hollywood nod just to confirm their excited suspicions, which I'm certain gave them all a cheap thrill during their otherwise routine ride to the market.

The bus was almost a full house but I found an empty seat half way down the aisle and flopped my slightly big ass on the double bench. The bench seat, like something you'd see in kindergarten class, was barely wide enough for the average overweight American. I squeezed myself against the window and began chewing on my knees that where propped only inches in front of my mouth.

The rest of the passengers were quiet and mostly kept to themselves. Thai people are naturally reserved and respectful and silently inquisitive. Not a one of them gave me a threatening glare.

A young couple up front, a boy and what looked like his twelve year old girlfriend, kept turning around to see the foreigner, most likely thinking they were on the same bus as Chuck Norris, discovering he was much bigger in real life. More handsome too, I thought, though my martial arts moves were a bit rusty since my last and only class back when I was about seventy pounds lighter.

I caught a few of the riders sneak a peek my way, probably wondering why such a celebrity was taking the poor man's bus into town. Maybe the whole thing was part of a new movie, a remake of those old Vietnam War flicks where Thailand was a jumping off point to wipe out the fucking Viet Cong. And a bad ass, pissed off hero would rescue captured American warriors who were wasting away in bamboo cages.

Don't fuck with this dude. He'll tear your throat out just for the fun of it. I grunted a bit just to confirm to these lowly riders that I was the real thing.

A young child, hanging onto his mother's long dress, every few seconds looked at me as if it was his first time seeing such a man. He was probably thinking, "Mama, what is that big white man doing on our bus? He might eat me." I smiled at the little squirt to let him know I wouldn't really eat such a scrawny kid. Then I flared my nostrils several times in his direction as I often do to entertain children and pretty little girls.

I can wiggle my ears too if it's of any interest to you. Cracks some people up. Oh yeah! Just for the record I can also move other things on command, but this is neither the time nor place.

The boy's dark eyes widened at my facial tricks and quickly hid his shaved head in his mother's lap and then began crying. Out of the corner of my eye I saw another passenger smile and turn away from the crazy foreigner. I think she liked me. She turned to her seatmate and giggled, no doubt thinking I was one crazy bastard with an uncanny ability.

I felt a hundred eyes looking at me, but it didn't bother me a bit. I was in the midst of a docile tribe. I just sat there trying to get comfortable without turning and worrying. I felt certain I would not be attacked on this bus. Mr. Cool all the way.

Hey, I'm making friends here!

The bus gradually hit its top speed of perhaps thirty kilometers per hour. Bicycles with families on them were passing us. The light morning breeze blew papers down the road faster than we were traveling.

I swear, if this tin can of a bus went any faster it would have shaken apart at its wooden seams. I renamed it the tin can bus after my first excursion on it with my gorgeous wife. I felt like a double vanilla milkshake after we had gotten off at the last stop, dizzy from the experience, my bones and derriere—which is French just in case you were wondering—were sore from the rock and rolling.

I'd bet twenty baht the bus was at least forty years old and not a thing had ever been fixed on it.

The windshield was cracked in two places, but see-through tape held it in place so the driver could have bifocal vision. The narrow high-back seats were worn down to their metal frames, which was in one way an improvement, making them easier to grab onto. The plywood ceiling was peeling in sections from decades of rainy leaks. Several electric fans hanging from the corners of the roof were in the permanent broke position. Others worked whenever they damn well felt like it.

I could even see the road passing beneath my feet through a hole in the rotted floor planks big enough to pass a watermelon through or to take a crap if the urgent need arose. I was pretty sure I had ridden this same bus back when I was stationed in the area some decades ago during the war.

If I recall it was a piece of shit ride back then too, but at least the fans worked.

Chapter 9

THE TIN CAN ON wheels kept making stops at just about every corner.

Newcomers would pack their baskets of food in the back open area as they headed to the markets to sell their merchandise from concrete booths or jammed street corners. In the city every empty spot with foot traffic was an instant marketplace. Every street corner became a grocery stall, every section of sidewalk curb a makeshift restaurant.

I saw mounds of dried fish with sharp protruding menacing teeth neatly arranged on round bamboo trays stacked in the corner near the back door. The skeletons looked smaller than the sunfish or bluegill I used to catch at the pond near our old house when I was a kid. The salted, sun-dried fish looked damn ugly and not a bit appetizing.

Bushels of morning picked fresh fruits were packed in large plastic sacks weighing more than the old bent women who had carried them on board. One contained mangos, another some white fruit that appeared to be a cross between an apple and a pear. A different bag held loads of red things with soft spines all over them. Still more held husks of corn, sections of raw sugar cane, stacks of tangerines, and mounds of pineapples. We were a produce bus in motion headed to the grand city.

Yeah baby!

There were bulky straw things covering who knows what and something that smelled like death warmed over that took up the rest of the storage space. I was glad to be in the middle of the bus with the windows opened and the forty year old curtains flapping away offering some relief from the morning heat and our traveling stench mobile.

At one stop a woman actually carried on one of those whicker cages with two live chickens in it and another one with a duck big enough to be a friggin' swan. The fucking duck wouldn't stop quacking, as if it didn't really enjoy the ride. Or maybe it knew what was in store for him at the end of the line. I couldn't wait to see him hanging by his limp neck at the meat market. The noise was so loud I was ready to begin squawking too, but thought it would be too juvenile.

Now we were riding the friggin'barnyard express!

At the speed we were going we'd have fresh eggs before we got to Korat. Maybe even a flock of those cute little chicks. I was waiting for a herd of goats to hitch a ride at the next stop and hoped to hell they wouldn't be searching for an empty seat. If that happened I promised myself I would jump off this traveling wreck and walk the rest of the way. I hold the line at traveling with goats sitting beside me.

Sorry, that's just how I am!

There was Thai music blaring from somewhere in the bus. The goddamn fans didn't work but the speakers blew out their music in ear-splitting surround-sound. The driver kept adjusting the volume on his rigged CD player loosely wired into the speaker system. He was having a jolly good time cruising down the crowded boulevard glad to have such a slow paced job listening to his favorite tunes, paying more attention to his live concert then to the road ahead.

The high pitched singing sounded like The Bee Gees with their collective nuts being squeezed whenever the chorus kicked in. I swear I heard glass bottles shatter all around me. Or the music could have been a lip-syncing of that singer, James Blunt, who, I am certain, wears his pants way too tight. Either way, I was developing a wicked fucking headache from the ungodly melodies.

The mellow cargo of passengers didn't mind the agonizing screaming blasting from the speakers. They simply swayed back and forth with the music, smiling all together as if they really liked it, while the death trap rolled along in rhythm with the screeching tunes. I blanked out the roar as best I could and found myself surprisingly swaying to and fro with the rest of the tone-deaf customers.

There were strands of pretty yellow and white flowers strung together hanging from the driver's rear view mirror, I guess as a gift to honor the road gods, a traditional offering assuring us all a safe and pleasant journey. I felt safer just seeing them. Maybe they were there to cover up the smell of shit coming from the pile of rotting food in the back.

A cheap plastic kitchen clock screwed to the driver's visor indicated 11:05. I knew it was earlier than that since I thought I had caught the nine o'clock bus, and discovered several minutes later that it was always 11:05. Here it seems anything goes except for time.

I was wondering who to pay my fare to and a few minutes into my ride to town my question was answered. The driver pulled to the side of the road, beeping his high pitched horn at a few three-wheeled taxis called tuk-tuks.

Really! I'm not making this up. Tuk-tuks are motorcycles with two wheels in the back and a small low rider seat large enough for two foreigners or eight Thai nationals with all their shopping bags. The drivers charge whatever the traffic will bear, which for obvious reasons is always higher for the tourists than for the natives.

Damn New York cabbies!

These tuk-tuk pilots speed down the road, weaving in and out of dense traffic, dare-deviling ten-ton trucks for a few feet of open space, barely fitting in between a thousand other taxis and motorbikes all jockeying for the same three feet up ahead. Passengers dare not extend their fingers beyond the confines of the three-wheeled rocket ships unless they have a pressing desire to be called Stubby McGee.

Riders suck in great quantities of fresh diesel exhaust and miscellaneous sputter kicked up from millions of competing vehicles, all the while holding on to flimsy handles and torn canvas tops praying that this isn't their day to meet the great Buddha.

These crazed maniac drivers, who I swear are on assorted drugs, take street corners as if they had graduated from the Evil Kneivel School of Racing, cracking up all along like a whacked out Dennis Hopper ready to make a death-defying leap over the Grand Canyon.

Though, as drivers, I must admit, they have three great tricks.

One is dodging the treacherous sidewalk curbs, which if hit by a side tire will flip the son-of-a-bitch over like a dead cockroach. I've seen tragic tuk-tuk crashes that left dozens of little people scattering for safety, running for their lives away from oncoming traffic that refused to stop. There was nothing left but an overturned three-wheeler and a gigantic salad bowl in the middle of the street.

Another of their tricks is trying to almost run over pedestrians who often make the near fatal mistake of crossing the street. For some unknown reason taking out someone's toe is considered good luck—go figure. People crossing any street did so at their own peril and if by chance one of them got hit or lost a big toe, oh well, the foot goddess was appeased.

But by far the tuk-tuk drivers' best stunt is stealing loose snacks from food vendors' hot plates set too close to the roadside. Last week I hired a tuk-tuk to run me around while my fantastic wife was shopping for underwear or something. From the back seat I scored a free hot dog on a stick when my driver, Pirate Eddie, just for the sport of it, was making a U-turn in front of an unsuspecting meat cart.

We both laughed our asses off at his skilled driving and my dexterous lifting of the popular snack. We were buds for life, gave each other a high five, and become blood brothers. I gave my new friend the ill-gotten shish-ka-bob as a trophy of sorts for his expert driving.

Besides, those things taste like shit!

I called him Pirate Eddie because of his glass eye that looked like one of those ten cents aggies I used to play with as a kid. I also admired his impressive black eye patch, half the times of which I couldn't tell if he had it over his good eye or the fake one.

The way he drove I suppose it really didn't matter. As far as I could figure he was one of those rare tall Thai men who forgot to duck while shopping on the sidewalks. We had loads of fun together that day and I shall miss him.

Pirate Eddie was one crazy bastard, may he rest in peace.

Chapter 10

Anyway, the bus driver stops his rig and gets his plastic change bowl out. He's the fare collector too on this one-man job. My guess is he's also the mechanic without tools. A true multi-tasker.

When he gets to me I tell him my destination. "Korat," I say in my best Boston-Thai accent, as if I've been saying it all my life. A commanding sense of clear-cut confidence works wonders when in an unfamiliar situation. He gets my drift, probably wondering what a dumb ass foreigner he has on his coach.

"That's the only place this bus is headed, you dumb shit," he said, shaking his tooth-challenged head.

Well, he didn't exactly say that, but I saw it in his eyes. I chalked it up to my broken but improving Thai.

Hey! Back off, I'm trying my best here.

I held up a twenty-baht bill and hoped he wouldn't screw me on the fifteen baht fare. To my surprise he handed me the correct change and I smiled back at him. In a matter of minutes the driver-toll collector-mechanic-wise ass finishes his rounds and we were off again at a screaming pace.

It was a twenty-kilometer trip to the big city, twelve miles to you foreigners. The leisurely ride could take anywhere from twenty-five to fifty-five minutes, depending on the driver, the condition of the bus, and the number of passengers, both human and otherwise, and which songs were playing on the loud speakers. But who cares. Time is not a very important commodity here when everyday is the same.

Hell, I was in no rush either. I was starting to groove with the tunes and rock with the rest of the paying passengers, content that I was fitting in and getting along so well with the Thai people.

A flashing thought went through my usually rational brain that I may have been turning native, or 'going bamboo' as some call it. There are some foreigners who have lived over here for so long they can barely speak their own natural language.

They walk like Thais, eat like Thais, dress like Thais, and live simply like Thais. They've assimilated into the local culture, forgone their quirky, obnoxious ways, abandoned their music, and haven't seen a James Bond movie in decades. In short, they've gone over the hill, gone 'bamboo.'

If such a metamorphosis ever came over me I decided right there that I would never change who I am. I'm determined to stay the same. I came into this world as Bob Swift, and that's how I'm going out. The old B.S. way.

I was fascinated by the traffic, the storefronts, and street vendors along the route, the crowds of people coming and going. There was a casualness of life, an air of euphoric contentment. Horns hardly honked. Cars, trucks, buses, bikes, and tuk-tuks entered and exited the traffic flow nearly without a smithering of road rage.

Older men riding samlars, a close cousin of the Chinese rickshaw, only a three-wheeled bike with a twenty-inch passenger seat, eeked out a living pedaling customers around for a few baht. They were at the bottom of the transportation chain, a rung below the tuk-tuks, but not very much faster than hoofing it on your own. The samlars are something like the laughable trikes with the big grocery basket on the back you see the old ladies pedaling their short chubby legs as they head to Safeway for their weekly social hour.

Life on the fast track, baby!

Everyone was engaged in commerce. It seemed like every individual worked, either selling something, hauling something, or making something. Thai people have a true entrepreneurial spirit. A strong sense of free will and self-determination. A pride in having the freedom to do whatever they damn well felt like doing.

Which in my book ain't all bad.

I guess they understand the first economic rule of life. If they don't work they don't eat, which is quite an incentive for meaningful and full employment in my opinion.

Our welfare system back in the States should check into this unusual form of self-reliance. Work equals food. Laziness equals starvation. True personal effort equals rewards. Lack of ambition equals a healthy government handout. Pretty deep, huh?

Nay!

That kind of system wouldn't work back home. The people in charge won't go for it. There's too much free cheese to give away to the no good, lazy bastards who spend their days on the couch watching Opah, or Dr. Phil, or that instigator Jerry Springer, waiting for the welfare check to be delivered, while me and my friends are out busting our asses everyday for these fucking low-lifes.

Besides, if it really did work, the Democrats would have nothing to do.

Here it seems everyone gets along and no one bitches about the traffic jams or long waits at stop lights or even waiting for the hordes of day shoppers worming their way across the boulevards. There are no middle fingers thrust in the air, no nasty looks of contempt, no gun carrying son-of-a-bitches looking to settle a score, as the local citizens make their way toward their destinations in slow motion.

No one complains about their work, or moans about the unfairness of life. There's no griping about the meager wages, the long work hours, the aches and pains of living, the hand they were dealt. They simply do what they need to do live.

Gradually moving along we drove through a small village named Dan Kwean. I had been sitting on the bus for nearly fifteen minutes and we had barely gone two kilometers. Hell, if I turned around and looked out the back window I could still see the rooftops of the houses where I lived.

Dan Kwean is a world famous region of fabulous Thai pottery and ceramics manufactured right there on the spot just minutes from my retirement home. Made from local heavy clay the pottery is kilned in aged, stone-arched, wood burning ovens just as the practice of pottery making had been done for thousands of years.

I bet they could cook pizzas in those things.

There are miles of vendors on both sides of the street, some displaying their uniquely spectacular vases and fountains and statues in open-air fashion. Hundreds of other merchants in their covered patios and partly enclosed stores proudly present their wares, explaining to the browsing shoppers the quality of their hand-made pottery in a constant attempt to negotiate a sale.

Small, easy to carry trinkets were being purchased by hordes of tourists, both foreign and domestic, dismounting the huge, clean, air-conditioned buses stopping at the numerous stalls in frequent intervals. I was immediately jealous of their rides.

"Twenty baht for your clean, air-conditioned, animal free seat to Korat," I yelled out to the lucky bastards. But there were no takers.

Local citizens were buying statues for their homes and yards, and religious renderings to honor the spirits that lived amongst them. Boxes and boxes of exquisitely glazed handiwork were packaged for shipment to all corners of the globe. Even large twenty and forty-foot shipping containers were being loaded to be trucked out to transport ships waiting at the Gulf of Thailand south of Bangkok.

The world loves this stuff!

Raw red clay pots stacked in towering piles were magically and tediously transformed into beautiful vases. Under the steady hands of skilled artisans, young and old, the pieces gradually came to life with colors and glazes. Many were patiently painted with delicate lotus blossoms and fierce protective dragoons and fluttering red butterflies.

Demon-like configurations stood in long rows waiting to adorn business entryways. Mythical idols of half human, half animal figures dominated sections of the showcase, a tribute to Thai, Chinese, and Indian tales of the past. Fish ponds and elaborate fountains of every possible design offered the sense of tranquility so often sought after in the Far East.

A thousand different wind chimes gently moved in the morning air singing their songs of the earth. It was truly a sight to behold. I was amazingly impressed, which if you know me by now, is no easy feat. And I was only looking at these pieces of art through the grimy windows of my bus.

Massive concrete panels as large as ten by fifteen feet, intricately pieced together like giant jig saw puzzles weighing untold tons, depicted scenes from Thai folk lore, or revered gods directing mere mortals, or Asian elephants working in the forest lands. Folks back home would certainly be fascinated by the varied colors and designs and shapes and sheer variety of such workmanship. It was no wonder this place was known and sought after throughout the world.

My bus continued its low speed pursuit and took the long curve up ahead leaving the pottery village of Dan Kwean behind us. I decided to spend some time there later on when I had some extra coin.

Don't laugh. I wanted to buy one of those handmade wind chimes that sings its song of the earth.

A gift for my deserving wife, of course.

Chapter 11

I SETTLED INTO MY ancient spring-punctured seat, trying to block out the rattling noise and bumpy ride, and that's when I felt something sharp sticking up my ass. A little shift of the old cheeks and I was sitting pretty again.

Without drawing any attention to me I pulled a casual check of my glutimous maximus and was more than pleased to discover no penetration down there. No pain, no problem. I just had to remember not to move too far left again, otherwise I might be the new bus singer crooning a Thai version of "Rocketman" at a much higher octave than Elton John could ever hit.

I thought about my good buddy Hank back home who bid me farewell on my voyage of a lifetime as he instructed me about my photo taking sessions with the babes of Thailand.

Hank the Love Shank, as he often referred to himself, would love it here.

The laid back atmosphere, the easy going slow pace of living, the inexpensive life style, the wide variety of foods, the drop dead gorgeous women. There were two things Hank loved most in this world. Money and women, and in that order. Nothing else really mattered to him. He figured if he had the dough then everything else would follow.

Smart man, that Hank. He made a pretty good living and as a single man, for the third time since I've known him, he had the distinct advantage of hunting for women in the wide open range, or wherever else they might be found.

He would have a friggin' field day here!

I've known Hank for nearly twenty years and have been friends with him for most of that time, off and on. Actually, his name is not really Hank. I'd venture to say that I'm probably his best friend in the whole world, having gone through good times and bad over the years, and he still to this day refuses to tell me what his real Christian name is.

That's right! Fucking weird, huh?

Like maybe it might be Sue or Billy Joe or Freddie, something stupid that he'd be ashamed of. I can only imagine his real name must be down right awful if he's so damn self-conscious about it. Probably has one of those neurotic complexes from when he was a kid when the other children in the fourth grade made fun of him.

He keeps telling me he dropped out of grammar school to become an ironworker but I can't believe everything he says, especially if he won't even tell me what his parents called him.

Come on buddy. We're friends. You can tell me. I promise I won't laugh.

In our first years as friends I kept asking him about his name. It was bugging the hell out of me. He wouldn't say, refused to answer me, and simply brushed off my questioning every time the subject came up.

Come on man, tell me what your fucking name is!

Then without any satisfaction, whenever he wasn't paying attention or was focused on some part of a female's anatomy—which was most every waking moment of his pathetic life—I tried to trick him by calling out strange names, the ones I would never ever want to be called.

I'd yell out, "Hey Vern!" or "Watch out Bubba!" or sometimes even, "Duck, Leonard."

He never fell for the ploy and refused to show even a slight reaction to any name I tossed his way. The bastard!

He was a crafty son-of-a-bitch!

"Hey man," I screamed at him in frustration one day. "If you won't tell me your given name then why in the hell do you go by Hank?"

He at least owed me that, I thought.

So at lunch one day he told me.

"I have a brother," he said. "His name is Darrell, a few years younger than me. Haven't seen him in a long time now. I think he works at some recycling plant crushing aluminum cans or tearing pages out of old phone books one at a time, or something like that. Anyway, he's a little slow in the head."

Hank touched a finger to his temple as if I didn't catch his drift. "He could only count to six, and never learned more than three vowels—a, i, and u, and sometimes y. I could never figure that out. He's truly a dumb son-of-a-bitch, but hey, what can I say, he's still my brother."

I know how that is. I have cousins like that living back East. I haven't seen them for a very long time either. None of them could ever pass their driver's license test because some of the words had more than four letters, so they have to bum rides to and from work and back to the VFW bar every night. Poor guys.

By now most of them are in their forties and fifties. Hell, even one of them, not from my side of the family, is named Daryl. Close enough in my book. But I'm pretty certain he can count beyond six.

Sometimes I really believe that ignorance is bliss, as the saying goes.

Ice cream time!

My friend what's his name continued his story.

"Well, every morning my brother Darrell would run out of the house dragging his Batman and Robin lunch box to catch the short yellow bus to school and he'd yell back at me, 'By Hank,' since he couldn't say my real name, you know, because of the vowels. And the name just kind of stuck."

I didn't really believe the lying bastard but listened to his story without interrupting him. Maybe he'd slip up.

"I think half of him ran down his mother's leg while he was being conceived and so he wasn't all there, if you know what I mean," Hank said, swirling an index finger around his ear and giving me a wide, shit-eating grin.

My good friend was a disgusting pig talking about his brother's mother that way, but I have to say the first time I heard that story I cracked up like a friggin' idiot.

Right Rodney?

Hank, I have to say, is an equal opportunity hound dog. I mean he has that uncompromising leer whenever a beautiful female walks by that says in no uncertain terms, "I'll do you right now in the middle of the street." And he would too if the opportunity arose. Damn social conventions. Cops too.

I swear, this boy embarrasses me in public on a daily basis whenever there're women nearby. It's gotten to the point where I can't go into some local restaurants with him any more. I don't know how many waitresses have quit because of him. But I have to give him credit for the ones who keep coming back. He must be doing something right. Oh yeah, there's a few stores I can't go into with him too. The bank too. And the coffee shop down the street.

"Let's go to lunch," Hank would say to me everyday when we tried to escape the office.

"No thanks, I'll eat at my desk."

Less humiliating that way.

He really believes that every hot chick wants him. I mean he really, really believes it. Did I mention that he's a shameless pervert. Mr. Hot Shit. I never wanted to hurt his feelings because he's my best friend, but here it is Hank, or whatever your fucking name is. If you lose the stupid mustache you would be a spitting image of the guy on the Indian head nickel. You know, Chief Whatshisname.

No offense pal. I'm just not sure the girls are into that look.

In my professional opinion I believe my pal Hank is truly delusional, but in his defense I will say that beneath his perverted shell he is basically a good guy. I mean, I've seen him buy pizza for little kids near the schoolyard and hand out candy at the bus stop. I even happen to know he's generously sponsored the girl's high school soccer team on more than one occasion. A man who does those kind of things can't be all bad. So I continue to humor him.

Yeah, old buddy, they all want you.

That so, Clyde?

Over here it would be a major step up for you my friend. It's a completely different league of honestly gorgeous ladies. I've known you long enough to realize you have absolutely no scruples when it comes to sleeping with strange, and sometimes very weird women. Don't try to deny it, brother. I know. I've seen some of the ones you've dated.

Up close too!
Anyway, I'm still taking lots of pictures for you, old pal of mine.
Maybe when I get back we'll put together that calendar.
How's that sound, Albert?

Chapter 12

I WAS SHAKEN FROM my daydreaming when the bus stopped to pick up yet another passenger. I automatically looked out the side window onto the crowded sidewalk and was instantly awed by what I was seeing.

I could not believe my tired eyes! I lifted my cool shades to get a better look.

Fantasy had turned into reality. There really was a Santa Claus. My guardian angel had finally watched over me despite all the misunderstandings we've had over the years. The most fabulously stunning young lady I have ever seen in my entire life—except for you my dear beautiful wife who I will always cherish and will love forever and ever—was boarding the front of the bus.

Oh thank you Clarence! You're the best angel there ever was.

It was like a scene straight out of the movie *10* when the drunken Arthur first sees Bo Derek in her delightfully revealing wet bikini coming out of the oh so cold ocean when every man in America, like Arthur, instantly falls in love. At that very moment the highest of standards had been set which few women in existence could ever come close to. Men like me and Arthur were ruined.

"Oh…my…god!" I uttered to myself.

I was enthralled with the girl's unspeakable magnificence. The brilliant aura of her majestic beauty halted my breathing. I was mortally struck by that stupid little guy's love arrow. Watching her was like an up close viewing of the classic and glorious arts of Michelangelo, Monet, and Little Debbie. I was mesmerized, speechless, dumbfounded. I was utterly lost in her glowing presence.

The vision boarded my chariot and gingerly leaned over to pay the driver. His crooked jaw fell open at the sight of this fabulous female. I swear he lost the rest of his teeth as he foolishly attempted to smile.

Bo Derek had nothing on this girl.

Time stood still.

Life had just begun!

Heaven had opened its gates and let a winged angel descend among us mere mortals.

The gorgeous creature looked toward the back of the bus. She stood there, a model of perfection. Her heavenly face could launch ships crossing uncharted seas, or in this case an old tin can of a bus, which still was no easy task.

She had deep set almond shaped eyes enhancing the beauty of her classically elegant high Asian cheekbones. Her full pink lips suggested a demure but confident manner and glistened with wet sensuality. Her skin was dove cream smooth and reminded me of those little China dolls they sell in the market. Her long jet-black hair lustered with the sheen of a goddess and freely fell to the small of her back, which absolutely drives me crazy.

Long hair gets to us guys, but you already knew that.

Her half smile thrown my way almost knocked me out of my seat. Her perfect white teeth were like the untouched snow on high mountain peaks. Her smile was as radiant as the new day's sun. She was absolutely astonishing.

Then I felt something sharp jab my butt!

The young woman appeared to be only sixteen years old but I was sure she was of age. Or as my buddy Hank would say about her underage, youthful appearance, "Just right!" all the while grinning like a toothy Cheshire cat that just devoured the delicious canary.

The fucking letch!

She wore a light blue, sheer summer dress trimmed at the hem with lace. A black cloth belt pulled tight just beneath her small but adequate supple breasts accentuated her petite figure. Some would say her dress was too short and maybe too tight, but I thought it quite proper in revealing a pair of fantastic curvaceous legs slipped casually into matching blue high heels.

She wore rings of gold that sparkled on her delicate painted fingers. Golden bracelets tinkled on her slender wrists as she moved closer. Simple gold earrings dazzled beneath wistful strands of lovely hair. A thin gold chain clasped to a Buddha locket hugged her thin neck and rested softly in her cleavage.

I was ready to convert right there and then.

"Wow! Where the hell did she come from?" I quietly asked myself.

I quickly turned around, nervous as a whore in church. There were no empty seats except for the one next to me.

"Oh no!" I squeaked.

It was the instantaneous dumb reaction of a married man out on his own trying desperately not to get himself into trouble. I knew something like this was going to happen. I just knew it. Now what?

How in the world does something like this happen to a guy like me? How can I explain this intimate encounter to my dear and loyal wife? How in the hell was I going to make it through the entire trip to Korat? My feeble mind was racing like a clock on steroids.

Then I righted myself, remembering I was still a man. I stopped asking foolish questions and thought out loud, "Oh yeah!"

This angel of the Orient slowly moved her slender body down the aisle while all eyes on the bus turned toward her. Every man and boy-man lusted after the vision before them. Every woman looked upon the image of female perfection in snaring envy. The children stared in wonder at the maiden of Thailand, such beauty still alien to their young eyes.

Even the two caged chickens stopped clucking for a moment in honor of the new passenger. Thank god too, the fucking duck quit quacking as this irresistibly attractive femme fatale walked the aisle closer to my loveseat.

Her elusive scent drifted my way and forcefully grabbed my senses. I felt as if ten thousand blossoming flowers had enveloped over me and transported me to a land never before visited. The gorgeous vision thrilled me with yet another silent smile and an ever so slight nod as she sat down beside me like a whisper moves the wind.

I smiled back and thanked the heavens I was wearing my Hollywood shades to hide the doe-like look in my eyes.

There really was a Buddha!

I scooted over against the window and locked my knees against the confining seat just six inches in front of me. I felt like a friggin' Butterball turkey tied and prepped for the Thanksgiving oven. It was so tight I was jammed in my seat like a Jap in a subway at rush hour. The girl put her sculptured hands on her lap and demurely tidied her tight dress, which reached up just inches from every man's dreams.

Even dirty old married guys like me.

She had a presence to her that I could not explain. Unable to control my male instincts I kept glancing at her long hair, her skin-tight dress caressing every soft curve of her womanhood, the smooth cocoa skin of her incredible arms and sculptured legs. There was the perfumed scent of sensuality floating off her perfect neck and other places I dared not think of.

Or should I dare?

It was as if we were both sitting in the Garden of Eden, the only two souls in the vast universe, waiting to take our first bite of the forbidden fruit and asking for forgiveness later.

I casually wiped beads of perspiration from my pale and nervous forehead as if not a thing in the world was bothering me. In fact, beneath my calm demeanor I was sweating like a stuffed pig the day before Chinese New Year.

This had to be a test, I thought.

"Do you know my wife?" I wanted to ask the sweet little thing pressed against my numb leg. But my mouth was too dry to say anything. My tongue, twisted like a two dollar pretzel, could not work. I couldn't believe I was at a loss for words. I was shy, afraid, stupid. I don't know. All of the above.

"Think man, think!" my brain nudged me on.

Hell, I was a famous movie star and couldn't come up with anything clever to say. I was lost in the moment, petrified, star-struck. How could this be happening? Where are the fucking writers when you need them?

I tried to remember that phrase I taught myself. "How much baht for one hour?" I forgot the Thai words but knew exactly how to say it in my mind. How would she respond?

Do I feel lucky?

What a bad, bad boy I am.

Son-of-a-bitch, I should have studied harder!

This was going to be the longest friggin' ride of my life.

Chapter 13

The young lady's left leg was rubbing against my cargo pants. I caught her looking down with an innocent up-turned smile on her fresh face. Up close she was even more beautiful. Maybe my friend Hank was right in situations like this. Maybe she wanted me.

I could only wish!

My cell phone was bulging out of my lower pocket and I was convinced she felt it hard pressed against her thigh in our confined seating condition. I thought of other bulging things and was certain she had never heard the phrase, "Is that a cell phone in your pocket, or are you just happy to see me?" But for some reason it just naturally popped into my mind.

"Oh no! What if my wife called me?" I mumbled to myself, caught in my own bundle of guilt.

What if she was checking up on me to make sure I wasn't bored at home or out doing something I wasn't supposed to be doing? She didn't even know I had skipped bail. I was left home by myself with lunch money and a new *Sienfeld* DVD set, seasons 1 through 5 with English subtitles. I was supposed to remain in the safety of our home, take my nap, and not drink too much.

If the phone rang there was no legal room between the girl's liquidy smooth thighs and my sweaty white legs for me to retrieve it without the inference of carnal knowledge between two consenting strangers. None that a judge and jury would acquit me of, anyway.

Hell, just my thoughts would be enough to throw me in jail. I'd have to let the phone ring and ring and answer it some other day. Or if I did draw on my manly courage to squeeze my trembling hand down there to grab and caress the phone I'd have to lie like a hooker in a line up to my dear wife. I'm sure she would understand, considering the circumstances.

I'm a bad liar, although I am getting a little better at it. Many years of married life have given me lots of time to practice. That's why I don't play poker with the guys or go out to lunch with Hank any more.

"Yes dear, I'm fine. I watched my show. That Kramer dude is a riot, especially when he speaks Thai. Yes, I got it. Thank you for the lunch money. I decided to take a nice quiet ride on the bus to Korat all by myself. There's nobody with me and I'm being a good boy."

Please don't ring!

Just as I was worrying about my phone and what it was so nervously pressed against I felt another problem emerging.

A very big problem!

That's when Big Slick woke up from his slumber, wondering what all the commotion was. He smelled something delicious, and to my horror I think he was hungry, since to the best of my recollection he hadn't been fed in a while. It was two weeks last Tuesday if my memory serves me correctly.

The twins shook the sleep from their eyes too, scratched their thick beards and nudged their big brother on to find out what was happening next door.

I was instantly reminded of my wayward attitude toward undergarments and immediately hated my French teacher.

Sacre bleu! This was going to be the death of me.

My nemesis had joined the game!

If Big Slick could speak he would have said something like, "Hey you. Yeah you, with the big head. I'm talking to you, you dumb shit. Let me out of here. I've got people to see and places to go. Slicky likey what he sees. You holding out on me, or what? Now let me loose you chicken ass son-of-a-bitch. I got work to do."

But thank god he can't speak, not out loud anyway. Although in too many situations he tends to take charge with the determination of a natural born leader ready to conquer the world. Like Attila the Hun, he uses his almighty power and devious cunning, deaf to the crying pleas of mercy in his relentless pursuit to add more notches to his formidable staff.

If we had the time I could show you the scars. They're hideous!

He's been a real pain in the fucking ass ever since I can remember.

It first began when I was about two years old taking a bath in the kitchen sink with my little sister who wanted to know how the funny looking squirt gun worked. Of course Baby Slick, the show off that he was, just had to show her and took it upon himself to shoot her in the eye. After that our mother made sure we took separate baths. I have a sneaky suspicion that's part of the reason my baby sister became a lesbo.

Then there was my twelfth birthday, when after the cake was gone, the gifts unwrapped, the party was over, and my friends Tommy and Ralphy and Billy had gone home, Slick fell in love with my pillow almost every night.

Even now I hate pillows of any kind!

Fucking disgusting habit!

The most embarrassing moment of my young life, however, was when the whole family went up to Hampton Beach one summer. Of course being thirteen years old I couldn't take my eyes off the pretty girls in their skimpy bikinis strutting their stuff up and down the shore.

Bunch of teasing sluts!

Slick also noticed the cuties and quickly protruded his small head into the outer layer of my loose fitting swimming trunks. Hell, I was walking along the sandy beach like I was advertising a friggin' pup tent. I could have hung oversized beach towels out to dry on the stiff little guy.

And finally, I don't even want to go into the predicaments the little pecker put me through during my first two sophomore years in high school. Hell, it wasn't my fault. I had no idea the perky cheerleader who loved to party and was maybe a little bit drunk, was the chief of police's daughter. Besides, her pom-poms weren't real. But do you think Slick cared?

No fucking way!

Then in the Air Force he finally started to mind his own friggin' business, probably because of the open men's showers, if you know what I mean. That is until our first tour of duty together in the war zone.

That's when all hell broke loose!

Big Slick had developed some sort of death wish and tried to kill himself through over exertion. He was like a friggin' vigilante. He could have taken down an entire female army and ended the war in no time if left on his own. The VC women were lucky he wasn't sent out on a search and destroy mission. Most Monday mornings he found himself at military sick call, along with his other perverted pals, looking for a miracle cure. During our tour we both learned there are some very strange and scary dick rotting diseases in the Far East.

Hey! I told him so, but do you think he'd listen to me. He didn't give a shit!

"You're not the boss of me," he'd remind me and then head to the door in search of a good time. I always had to tag along with him, sort of like a blind chaperon, so neither one of us would get in trouble.

He was a lost cause until we got married, and eventually he slowed down. After that he rarely raised his ugly soldier's head, and even to this day still bears a grudge against me for taking him out of circulation.

So as you can see, I've always had problems with that prick down there.

"Shut the fuck up and take a friggin' nap," I yelled down at him so only he could hear me.

"You too," I snapped at the little ones. The bastard sons-of-a-big prick.

Sometimes Big Slick would win. He was unpredictable in circumstances like this with such a magnificent beauty so near. Other times I would overcome. It was a constant battle and this time I insisted on taking control.

He puffed himself up into this grotesque shape as if he were preparing to attack, to make a lunge at his innocent captured prey sitting beside us, much like a peacock displays its impressive fan of plumage in an attempt to scare off its predators or attract a hot date.

"Fuck you!" I screamed at him once more.

"Blow me!"

"Jerk off, you prick!" I said, as angry as I'd ever been with him.

"Lick my balls!"

"You're a real asshole, you know that?"

"You're a fucking pussy!" Big Slick yelled back.

He was relentless. The smell of victory was way too strong, like an addiction to pure sweet, alluring drugs, so this time I squeezed my knobby knees together, strangling the son-of-a-bitch such that he had no air to breathe and no room to roam. After giving up he finally cooled down and wimped back into his cave to shake it off.

I heard him utter one last word.

"Bitch!"

Today I was the master.

No means no!

Having taken care of business with the three horny intruders I turned to my girlfriend in the blue dress to say something cavalier in Thai. Something nice and poetic, or perhaps a bit romantic. The time had come. I wasn't even going to mention anything about money.

"Sawad…."

Before I could spit out the word she rose from our loveseat to get off the bus, barely giving me a farewell smile. My heart imploded. The angel had left my side. All that remained was a mild scent of her presence and the worn indent of her body on the torn seat beside me.

I was left alone, devastated. The girl of my dreams had simply up and gone away without uttering her sweet good-byes. My plans were shattered. My heart was broken. My lustfulness suspended. How could she so quickly break off such a romance? How could she leave me, hurt me, after all we've been through? How could she do this to me? It was then that I realized lost love is so bittersweet.

By the fortunes of fate, and some help from the damn bus driver who pulled over to let her off at the next stop, I had relinquished my love and passed the test of temptation.

What a good boy am I.

Son-of-a-fucking-bitch!

That's when I felt a little foot kick me in the nuts.

Slick was still pissed off.

"Fuck you!" I said, putting him in his place, pissed off at myself more than at him.

Okay honey. I thought about my understanding wife, you can call me now.

I remembered my camera in one of my pockets but by the time I got my locked knees released the girl in the blue dress had disappeared and the only image I would ever have of her would be in my feeble, deprived, lusting mind.

I'm sure Hank would never believe me.

Chapter 14

A **FEW MORE PASSENGERS** got on my bus, the train wreck to hell. But I didn't really pay much attention to them, or to the rest of the crowd for that matter. I was depressed, lost in my grief, unable to erase the new love of my life from my mind. The entire trip was shot to hell.

We were about halfway to the city by now. I stretched out my legs to the side and rubbed my sore kneecaps. A tingling sensation came back to my feet and I felt dizzy from the blood rushing from my head. I was despondent at how quickly I had lost my fantasy love, how the best things in life are so fleeting.

Then someone sat beside me. I looked at the person and kindly, but half-heartedly said, "Sawadee."

I really wasn't in the mood to talk, but hey, that's what I do.

In my travels I've heard of these kind of people over here in Thailand. Guys who dress up like women and try to pass for the genuine thing. They go all out too. Long flowing hair, painted fake fingernails and fake you-know-whats to show off some cleavage, which everyone knows is a sure sign to snag a guy.

Cleavage absolutely rules!

Full makeup, sexy clothes, sparkly accessories and jewelry, cheap French perfume, loose body movements, a little ass swinging. They come with the whole package.

Well, almost!

Looked and smelled like a girl to me.

"Harro," this person in the next seat addressed me.

A strange look twisted my usually jolly face. Well, I want to be a friendly guy. You know me by now. I like the Thai people. I am beginning to enjoy my visit here. And I sure as hell am easy to get along with. So why in the fuck did this friggin' queer sit next to me?

It was another test, no doubt.

The great Creator is always testing me by putting obstacles in my way or arranging tempting situations to see if I fuck up or do the right thing.

Like when I lost the mortgage payment a few years back on a sure bet at the races but the damn dog stopped chasing the rabbit to take a shit right there on the track. I fibbed and told my understanding wife how I got mugged on the way to the florist. She bought the story but I felt so guilty the next day I got her a rose bush. Later she found the crumpled up betting slip in my pants and gave me holy hell on laundry day.

Sometimes I think the Great One is in cahoots with my all-knowing wife.

I was both repulsed and curious at the same time at the sight of the person next to me.

"Sawadee," is all I said for a second time, nice guy that I am.

Here we go, I thought. He asked me, in pretty damn good English, I might add, "What is yo nam?"

Okay. I was going to be polite, but this wasn't going to be a long-term relationship. I'm straight and not into kinky shit like that. I'm also happily married to a wonderful and precious woman.

"Hank," I told him…or her. My buddy Hank would have gotten a real kick of out of that one.

There was a long moment of silence. I guess I was expected to ask his name too. This is tactful Bob you're seeing now. Be nice Bobby.

"What is yo nam?" I finally asked.

He was glad I asked.

"My nam is Ice," he answered with a nice big smile, thrilled down to his panties that I was showing some interest in him.

"Ice?" I said with a surprised and somewhat confused look. "What kind of fucking Thai name is that? What are you, a friggin' rap star or something?"

Well, I didn't actually say that, but that's what I was thinking.

"That's an unusual Thai name," I said in a strained politically correct voice.

"Yank yo."

"Not on your life, pal." This was getting too weird. I looked around for an empty seat and remembered queer boy had taken the last one.

"Why do yo come to Thailand?" the person asked me, I guessed trying to make conversation or to solicit me. Not interested bub. I ain't switching teams for you or nobody else, no matter how good you look. I have a wife and a girlfriend, you know.

That did it. I wasn't quite sure until that very second. I knew she was a he.

He sounded like Barry White with that deep well of a voice.

"Hey baby, want me stir your drink?" he used to say from across the room. Or, "Let the Love Master get that door for you, honey." That's all jive talk if you ask me. Part of the myth that black guys have a bigger root of life than us regular white men. Strictly hype I tell you.

How do I know? I'll tell you.

I was in the barracks latrine once taking a leak way back in my younger years while serving my country. My good friend Pitts, which is not his real name in order to protect the guilty and to maintain his bogus reputation, was from Philadelphia and was as black as they come.

He was standing at the next urinal holding himself against the wall like we do when we've had too much to drink. I happened to look over in a weak, adolescent moment of my youth and noticed his whizzer was no larger than mine. And voila! Real proof! It's just a bullshit lie that black men continue to push to try to pick up women.

Now I ask you, how in the hell is this friggin' faggot supposed to pick up guys talking like that? I can see it happening in a dark bar late at night after a few bottles of Leaping Deer whiskey or a case of Singha. I mean, even I might fall for such a charade if I were young and stupid and drunk and was lonely in a dark bar very late at night right after pay day not too far from my Air Force base back in early March 1970 right before my twenty first birthday.

These Thai queers look pretty damn good though, in the evening when you're drunk and horny. But hell, they shouldn't say a goddamn word. My advice to them is don't open their damn mouths unless they're ready for business. It's a damn easy giveaway before opening the package. Although I have no doubt that once a deal has been made the poor deceived john, drunk or not, would eventually discover there were too many boys in the same room, if you know what I mean.

One of my unit sergeants got shit ripping drunk back in the seventies. He was enticed by a ravishing female that me and some other subordinate peons set up as his blind date at The Pink Banana, which back then was a popular bar in the red light district of Korat. I even frequented the establishment on several occasions myself and am ashamed to say I got myself into one heck of a jam with a few of the local working girls.

They get so bitchy when you don't have any money.

Anyway, the guy's girlfriend happened to have an Adam's apple as big as a grizzly bear's, but our sergeant was too buzzed to notice, which we had counted on. The next day he transferred out of our unit without even going to sick call or saying goodbye to his old buddies. I sometimes wonder whatever happened to Chucky Baby.

Did I mention he was a real asshole?

Come to think about it, my queer boy sometimes actually sounded more like Barry Manilow, who, if you want to know the truth, I've often wondered about. Come on, have you heard him sing? My boy even looked a little bit like him too. Which reminds me. I need to get the new Manilow CD for my brother-in-law. He likes that kind of gay shit.

I figured I'd better answer the inquisitive freak just to fucking shut him up.

So I told him.

"I came to Thailand to see my girlfriend. She's the pretty one in the blue dress who just got off the bus. You're sitting in her fucking seat!"

I don't think queer boy understood everything I said because he smiled at me and kept talking.

"Where are yo fom?"

I bit my upper lip. To tell you the truth I just about had it with this guy. My typical patient demeanor was wearing thin. What am I, the fucking welcome wagon guide? But I decided to answer him anyway.

"I'm fom the United States. New Jersey, if it's any of your fucking business," I said, just to be safe.

I looked down at his cleavage. Nice small rack. Hey, I couldn't help it. It's a rule. Whenever there's any hint of breasts or cleavage showing a guy has to look. It's not my fault honey, just basic human male biological science. Sort of like a man law.

By now Slick was curled up like a lazy dog sleeping in front of a warm fireplace on a snowy New England night. He opened one eye to see what was happening this time. He took a quick sniff of the pretty queer boy sitting right next to him. Not the least bit interested, Big Slick shook his head in disgust at the fat guy up top and went back to his cozy nap, mumbling sometime under his breath.

"You whore," were the last words he said before dozing off once more.

The boy smiled again. He had nice teeth. Nice shiny long hair too. But I think he finally figured out that he was barking up the wrong tree and he shut the fuck up, then thankfully got off at the next stop.

"So long faggot. Better luck on the return trip," I said to myself.

More people boarded the downtown express.

All of a sudden the bus drastically tilted to one side at such a treacherous angle causing me to think we were going to tip over and scatter short Thai people all over the roadway, not to mention the piles of stinky dead fish.

If we were on a ship I would have donned my life jacket and jumped overboard before the son-of-a-bitching thing rolled starboard into the sea and sank to the bottom drowning two captive chickens with it.

I looked out front and saw Mrs. Sumo, of the diaper wrestling family crowd, haul her monstrous frame up the narrow stairs. The bus driver's beady eyes nearly popped out of his head as he looked at his newest customer. It immediately occurred to me he was calculating the women's fare in poundage, kilos to be exact, and came up with a figure of four times the normal rate, which I thought was quite fair considering the extra fuel and wear and tear his coach would incur.

She banged her way along the aisle, crashing into the poor little Thai passengers on the outside rows with each lumbering step. I felt sorry for their injuries, but hey, that's what they get for sitting in the aisle seats when the fat ones come aboard.

A few of them were slightly maimed by what looked like a herd of elephants all under one tent desperately trying to reach a watering hole. However, most likely the riders would recover from their bruises in a short time, but would no doubt remember where to sit on the next trip.

But one guy nearly lost an arm when Thunder Thighs, attempting to make her way toward the back, turned around sucking in his right forearm clear up to his shoulder blade with her enormous butt cheeks. I'm pretty certain he lost his watch and a bag of roasted peanuts during the encounter.

It wasn't until she had miraculously squeezed past his row until the dangling appendage was finally released with a friggin' disgusting slurping sound as it snapped back into its socket like a toy rubber ball bouncing back to its paddle. The man remained quiet throughout the ordeal and merely looked out the front windshield not wanting to miss his stop. I'm sure the poor guy could never work again, although perhaps he could be a one-armed proctologist, having just gained some valuable mobile experience in that field.

From afar the plump lady eyed the empty seat next to me. She looked like Jabba the Hut, if you've ever seen that movie. A huge squeamish slug, larger than Miss Piggy even, searching for its next meal. She glared at me while licking her chops. I felt like a large Domino's pepperoni pizza with her name on it as she waddled closer and closer.

The slowly advancing broad was one hell of a big mama! King Kong or Godzilla would give way to this monstrous sack of blubber.

"Hey! Aren't there any other fucking empty seats around here?" I cried out. No way was this fat bitch going to sit beside me, or on top of me. Not after what I've been through.

I should have gotten off with my girlfriend.

Before two-ton Louise got to my seat I rose and went to the back of the bus, content in safely standing for the rest of the trip with the trays of shitty smelling foods beneath my feet.

It was better than being flattened to death!

Chapter 15

THE BOULEVARD TRAFFIC WAS getting heavier, the exhaust fumes thicker, the temperature hotter, and more people were crowding onto my bus. All clear signs that we were getting closer to downtown.

Standing in the back holding on to a pole for dear life I was reminded of the fermenting fish and other stinky things shifting around. I checked the bottom of my new sneakers to make sure I hadn't stepped in dog shit. The two chickens in the basket had ended their ruckus and settled down to a steady clucking. I swear one of them was a rooster and, after having his way with the other chicken, was enjoying a well-deserved cigarette break.

What a fucking life roosters have! All the fun and no long term commitment.

By now the bus was stopping about every thirty seconds and kept filling up. There was standing room only and not much of that. I looked around to see if anyone was paying attention to me. But I was already old news.

How quickly they forget their movie idols, bored looks on their faces. You know the look, like when you're with the wife in the grocery store, pushing the friggin' cart like all the other bored to death husbands, hoping to hell your wife will let you buy your favorite ice cream or something.

No respect!

And that's when you have the wicked urge to pass gas just for the fun of it. What else can you do there? Look at fabrics for new living room curtains? Wow! That's loads of fun. They don't let you crack open a beer while you're shopping or sneak open a pack of Oreos, which I think is discriminatory. I see kids eating candy bars in the store all the time.

Hell, if they allowed us men to toss back a few cold ones while shopping there would be more guys willing to go to the store with their wives. That's a guaranteed good-for-the-old-economy absolute fact.

You'd hear more of, "You need any more Tampons, honey? Let's go down to the grocery store." Or, "I think we're almost out of toothpicks, dear. I'll go to Safeway." How about, "Take your time sweetie pie. There's no need to rush. I'll be sitting at one of the picnic tables in the beverage section watching the game with a couple of guys I know. Tell me when you're ready to check out. Okay honey?"

I swear, sales would skyrocket, marriages would grow stronger, male-female relationships become more solid. Family time at the grocers. It would revolutionize going out together. Women's need for shopping, the biggest problem between husbands and wives, besides money and sex, would be completely accommodated, actually encouraged. There would be fewer divorces, fewer arguments, even fewer accusations like, "You never take me out," or "You don't spend enough time with me."

I think I've discovered something here!

So anyway, you're being completely ignored and you go down the bread aisle after you drop a deadly but silent one and look back to see if any poor sap walks into the toxic but invisible cloud.

Farting in public is kind of like fishing. Sometimes you catch one, sometimes you don't, and that's the fun of it. It all depends on the bait, like if you had Mexican food the night before or a bowl of my fabulous wife's award winning, hot as hell, ass tearing chili. If the first toot doesn't work you chamber up another shot and go to the cake mix aisle and try to drop a few old ladies reading the Betty Crocker cake mix boxes.

"Grandma down in aisle seven!"

Any semblance of respect might be gone but at least you can have some self-righteous juvenile male fun.

There must have been a hundred people on the old can at this point. I wondered if the tires would pop, or if the rusted chassis would hold tight, or if the rotted floorboards could bare such a load. The friggin' greedy bastard driving the bus was getting filthy rich at fifteen baht a head and would stop for anyone.

In the back I was getting edged out of my space and decided to do the old bored-husband-shopping-with-the-wife trick where beer is not allowed. I actually learned this technique back when I was about ten years old. My great Uncle Joe, who was a master flatulator, taught all us boys the finer art of fun and tricks with flatulence.

"Here, pull my finger," was his famous but over used line. Of course us kids loved pulling U.J.'s finger. It was the highlight of his visits.

We looked up to Uncle Joe as our in-house hero. He could wipe out a whole donut shop on a Sunday morning with one long, steady, drawn-out blast. Family cookouts were cut short when he was at his raunchiest. Taxi drivers who knew Uncle Joe and his gastric talents refused to pick him up.

He was truly a disgusting pig.

All us kids wanted to be just like him!

I was in church one hot summer day and the pews were crowded with sinners. I was gasping for air in the stuffy holy place and almost passed out. So I purposely let out a little boy fart, which frankly surprised me at its deep, thunderous sound as it hit the wooden bench, ricocheted off the back of the seat, and reverberated throughout the church.

I swear it never sounded that good at home!

At that very moment in my life I knew I was a man.

Even Father Donnelly's sermon to steer us from the ravages of hell was interrupted for a minute or two while the entire congregation had to standby for the odorous smell to pass and the echo to fade away before they could continue being saved. My mother swatted my arm so hard it hurt for a full week. If she was going to be mad at anyone it should've been at her brother Joe for teaching us boys such a disgusting habit.

Back on the bus my stomach was rumbling pretty regularly by this time from the fucking spicy hot rice, the curried chicken, and peppered pork I had eaten the night before. Vinny's suicidal hot wings had nothing on authentic Thai food.

So I thought this was a perfectly good opportunity to share one more of my talents. I could kill two birds with one stone, as it were. Relieve the very uncomfortable pressure percolating inside my upset gut and earn me some more standing space in the back of the bus.

The bus was still rocking and rattling, so when I released the bomb of all bombs no one could hear it. I stood silently, snickering to myself like a fool, as we do at these memorable moments, waiting for it to hit my fellow passengers. It didn't take long before their grotesque facial expressions proved my intended targets had been struck.

My Uncle Joe would have been proud. That's the really fun part, watching your victims' reactions. Seeing them gag like they just swallowed a maggot and suspiciously look at their closest neighbor out of the corners of their eyes. But to be politically correct and not be accused of being a fucking pig myself, I too turned up my nose with a horrid look on my face.

"Who's the fucking stinking asshole here?" I wanted to shout out so no one would even consider blaming the foreigner.

Works all the time!

A bunch of the passengers lifted their flip-flops making sure they hadn't stepped in dog shit. Then they looked down at the piles of fermenting fish on the floor and naturally assumed the market banquet had let loose. The funny thing is they all hovered closer to me trying to escape the rotten smell. I have to say in all honesty, that was probably one of my best performances to date, although it didn't get me the extra space I was after.

Instead I was gradually being forced out of my safety zone from the pressure of new arrivals coming in the front door.

"Hey," I yelled forward, "We're full. Take the next fucking bus." But no one heard me, or understood me. Before I knew it I was hanging out the rear door, one foot on the bottom step and one arm holding a death grip on a splintered railing. The other seven guys hanging out with me simply smiled as if they were thinking, "Isn't this fun, you damn whimpy ass foreigner?"

I smiled and said "Sawadee" to my fellow dare devils as if I did this sort of thing every day and thought nothing of it. "You guys want to do something really friggin' scary?" I wanted to ask them. "Try to buy lunch, hold the pickles, hold the fucking lettuce, at the Burger King across from my office at high noon. Have it your way. Bullshit! Now that takes balls, my friends."

I was losing my grip on the rail as we were nearing our destination. The bus driver kept swerving his overloaded crate toward the curb, forcing me and my surfing buddies to pull in a little closer to avoid smashing into street signs and parked tuk-tuks.

That's how close we got to disaster. We were so close I could have swiped a cold bottle of Pepsi from one of the street vendors. It was getting quite warm, though the breeze on the outside of the bus was actually very refreshing. However, there was a two-baht deposit on the bottle and I didn't have the correct change so I decided against scooping up the cold drink.

I think the driver was just doing it for kicks to see how quick we were. The inside passengers were getting their jollies too watching the show, the bunch of sadistic little brown bastards. All except for Jabba, who was wedged into my old seat so friggin' tightly she couldn't move a flab of fat and would probably need the Jaws of Life to extract her humongous mass from her seat.

Whenever the side of the bus nearly scraped something solid the entire traveling crowd in unison would yell something that sounded like "Ole," as if it was a goddamn bullfight or something. After all, we had already paid our fare, and if the bus lost a few passengers, then fuck 'em. They were close enough to the end of the line anyway.

Finally, thank god, we came to a complete stop.

"Everybody off," someone yelled, or something to that effect. Two Thai men helped me unwrap my white knuckles welded to the railing and I was released to the sidewalk. I smelled something disgusting in the air and at first thought I shit myself, but realized the old lady with the fish had just exited the bus.

I would have gotten down on my knees to kiss the dirty pavement but there were too many witnesses, and as an action super star I had to keep my composure and be cool. So I matter-of-factly thumbed the sign of the cross and stood up like a man.

Chapter 16

Ah, Korat. The second largest city in all of Thailand. The commerce center of the region. The bread basket of the country. Home to nearly a million people. The end of the bus line. The ultimate destination of this sole traveler.

Against all odds I made it!

Situated in the northeastern plains of the country, Korat was the site of large American Army and Air Force bases heavily supporting the war effort during the Vietnam era in conjunction with the Thai military. Lots of the younger GIs, after getting laid here for the first times in their lives, married their Thai sweethearts, moved back to the states when we finally gave up on the war, and eventually wound up back in this very spot, some to visit, others to live permanently.

A few, I'm positive, returned to hide out either from the Army, their ex-wives, or the IRS. Any of which could easily find the deserters by simply hanging out at one of the many local bars during happy hour, or Happee-Happee Time, as it is generally known by the natives.

A few of the expatriates looked like refugees from the hippie town of Bisbee, which is not too far from my home back in Arizona. They sport long dirty ponytails, fucked up goatees, back packs with all of their worldly belongings, and a spaced out look on their wrinkled faces behind the granny glasses. Yep, Bisbee is a regular Woodstock in the desert mountains within ear shot of Old Mexico.

Apparently even the freaks can get a visa.

There's a time tunnel on the road into Old Bisbee, which was a huge copper mining town years earlier, that takes you from present day back to the 1960s. Now it's inhabited by the dropouts from California and other welfare recipients. Groovy, man. Bet they were living here in Thailand for the great weed and plentiful female companionship. Peace, brother. Where are the fucking Twinkees, dude?

There were some soldiers, I knew, who made certain they never came back to this beautiful country, content with shooting off more than their guns while stationed here and leaving their mark throughout the countryside like Johnny-fucking-Appleseed. Some of the guys promised their Thai sweethearts that they would return after the war to take the young girls back to the States, their ticket to paradise.

It hardly ever happened. The cowards forgot to mention they had a wife, four kids, and a dog someplace in Oklahoma and couldn't even find a fucking decent job when they left the military.

Once a fuck up, always a fuck up!

Ah, the ugly American. No wonder most of the world hates us and just wants our money.

The trials and tribulations of war.

Most of what happens in wartime is a horrific nightmare of human brutality, wasteful devastation of untold deaths on and off the battlefield, the tearing apart of families and nations. All vile and destructive events unless you happen to own major stock options in crude oil and futures in copper and brass. Then life is good, damn the torpedoes, full speed ahead and pass the scotch.

But there are some good things that come out of worldwide conflict. Like the great weed that was as easy to buy as a bowl of fried rice from a sidewalk vendor for only five bucks for a gigantic trick-or-treat bag full.

Just kidding honey!

I meant to say, like me finding my dear wife, marrying her, and having a wonderful son and a beautiful daughter together who will be the joys of my life up until the day I keel over.

Now, all these years later here we are, my wife and me, staying in our own small bungalow vacation home not ten miles from where I was once soldiering and fraternizing with the indigenous personnel.

Go figure!

Korat is a spread out, overpopulated, thriving metropolitan area whose economic base is built on the vast stretches of farmland surrounding it, and the unbelievably huge factories that produce plastic ware, electronic components, food products, and consumer goods for Thailand and world markets. I ask you. Where would we be without hand-carved chopsticks and elephant embossed throw pillows?

Many of the outlying farms are small family owned pieces of land that have been passed down from generation to generation, planted with basic crops like rice, sugar cane, peanuts, potatoes, and many varieties of fruit. My wife's family at one time owned a sizeable parcel of fertile farmland, but over the years the younger children have sold it off in pieces, tired of the farmer's life. In return they traded their sweat and toil in the fields for a more regimented sweatshop in the factories.

At any rate the Thai people work hard for a barely sustainable salary. You have to respect them for their unrelenting work ethic and search for a more comfortable life.

The factories, located about every mile or two along the highway that runs into Korat, are massive structures with three to five thousand employees each, mostly young people, who produce great American imports and work for only six or seven dollars a day. Hell, a six-pack of Bud Lite costs more than that. Maybe that's why they drink Chung Beer.

Ah, ain't cheap labor great if we can save a buck on a toaster oven?

The city is over run with merchants, from the little unlit shacks selling garments made in even poorer countries like Cambodia and Laos just across the border, to the mall-like stores that put to shame our fancy shopping centers back home.

Then there are the food vendors. Every friggin' corner, every bus stop, every open spot of a sliver of fucked up sidewalk space is homesteaded by people cooking hundreds of different foods, most ready to eat for a country on the go, and none of which would ever in a thousand years pass a surprise health inspection.

I knew where I wanted to go first.

There was a restaurant about two klicks down the street from the bus stop. It had pretty good food, provided you liked spicy rice and weeds. The place was also relatively clean, and actually had a bathroom. It reminded me of the Golden China Buffet restaurant back home on the older west-side of town, only this place was much cleaner and had a friendlier staff. And it was a favorite hangout for many of the foreigners who called Korat their new home.

It was sort of like a home-boy club, only the boys were from all over the world. My wife and I ate there one day last week when we first came to shop and I was fairly sure I knew how to find it.

I headed down the crowded, uneven sidewalk into the mesmerizing world of merchants. I made certain every one of my cargo pockets and secret compartments were zippered shut, buttoned tight, Velcroed closed, and otherwise completely secured before entering the shopping zone.

I knew anything could happen to a lily white, unaccompanied visitor with no back-up, unable to defend himself from all corners, with a limited handle of the local language, a load of cash in his pockets, a cell phone he didn't know how to use, and no idea of what the fucking Thai word for 'Help' was.

I was aware of the possible dangers lurching ahead of me. I had heard stories of wild teenage gangs mugging innocent foreigners like myself out on their own, beating them up, stealing everything they carried. They'd leave the retched victims with nothing but their underwear in the back alley of a Happee-Happee bar begging for change to high tail it out of town. But I had the goods on them there and was more concerned with the fast talking merchants trying to swindle me out of my precious few bucks.

Then there were the marauding threesomes of pretty queer boys all dolled up roaming the streets, even in the harsh light of midday. These trios of perversion, a few of them who looked like Britney Spears from the waist down, who because of their Barry White voices were unable to score even with the grossly drunk foreigners. They lived a horrible life not knowing which bathroom to use. So in order to make a living they would attack us straight guys, take advantage of our naivete, and do what they did best for only a hundred baht each, which I'm told is quite a bargain.

I adjusted my sunglasses, stood tall like the bad ass hombre that I am, put on my best don't-fuck-with-me-bad-boy face and entered the battlefield.

Chapter 17

AT THE FIRST DAMN street I attempted to cross I forgot these friggin' kamakazee drivers drove on the wrong side of the road. I didn't see him coming around the corner like a bat out of hell. A fucking crazy son-of-a-bitching tuk-tuk driver aimed directly at my feet in the crosswalk, and, barely missing my right toe, went on like a banshee howling something that sounded like, "Almost got you, white boy!"

But I couldn't tell for certain because of the loud clacking noise coming from his Toro engine and the even louder this-bar-will-never-close roar from a configuration of at least eight drunken assholes stuffed into the three-wheeled wagon. What asinine behavior, and it wasn't even noon.

"May the friggin' taxi gods flip your damn toy cab over in the middle of rush hour traffic," I responded in kind.

I wasn't discouraged though, and pressed on, safely making it across the street then meandered through the maze of merchants along the narrow sidewalk. Hundreds of vendors plied their wares. There was clothing of all types, with an unusually large selection of tee shirts and boxer shorts with out-dated popular American slogans like, 'Where's the beef?,' 'I'm with stupid,' and "Speak into the mike,' with a big arrow pointing to the crotch.

The best tee shirt I saw had an air brushed picture of a big penis pulling a large condom over his head with his tiny arms. The caption read, "Give me cover, I'm going in." At first I was going to buy one for Hank, but then I thought I'd save the cash for something better for me. Sorry pal. Walking through the mish mash of merchants was like trolling through the dusty outdoor dirt rows of the K of C's Saturday flea market.

There were tons of fresh foods for sale, much of it prepared on sticks to go, of course. They had hot dogs on a stick, grilled bananas and sweet potatoes on a stick. Fish on a stick. Deep fried bugs like spiders and crickets skewed on a stick. They even had pancakes on a stick. You can't tell me you've ever seen that before. These people had an overwhelming fetish about foods on a stick.

There were lottery merchants with their portable folding tables and large briefcases displaying the lucky numbers. Gold dealers worked the flashy more premium corner stores. Vendors were selling cold drinks like sweetened iced tea and Pepsi in baggies with a straw tied closed by an elastic band. No deposit, no return.

Others were hawking cell phones, fish still flopping in their baskets, and whatever else you were looking for in the market. I couldn't believe the prices on genuine Rolexx watches and Guci handbags.

It was a shopper's delight!

I was especially fascinated with the booths carrying black market DVDs. Some of the movies were still being shown in the theaters back in the States while here I could purchase a copy of new movies for as little as thirty five baht, or about a buck. I bought a Steven Segal flick, one that I had only seen twice, and a new James Bond DVD with that blond guy in it.

There were even slabs of fresh cut pork and beef meat on open air tables, spread eagle chickens skewed on the grill, quail eggs by the kilo, and orange ducks hanging by their limp necks. Fucking squawkers.

I saw rows and rows of whole fruits, and cut up bite sizes iced in handy wrappers for the traveling shoppers. Watermelon and pineapples, oranges and pears, mangos and papaya, mangosteens and persimmons, star fruit and bananas, coconuts and tamarind, jack fruit and tangerines, and the rotten smelling dorian which had such a horrendous stench even the flies avoided it.

I strolled by full pig heads, sans bodies, smiling from their shelves wondering what the fuck happened. And there were buckets of eel-like slimy, slithering creatures, and pails of turtles and snails and crabs and things.

Oh my!

There were also—I'm ready to vomit here—trays of fried and grilled insects for the discerning gourmet in search of a crunchy kind of appetizer with a gooey surprise inside. I quickly walked past piles of cooked crickets and grasshoppers, deep fried scorpions and hairy spiders, steamed ant eggs and—puke—gigantic flying water bugs, aka cockroaches, about four inches long.

Needless to say I wasn't very hungry. One of the bug vendors tried his best to sell me some of his crispy critters with a demonstration of his which probably works for the less squeamish insect shopper.

"Handsome man," he called out to me.

Of course I had to stop.

"For you special price." He stuck his hand into a large vat of freshly steamed water bugs and selected a nice large shiny one. If I were to measure this sucker, which was highly unlikely, from the tip of its antennae to the ends of its back legs this specimen could have qualified to be a licensed tuk-tuk taxi.

Making sure I was watching him so I could learn the technique of chewing a fucking bug, the salesman quickly snapped off the cockroach's head, and lightning fast sucked out its inners like you would suck on a big, juicy, buttery crab leg.

"Ummm! Wery tasty," he laughed, knowing his disgusting behavior was making me sick. Some sort of green sticky slime oozed out the side of his mouth as he continued to enjoy his gross snack. Sadistic bug eating bastard.

"Okay, I'll take a kilo of grasshoppers and half a kilo of those scrumptious ant eggs. I'm having company over tonight. Skip the crickets. The legs get stuck in my teeth. Hey, what the hell, throw in a bag of cockroaches too, the jumbo ones. Let's get crazy."

Yeah right, like that's going to happen. Thanks for the show my friend, but no sale today.

Traveling down the rows of crap I noticed several guys with patches over one of their eyes. At first I thought maybe there was a pirate convention in town but then I realized that was foolish. Thai pirates wear makeup and fake boobs, not eye patches. I thought it was a curious look but disregarded the fashionable trend. I kept moving along and was reminded to always watch my step.

The sidewalks were multi-leveled. They weren't designed that way but over the years they had heaved and cracked and separated into a hazardous maze of hop-scotch panels. Large sections were missing, just gone, as if, oh well. Portions were weakened so poorly it was unsafe to step on them. Thais knew that, regular shoppers avoided them, more astute patrons stepped around them, but stupid foreigners learned about the treacherous Thai sidewalk system the hard way.

I kept wondering why a number of shoppers were veering around certain spots until I saw a visitor, easily identified by his black socks and sandals and camera hanging around his fat neck, fall into a large unmarked hole. It was as if he were swallowed by the gods of the underground for failing to watch his step and for his impure thoughts toward the hordes of young and pure Thai girls wearing short skirts walking directly ahead of him.

Everyone simply went around the disgraced foreigner who got exactly what he deserved, as if he were simply part of the city's fix-the-pothole-problem. I looked down to make sure it wasn't anyone I knew and made certain to steer clear of the cave in. Then I tried, for safety purposes, to forget about the ladies in front of me and only think about baseball for the rest of my trip.

There were hundreds of small clothing stores hidden off the walkway and too many day vendors hawking their threads to anyone who came within shouting distance. Being a diehard baseball fan I stopped to look at an assortment of baseball caps hanging from the rafters of an old building.

Cool!

They had official major league shirts and caps. I love baseball, especially my old team from Bean Town and the amazing young players in Arizona. For only twenty five baht each I picked up a Boston Red Socks hat and a purple Dimondbacks cap as great souvenirs

Yeah, I know what you're thinking. I thought the very same thing myself when I first saw them. Since they were such good deals I bought two more for my buddies back home.

I was surprised to see a lot of the clothing had American logos and designs on them. Most prevalent were silk-screened pictures of Disney characters. Mickey, Goofy, Plato, and the gang. Thai people must have a thing for those guys. There were also a lot of Playboy logos on shirts and pants and bras and panties. I kind of liked some of them and wondered if I could find a copy of this month's magazine someplace.

Wouldn't it be funny if the Disney crew and the Hefner playmates got together over here to open a theme park of sorts? Mickey and Goofy could hook up with Tiffany and Amber while old man Hef was taking his nap. There'd be some hell of amusement rides. Then Minnie and Cinderella would break in on the action and cause a major ruckus. It'd be loads of good clean family fun with several million or so ready fans.

I saw a couple more people with those strange black patches over their eyes and wondered what the hell was going on. I kept walking, side stepping the holes beneath me and avoiding the low hanging awning poles. Many of the merchandise hangers were held down by poles that were only about five feet high, a safe distance for most Thai people, but a sure fired trap for many unknowing foreigners and tall Oriental bastards.

Up ahead I saw a rather tall man go down like a hundred-kilo sack of rice just as he was entering a fried banana tent. He had fallen victim to a canvas covered pole swinging about eye level that had some sort of thirty year old advertisement for the 1978 Southeast Asian Games, sponsored by Singha, the 'King of Thai beer since 1933.'

I ran to his aid and attempted to help the guy up while the other shoppers were politely stepping over him. He yelled something obscene to me, in Russian I think, as if I was to blame for his dumb ass maneuver. So I dropped the ungrateful bastard back into his hole and went on my merry way. The damn Russians never did appreciate our help. He eventually shook off his wound, pulled himself out of the pit, and held a hand over his injured eye.

Fortunately for him the fried banana vendor also had some nice eye patches in black for sale next to his grill. The fat jerk was happy to buy one and be on his way.

Chapter 18

I stopped for a moment in front of a jewelry store that sold mostly Thai gold. It was one of many such establishments along the walkways that carried the genuine, one hundred percent, solid through and through glimmering soft metal of the ages.

There were at least eight young Thai ladies working the counters and assisting customers. I was about to stop in to say hello to the girls, but I really had no business browsing in a gold shop. I had no money to speak of and no intention to purchase any gold, but I thought it was about time to begin taking more pictures of Thailand's beauties.

"Sawadee pooying swai," I said to three very attractive female clerks who were straightening out the sparkling rings and shimmering necklaces in the open glass cases. The girls simultaneously looked up at me, obviously thrilled down to their Playboy panties to see me enter their shop and hear a handsome foreigner speak almost perfect Thai.

"You are indeed three very lovely ladies," I repeated in English just in case they had trouble with my Bostonian accent. I bet you thought I was bullshitting you about my ability to speak Thai. A wise man never reveals all of his talents until they're needed.

Always keep them guessing!

Each one of the lovelies returned a polite bow toward me, no doubt anticipating a large sale from such a worldly gentleman. "You like gold, handsome man?" one of the cuties asked me.

Oh, they are so good!

"Well, hell yes I like gold," I answered.

The one in the middle gently took my left hand to try some fabulous gold rings on my fingers. The sight of my wedding ring choking my ring finger didn't deter her one bit. Maybe she wasn't going to hook a well-to-do husband today but she sure in hell was determined to sell him something.

"This one wery nice," she complimented the spectacular piece of jewelry while she slipped it over my thick knuckle as if it were part of her wedding ceremony. Up close she was even prettier and her slender hands were oh so soft and comforting.

I lifted my bejeweled hand and admired the intricately carved ring. It was wery beautiful. It was also wery expensive. I felt bad leading the girl on, getting her innocent hopes up, teasing her with the anticipation of a whopping sale. So I did what any decent, up front, selfless, courteous gentleman customer would do.

"Let me see that one over there," I said, pointing at an even larger and much more expensive ring embedded with diamonds. A huge happy smile shined on her pretty face. The second ring was quite radiant. I felt like a rich gigolo flush with the luxuries of wealth and the dedicated attention of gorgeous women. Fanciful thoughts danced in my mind as I was shamelessly being flaunted upon, most likely because of the 50,000 baht price tag hanging from my ring finger.

While I had the full attention of the trio sisters I decided to ask them one more question.

"Do you mind if I take a picture of you three?" I figured since the girls were hyped up on a potentially huge sale they would do just about anything for me. A long time ago I learned the secret of success. Always ask for what you want when the other person is near their peak of happiness. Like when you buy your wife a new car. It just about guarantees some good loving.

Works every time!

The sweeties hugged each other behind the counter as I took a terrific snapshot of them for my calendar. Later I'd worry about which month they would dress up. But for now I was enjoying their carefree giddiness and every minute of their affectionate display.

"Thank you ladies," I said as I returned the ring. "I really don't see anything I care for today," I told them, bursting their visions of a fabulous sale. They bowed back at me in thankful honor of my brief but unsuccessful patronage just as another sucker with a big black camera hanging around his neck entered the store.

Next!

Everywhere I went there were tons of workers attending buyers in their shops. The level of customer service was beyond belief and, I must say, very nice to look at.

There was none of this, "I'll be right with you as soon as I get off the phone with my boyfriend," kind of shitty service we're used to back home.

Here a clerk will stick with you until you buy or scram. I mean, you could spend hours with one of them, asking to see this and that, taking their picture, trying things on, or inquiring about the prices. And then you finally tell them that you're just browsing but thanks for their time. They don't give you the you're-a-real-friggin'-asshole-for-wasting-two-goddamn-hours-of-my-time look.

I enjoyed watching the constant and varied traffic going up and down the busy thoroughfare. The number of motorbikes still amazed me. Some carried tall boxes of strapped-down merchandise back to their places of business, or cases of bottled water, or bundles of flowers, or pottery. Others breezed by with three or four youngsters on board heading to school. Still more transported a single passenger on the back of their one-man motorcycle taxi cab.

How friggin' cool is that?

They'd park wherever there was a foot of open space, between the tuk-tuks and samlors waiting for a fare. Large trucks filled with various products or cases of beer moved smoothly along the road barely missing the smaller traffic. Huge buses, single and double-deckers, rolled along as if there was all the space in the world in the crowded street. Small pick-up type buses slipped through the ever-constant moving maze dropping off and picking up travelers heading to different parts of the city.

Food vendors on foot cautiously pushed their carts laden with cold fruits and fried meat snacks and flavored drinks and ice cream through the downtown area, hugging the side of the road as best they could, but still having every right to be part of the traffic. Thousands of cars and king-cabs or full size pick-up trucks, mostly new and mostly Japanese imports, flooded the byways as everything was in motion and commerce thrived in this growing city.

It was a friggin' circus out here!

The one thing I did notice was that everyone smiled.

Whether you bought from them or passed them by, the people warmly greeted you, or smiled, or nodded a friendly gesture. They smiled when you entered their store or shop and they smiled when you left. They smiled when you bought their food or merely looked it over. They smiled when they passed you on the street or squeezed by you amongst the crowded sidewalk vendors. They smiled at you while laying down in their tuk-tuks or reclined on their parked motorbikes. They smiled when they ate and when they waited to cross the road.

The Thai people smiled all the time.

The country is rightfully known as 'The Land of a Thousand Smiles.' I can understand why.

But what I wanted to know was why in the hell were these people always so friggin' happy. They worked outrageous hours that would knock most Americans flat on their asses. The Thais made very little money for their efforts, enough to get by but not nearly enough to splurge. They survived the damn hot and sticky and sometimes downright miserable weather.

I had to find out why they were always smiling.

It would be nice to be happy most of the time, I thought, like these people all around me. The majority of people I know back home aren't really happy. They simply trudge through their monotonous and boring lives, hating their jobs, tolerating their families, begrudging their neighbors, regretting choices not taken. The smiles are few and infrequent, and not so genuine.

One day I'd like to be able to contently smile like these Thai people do everyday.

Moving closer to my intended destination I kept looking at the diverse merchandise along my path, still making sure I wasn't going to fall into a sidewalk crevice. I should have known better but I made the stupid mistake of not watching where my head was going. I walked right into one of those low hanging awning poles and got knocked down to the ground like a drunken soldier on R & R. I shook off the hit and found myself at the bottom of an open sewer pipe, a big friggin' bump on my forehead.

No eye patch for me, but it hurt like a son-of-a-bitch!

A big burly guy walked by me and looked down with an air of contempt. "Fucking Americans," he said without bothering to help me.

"Fucking Russians," I yelled back from the hole as he limped away. "Commie bastards." I didn't need his damn help.

I was ready to brave the traffic and cross the road toward the restaurant I was in search of. I waited at the final curb and paid particular attention to the crazy tuk-tuk drivers careening around the corner. There was an old lady squatting on the sidewalk selling smelly dried fish to a stream of hungry customers. She looked up at me and peered over her wide-brimmed straw hat. To my astonishment she was the same woman on the bus with the stinking cargo that got blamed for my odorous mishap.

How in the hell could she have traveled this far and set up shop before I even got here? I asked myself in disbelief. She saw the recognition in my eyes, and seeing that I was flying solo for a change blew me a soft kiss through her toothless mouth and blinked her eyes like she was the fresh catch of the day.

"Not even if you were eighty years younger and had all your teeth, honey," I said beneath my breath. I quickly turned away and stepped into the street, which despite the risk, was a much safer place to be, knowing how damn fast that woman could move.

I made it across the street and entered a large common area of a park before I crossed a second road to my favorite restaurant. There were lots of people seating inside and I noticed several white guys nursing their drinks.

I was safe at last and with my own kind.

Chapter 19

The eatery was located on one of the busiest traffic corners in the city. Its wrap-around front plate glass windows offered a great close up view of the constant hustle and bustle on the outside.

In the joint there were about twenty-five wooden tables with brightly colored plastic chairs arranged haphazardly around them. At a quick glance I saw at least half of the tables were occupied with diners having an early lunch or beginning to drink their day away.

There was a long counter with several gas burners where three women were cooking large pots of rice and woks of stir-fired noodles. Smelly soups and spicy concoctions simmered away emitting clouds of treacherous steam into the dining area. Two slightly over weight kitchen helpers were chopping up piles of greens and veggies. Dangling chickens and slabs of pork hung from hooks above the stoves.

Lunch at the Olive Garden was never like this.

Some of the patrons, with their light skin, were no doubt foreigners. As I said before, this is one of their hangouts. It's a club of sorts for the motley crew of aging men enjoying the front row view of women in their short skirts and tight jeans strolling by.

Some of the diners were no doubt long retired soldiers living on their more than sufficient pensions that accorded them a comfortable living in a simple way. Others were rather ugly old guys looking for love and could actually find it here for a reasonable price. Several were simply early drinkers getting a head start on washing away their sorrows and the heat of the day.

I loved this friggin' place!

A few of the men had pretty little Thai ladies sitting next to them. Wives, girlfriends, or short time companions. Maybe even all of the above, which believe it or not, is a fairly common and somewhat accepted practice here.

The fucking lucky scoundrels!

The strong aromas of spicy soups, jasmine rice, fried noodles, dried fish, and shrimp paste condiments filled the restaurant air. Just grilled Thai hot peppers that would cause the Scoville scale to burst into flames made several diners inside drop to the floor in a futile attempt to escape the pungent burning sensation. Passersby began coughing their brains out as the powerfully searing odor rose from the gas stovetop near the entranceway. The air was filled with the smell of mixed pleasures and cutting spices.

I didn't really feel like eating at the moment.

The establishment sat across from the most famous monument in all of Korat and the northeast region of Thailand. A large statue dominated the well-maintained park and outdoor forum with marble-like pavings. It was built and preserved as a tribute to the great lady-warrior Thao Surannaree, the Princess of Nakornratchasima, or Korat as it is more commonly called. She had saved the region of this country from marauding invaders determined to control and dominant the land of these free peoples.

The great statue was placed there to honor the city's heroine, who with her courageous army successfully turned back the vile outsiders. Even now, some hundreds of years after the long and great battle, small portions of the old fort which she and her followers defended still stand next to the monument in the center of this grateful and modern city.

I sat at an empty table along the front windows with a perfect view of the park and memorial across the way. A middle-aged lady wearing an orange apron came over and waited for my order. It was too early to eat, plus I was still heaving from the caustic grilled peppers, so I asked for a bottle of water with some ice. She knew this because I pointed at a bottle of water and a bucket of ice at another table.

She smiled and turned to get my drink probably thinking to herself, "When will these damn foreigners ever get it?"

My stomach was still feeling a bit queasy from last night's spicy feast and the ice water eased the rumbling. I figured I had plenty of time and would eat lunch later. But for now I only wanted to just sit down, relax, enjoy the breeze blowing through the open restaurant, watch my fellow diners crawl back onto their plastic chairs wiping their tearing eyes, and enjoy the sights all around me.

Hell, I was on my private little vacation and was in no rush.

Hundreds and hundreds of Thais surrounded the monument to honor the great Princess. They had come from far away by bus and pick-up truck and car and foot to give thanks to their ancient savior. They had come from down the road and across the street to pray and give worship.

The people bought flower wreaths and single blossoms from stalls set up along the perimeter to leave at the foot of the great statue. They knelt before the idol and gave silent prayer in appreciation of their lives and their heritage preserved by this god-like woman of centuries past. They burned incense in reverence to the one who had assured them, in their very simple lives, of their uniquely Thai culture.

In droves the devout believers kept coming to honor their heroine and themselves. Even people driving their motorbikes or cars and trucks naturally put their hands together for a brief second while passing by the monument. Others simply hit their horns for one short beep in recognition of their heroine.

I sipped my water and watched the gathered groups of people at the steps of their holy place. Even from a distance I could see the humility in their faces and the unconstrained love and pure adoration in their expressions. I had a sense of being uncomfortable sweep over me as I observed the procession of believers. I had the feeling that I was watching a secret ritual reserved for their eyes only. I felt like I was eavesdropping at a place I shouldn't be.

I was awestruck and curious.

I was seeing something that occurred every day here in the middle of this third world city which reminded me that I was indeed a stranger, an outsider who could never understand how the people before me acknowledged their roots and cause for being.

To tell you the truth, I was envious.

These Thai people had someone to worship. Not a god, but a true hero.

I had a Cy Young award winning baseball pitcher and a president who I really didn't care for too much. That was the miserable extent of my heroes. In America we have movie celebrities and sports superstars who we worship and love. We have politicians and performers who are somewhat respected and periodically supported.

All fluff, no substance. But we have no real heroes. They're all gone. We have no one we truly revere. There is no one left deserving of our uninhibited love and adoration.

What a fucking sad predicament!

Gone are the John Waynes and the Ted Williamses and the JFKs. There are no more Harry Trumans or Red Skeltons or General Pattons or Louis Armstrongs.

Instead we idolize big screen actors who help tear apart the moral fiber of our great nation. We worship millionaire sports celebrities who themselves only worship their own multi-million dollar contracts, having converted the games into mere business arrangements. We have allowed our governing agents to feed at the civic trough and work their own final agenda with complete disregard for their constituents.

Where in the hell have all the heroes gone?

"Where have you gone Joe DiMaggio, our nation turns its lonely eyes to you?" Simon and Garfunkle once sang. When I was a boy I used to look up to some high profile guys who were really good men. They had earned my respect. In my innocence I had admired them. My biggest hero was my dad who was truly a great man. But he's gone too. I wanted to be like him when I grew up. Now there is no one to look up to.

Sadly, we have become a country without good old fashion role models, and a nation without such heroes is a sorry state.

I respect the Thais for what they believe in out in the open. They revere their heroes. They love their long reigning king and the royal family. As a people they stick together in their basic and natural beliefs. They are proud patriots of their country, faults and all. For these things they believe in I think they are better off.

In all seriousness I have caught a small glimpse of why the people of this country seem to be always happy. They certainly do have something in their daily lives to be smiling about.

Chapter 20

Okay, enough of the history lesson and the soap boxing.

Back to the movie!

I looked around the restaurant and nodded toward two light skinned, blond headed fellow foreigners sitting a couple of tables away. They were up wind from the kitchen and appeared to be safe from the aerodynamic pepper particles. The guys were drinking beer together, enjoying an A.M. brew between two friends.

Apparently they had been here awhile, having already knocked off several tall bottles of the heavenly ale. So from where I was sitting they appeared to be okay. A couple of older guys hanging around, socializing, drinking beer, enjoying a great day in a tropical paradise. They couldn't be all that bad.

This was definitely my kind of place.

Except it was still morning, not quite noon yet, way too early to be drinking. It was unusual and intolerable behavior where I come from, except on Sunday mornings when everyone else is at church, and on vacation days where it really doesn't matter what time in the day you start drinking.

According to some people, drinking so early in the day is totally outrageous behavior, which shows a complete lack of self-control. It is completely irresponsible for grown men with families and mortgages and good jobs, burdened with a thousand other adult responsibilities, to be toasting the day away in selfish disregard for things that absolutely had to be done. It is a complete waste of precious time and hard earned money, and tears men away from more productive endeavors. Alcohol is the evil spirit that ruins men, destroys families, invokes confrontations, even starts wars.

It's the devil's doing!

Or so I've been told nearly every fucking day of my married life, to include my vacation days. Too bad drinking doesn't cause deafness.

The two drinking buddies nodded back my way and tipped their glasses in a friendly salute. It was obvious they weren't married and didn't have to live by the same restrictive rules as us committed men do.

Lucky fuckers!

The short, stocky, curly haired guy called over to me in a slightly inebriated tone, "Hello, how are you?"

Well, he spoke pretty good English, though with a rather thick accent, so I was ready to strike up a conversation. I liked meeting new people. I liked to discover different ways of life. I liked to learn more about the world. It was part of my outgoing curious nature, my strong thirst for knowledge, my search for new friends who enjoyed the very same things I did.

It was the perfect opportunity to initiate a scheme I have always wanted to try. The Chuck Norris thing on the bus was just practice. Sure, I faked out most of the passengers, even though my efforts in disguise weren't nearly up to par. Those morning riders were easy. They were simple, unsophisticated, low-income city bus travelers who wouldn't know the difference between Sylvester Stallone and Sylvester the Puddie Cat.

A smile here, a nod there, a convincing attitude that suggested otherwise. That was child's play. This time I would go into full character, no holds barred.

I was about to have some fun. I was going to be someone other than myself. I could be anyone I wanted to be. Hell, no one knew me here. Not a soul knew a single thing about me. They didn't know where I came from, what I did for a living, what kind of fun-loving guy I was, how much I earned. No one in Korat even knew my real name and it wasn't going to be Hank.

That's for damn sure!

So, with a quick snap of my fingers I could instantly and magically become someone else. I could turn into a person I never met before. He could be real or just a figment of my whacked out imagination. Old Bob Swift could be rich or famous, preferably both if I had my druthers. He could be ivy-league educated or royally refined. He could be adorably charming or statesman-like charismatic.

Anything I'm not I could become!

I could be a man I might like to be in an alternate world, if such things were possible. Like in Rod Serling's *Twilight Zone,* I could be the alter ego of myself from a far away planet. A reversed or mirrored image, whatever I choose. A clone of someone remarkably heroic or devilishly evil. I could be someone I would enjoy having a friendly conversation with and maybe shoot the shit over a couple of cold ones. I could talk about pressing worldly issues, high finance mergers and acquisitions, theories concerning the universe.

I could discuss more mundane matters, like should you put mustard or ketchup on your hotdog, or what is the perfect temperature to serve a cold beer, or even more important, what's the best way to turn on a women.

And while we're on that subject, I could find out where the hell the G-spot is.

These things and more are possible if one can only dream and believe in them. Let me show you.

Snap!

The old boring couch potato, senior desk jockey nearing a formidable retirement from some obscure little town in the mountains who is here on vacation trying to act cool was gone.

Vanished!

Banished to his safe and steady and predictable existence back home. Relegated to his four hours of watching idiotic television shows every evening. Left alone with nothing but his remote control, *TV Guide*, and *Sports Illustrated.* Sent back into his lackluster life where nothing really matters and even less happens. B.S. was forgotten in his passionless existence.

Poof!

Voila! A new me showed up in his place!

It was deliciously naughty and hellishly exhilarating.

Hey, come on!

Don't tell me the same feeling has never crossed your mind. Haven't you ever thought about being someone else? Putting on a mask? Hiding behind a new persona? Putting on the Ritz? Fucking with strangers?

Bullshit!

You're a damn liar if you tell me you haven't!

Haven't you ever wished you could be that cool guy in school that everyone liked? Or didn't you ever want to be the popular jock that all the girls were dying to date? Or perhaps it would be nice to be the tall dark handsome celebrity surrounded by millions of fans?

Wouldn't it be great for a change to be the rich guy who could afford all the luxuries and fantasies imaginable and spread the wealth amongst your loved ones and friends, enjoying life to the max?

What would it be like if for once you were the life of the party, the comic who could bring an audience to tears, the author whose words inspired, the prophet revealing the secret of life?

How would you feel if you were the hero in the crowd, the leader of the silent and meek, the benefactor of the oppressed? Wouldn't it be terrific if you could fix all the wrongs, or create fantastic time-saving devices, or invent the next super fuel, or discover sought after cures?

Fucking A it would!

Well, this was my chance. My one opportunity to enter into what I dubbed, "Operation, Blue Beard."

Chapter 21

I had briefly tested my plan on the bus as the action star Chuck Norris. With my stylish shades, my keen brilliant smile, and my don't-mess-with-me attitude I had pulled it off and fooled the spectators. I must say they were dazzled by my performance and at the time I wasn't even in full character. But Chuck Norris was old news, well out of today's limelight. He was too easy. I wanted to be more.

It felt good not to be me!

Shit!

I should have gone into Blue Beard mode with my girlfriend. Why in the hell didn't I think of that then? It was the perfect opportunity. I could have been a contender. I could have been the hero in the white hat walking off into the sunset with the girl. Why is it you always think of the good things to say when it's too late?

Happens every friggin' time!

I could have snagged my love in the blue dress with the smooth, suave, debonair, and irresistible moves of a Cary Grant or a George Clooney with his quirky smile. I could have made her laugh with cheap bus humor, which as you know, almost always works. I could have made her say "Yes darling," with sensitive poetry spanning the language of love. I even could have gotten lucky with a deep and sincere look into her beautiful eyes, communicating through unspoken words bringing us together.

"You make my toes curl," I should have told her. Or, "Wild thing, you make my heart sing." How irresistible is that? There's no damn way she would have left me after that. Or maybe I should have said, in a Latino accent, "You want to meet my little friend?"

No, that would be too forward.

How about, "Voulez vous coucher avec moi?" I'm pretty damn sure that would have done it. Sealed the deal as they say. There's no way she could have turned down such an offer. It's French too!

But noooo!

I wasn't thinking straight. I had battles on two fronts. I was fighting both my good-guy conscience and Big Slick all at once. Good cop, bad cop. Nice stable family man, and worked up, angry prick. The angel of righteousness sat on one shoulder whispering in my ear trying to keep me from temptation, and the fucking little diabolical devil was on the other shoulder prodding me with his sharp pronged pitchfork and hedonistic promises to go for the score.

What a fucking dilemma!

Opportunity knocks but once, and I was too enchanted with the women's beauty and exquisite presence to think intelligently. Or maybe I was just too stupid. So, distraught and torn in different directions I didn't have enough sense at the time to put on the charm, to be in role, to be anyone but me. Miserable, old me. And now she's gone.

Then he shows up in the restaurant. The new me.

"Howdy partner," he politely responded to the guys at the table drinking their beer and trying to be friendly. "Doing just fine I reckon, thank ya kindly. Just stopped in to cool off the old dogs and wet my whistle. Damn hot out there. Hotter than a hound dog in heat surrounded by a bunch of wet bitches, if you know what I mean."

The foreigners turned their eyes my way trying to figure out what the fuck this hombre was talking about.

"My name is Hans," the short one said. "This is Gretel," he introduced his tall, lanky fair-skinned friend who showed too many teeth. They both raised their nearly empty beer mugs my way in a half ass toast.

Sounded right suspicious to Jack, but what the fuck did he care if they were using phony names. Maybe even fake accents. They could have been from Old Bisbee for all Jack knew.

"Nice to metcha," Jack said, as he tipped the edge of his imaginary hat toward his compadres.

"Vee are from Switzerland on holiday here," the skinny guy said. This one sounded and acted a bit feminine. Jack noticed he also was wearing a fanny pack. Ball-less wonder.

"No shit? Ain't that up there near France and Germany?" Jack asked, knowing full well that Switzerland was closer to Italy. He wanted to see if these guys were being straight with him. That's a trick of the trade. Ask them a question you already know the answer to and see if they fuck up.

The foreigner sucked down his beer and poured the last of the liter bottle into his and his buddy's glasses filled with ice. Yeah, you heard me. Most places over here serve their bottled beer warm, warmer than elephant's piss. So you have to drink it over ice that costs extra.

That's plain wrong!

I mean, charging extra for ice.

"Ah...yah!" he said, with a slight hesitation in his voice revealing his dishonesty. Jack knew these guys were phonies but he decided to play along for the hell of it. He wanted to see where this charade would take him.

"Oh hell, where are my manners? My daddy would kick me in the ass for being so inhospitable," Jack said. "I'm Jack Corner. Crazy Jack to all my friends. You can call me CJ or Crazy Jack or just Jack. It don't make no shit to me."

The two men smiled, happy to have met a real American. Like many from the Old World they were enthralled with the mystic and lore of the American wild west.

"I'm from Montana," Jack bragged. "That's in the great United States of America, you know. Real purty country up there. Got me a nice spread, 'bout a hundred sections or so of grasslands right along the foothills of the great Rockies. I reckon it's probably bigger than your Switzerland, judging on my expert knowledge of world geography."

"You must be a cowboy," one of the European men asked, a sense of girlish thrill in his voice.

"Yep. Through and through. Was born with a hat on my brim, boots on these feet, and a burr up my ass." Jack slapped the top of his knee, cracking up at his own remark. "Ha. That's a bit of cowboy humor."

The Euro boys looked at one another as if they were thinking. "These fucking American cowboys are strange dudes indeed. Nothing like the John Wayne movies we're used to seeing."

"Run 'bout two hundred horses back on the ranch. Purtiest animals ever walked the face of this green earth. Stallions, pintos, mustangs, some mixed breed too. Dumb as rocks, though. Have a herd of beef cattle too. They fill up the whole valley from one side to 'nother. I come over here to get away from it all for awhile. The smell was getting to me, all them horses and quality steers. Then I come to learn the smell ain't much different over here, especially on the damn bus. More like low tide than piles of ripe manure. Same shit though."

The short guy had a big goofy smile on his sunburned face. He looked thrilled at the cowboy's remarks. "Queers? You got queers on your ranch?" Maybe he had the wrong impression about genuine American cowboys.

"Queers?" Jack yelled, shocked at such a question. "Hell no, partner! Where'd the fuck you'd get that idea? I got horses and close to ten thousand head of cattle, steers. You know, beef on the hoof."

Crazy Jack was getting pissed off even being asked such a foolhardy question. He was beginning to not like these Euro trash beer drinkers posing as friendly tourists.

"Ain't got a goddamn queer on the whole ranch. It ain't no brokeback-fucking-mountain. That's for damn sure. No-sir-ree-bob! We don't tolerate that kind of behavior back home. I seen it going on here, all disguised and made up to look like the real thing. They call themselves gay now, but there ain't nothing fucking gay 'bout it. S'pose that kind of thing's fine and dandy to the city folks and tourists round here but back in Montana it ain't cottoned to. Not one fucking bit."

Suddenly becoming uneasy, the two foreigners cringed at the cowpoke's remarks.

Then Crazy Jack remembered.

"There was this one time, though, back a few years when some queer boy got to working with the ranch hands. I guess one thing led to 'nother and the boys and me done caught him and my foreman doing the nasty in the hay barn, right in front of my favorite horse. Fucking disgusting behavior if you ask me."

The two beer drinkers' eyes widened.

"Yep, they were going at it like two dogs fighting over a greasy ham bone. So I fired the foreman and let him skiddaddle before I told his wife, who happened to be the ranch cook. Ugliest bitch I ever did see, but that's no excuse for such carrying on. Then me and a couple of the men threw the queer boy into the branding corral, still naked as a jay bird and crying like a school girl. We pressed him into the ground, snorting away like the spring calves do when they're roped and held tight ready for the iron. I pulled that ruby red bar out of the fire and spit on it to make sure it was blister hot," Jack continued.

"That poor queer boy was hollering and screaming like a two-dollar whore being mounted by my prized stud bull. By golly, I jammed that branding iron against his lily white ass cheek and heard it hissing and searing that boy's bottom. The young fella nearly passed out, for heaven's sake."

CJ was enjoying his story telling and noticed the two men were fidgeting as they asked their server for the bill. They had heard enough.

"We done sent that cry baby queer boy back to where he belongs, back to San Francisco. That's where they all live, you know. Even have girl queers there. Now what in the hell is with that? Never heard of such a thing. I hear they even have queer parades and get married to each other, and do all sorts of unnatural things. You can bet your bottom dollar he shows his bare ass with the nice crisp CJR branded to it, not a single one of his friends up that a way will ever dare step foot on the Crazy Jack Ranch again. And that's the way I want it."

Jack looked up from his sneakers and saw the two guys had left the restaurant. They were running down the street as fast as they could, each holding one another's hand.

"Well I'll be a son-of-a-bitch," Crazy Jack said aloud with a wicked cowboy smirk on his weathered face.

"Fucking queers!" was his final comment.

Chapter 22

Crazy Jack the queer hating rancher from Montana had left the restaurant too without anyone noticing, leaving me alone sipping my ice water and wondering where the hell he had come from.

What a friggin' rush!

This Blue Beard shit was turning into loads of fun. There were forty-seven minutes left to go before noon according to the chicken clock on the wall. I controlled myself and promised I would wait before cracking open the first room temperature bottle of elephant piss. The only question I had to deal with after looking around the place was who in the hell would step up next.

Not another minute had passed before I found out.

"I say there good chap," a tall skinny man with a terrible haircut came over to my table. "Wonder if you would be so kind as to let me borrow some napkins? I seem to be all out."

If his sissy ass accent was any sort of clue, he had to be from Old England where the men talk like girls in finishing school and dress like stuck-up prep school students trying to suck up to the headmaster. How in the hell did they ever conquer most of the world way back when? Being so sickly polite and all. Especially when they insisted on wearing those bright red uniforms, which made excellent targets and basically screamed, "Shoot here!"

That kind of hoity-toity behavior doesn't work with me pal. Go get yourself some cool cargo pants, a loud vacation shirt, and a little less pretentious attitude. Oh, by the way, lose the friggin' high top plaid dress socks with the leather sandals. They tend to clash and scream out, "Here I am, a complete flipping idiot straight off the tour bus ready for the picking."

I'm always willing to share, so I flared my nose, pulled myself out of a comfortable slouch, took a deep breath and said, "Jolly good," mirroring the asshole. That's what they say you should do. When you first meet someone new you should act like him, speak like him, stare like him, and fold your hands like him. This kind of mimicking will put the stranger at ease and make him like and trust you.

Kind of like having a conversation with a monkey.

I think this psychobabble is a bunch of horse shit if you ask me, and my days of mirroring this English dude had quickly come to an end.

I handed him the roll of toilet paper from my table. Yes, I said TP. Napkins on a roll. The tissue that keeps on giving. Two-ply and Charmin soft. Works well for going in and coming out. An all-purpose wipe. That's what many eating establishments use here. Hey, saves on ordering different inventory. And let's face it. It's just paper!

I think he was surprised and, frankly offended at my generosity.

"I can't use this!" he said, indignant at such a preposterous and totally uncivilized practice. No wonder this place is a member of the third world, he probably thought. Apparently proper Englishmen don't use shit paper to wipe their mouths. Go figure.

"Well, fuck it," I told him. "Use your friggin' sleeve."

Then I tore off a long roll of the TP and blew my nose like those old guys in the next booth do in restaurants that really gross you out while you're eating your salad with blue cheese dressing. A truly disgusting habit, by the way. Uncivilized too. I bet they do that in England!

So Mr. Prim and Proper returned to his table near mine and for some reason he still wanted to be friendly. I was about to blow my nose again and stare at the treasure left in my tissue when he started.

"You must be from America my good man."

Now I'm confused. Was that a fucking question that required an answer or was it a statement that, because of the smart-ass manner in which he presented it, demanded a little acknowledgment from my jolly good size-ten American foot up his tight British ass?

Be nice Bob, I had to remind myself. Not having the patience to count to ten, I counted to three. I never really liked snooty Englishmen except for that butler Higgins on *Magnum P.I.* I thought maybe I should simply ignore the uptight Anglo-Saxon and maybe he'd go away and bother someone else.

Or was it Mr. Blue Beard's turn again?

"You got it pal," I said, ready to fuck with this insolent red coat. Hey buddy, we whooped your ass back when you had a king and queen and a bunch of inbred faggy dukes and princes while you were trying to gouge us on the price of tea. You mess with the Colonies and you lose. Now who's the superpower?

I so wanted to put this guy in his place.

"Name's Chicken Eddie, from Nevada, just outside of Las Vegas," the newest member of my traveling troupe told him. "Ever been there?"

He pulled up his Oxford socks. "Can't say that I have."

Chicken Eddie just couldn't shake off this guy's air of indignity no matter how hard he tried.

"Well, you either have or you haven't," Eddie tried to straighten him out.

Fucking double talker!

"Never had the pleasure," the tall bastard answered.

"Well, you don't know what you're missing. It's a great town. You can get anything you want in Sin City. Just ask the taxi driver and it's yours," Eddie told him. "Tell him Chicken Eddie sent you. He'll take care of you."

"Is that so?"

"Yeah, that's so. Hey pal. What's your name?"

"Bradley. Bradley Butterfield. From Cambridge, Great Britain."

Now, why in the hell didn't that surprise Eddie? Is there anyone over there called Mike or Joe or Charlie? Hey you snooty bastard. I'm from Cambridge too. The new one near Boston. Maybe we're related.

Go suck on that one Uncle Bradley!

"Dear fellow. That is quite an unusual name. Chicken Eddie. How did you come by it, my young man?"

This guy was just full of nosy questions.

He asked, so Chicken Eddie was going to tell him.

"I run a chicken ranch in Clark County, outside of the Vegas city limits," Eddie said. "Damn good recession-proof business. Always busy through good times and bad. Never had a down year. I have so many customers I need to expand. That's why I'm here. Do a little looking around, hire some more help, something different, you know, to increase my business."

"Chicken certainly has become more popular ever since the mad cow disease and the concern about high cholesterol and fat in red meat," the Brit added.

"What in the fuck are you talking about pal? What fucking chickens and cow disease and red meat? I'm talking about pure pink meat. You know. Nookie. The stuff that every man craves. No cholesterol, just honest to goodness delicious pleasure."

It was obvious the Englishman was taken aback and was stuck on the street word 'nookie.'

Chicken Eddie saw that he had to explain more to this clueless chump.

"A whore house, you shit head," Eddie shook his head at the imbecile. "A pussy farm. A place for men to get laid without worrying about the M word. A den of pleasure. Are you getting any of this?"

"My goodness. I wasn't aware they had such farms or ranches or whatever you call them," the good chap from across the pond said utterly flustered and somewhat embarrassed by what he was hearing.

"Yeah right pal. Like you don't have them where you're from."

"I never…"

"Yeah, like hell you never. What, do you guys just stick your dick in a pencil sharpener and write about getting laid?"

This guy was such a prude Eddie wanted to lay it on real thick so the dandy could go home and tell fish tales about the outlandish behavior of American men and their chicken ranches in the middle of the Nevada desert.

Before Eddie pressed on he called the server girl over. It was ten minutes before noon, but fuck it, he needed a beer right now. These Brits and queers can drive a man to drink.

"Don't forget the ice sweetheart."

He wondered why the goddamn English all had bad teeth. "Get your fucking teeth fixed," he mumbled to himself. You people have that damn socialized medicine over there where you get taxed out the ass so you can have free medical. Use the fucking dental plan why don't you.

The girl delivered a tall bottle of warm Singha and a water glass filled with ice cubes.

"I have forty pros working for me twenty-four hours a day. Up to sixty on the weekends and when the really big conventions come to town. Like when the lawyers fly in for a long weekend or when the Amway group shows up or even when the Southern Baptists arrive in droves. Bunch of kinky holy bastards if you ask me. Anyway, I'm over here looking for some more recruits. The American taste is shifting from straight vanilla toward hot salsa and sweat and sour, if you know what I mean. Lots of beautiful women over here. A man has to keep up with the trends to stay competitive," Eddie explained the basic facts of his enterprise.

Apparently Mr. Bradley Butterfield had heard enough from Mr. Chicken Eddie. Insulted by the perverted American's remarks the Englishman got up from his seat and headed to the bathroom. Eddie was about to tell him to take the roll of napkins with him since the bathrooms don't come with TP.

"Fuck him!" Eddie said to himself while pouring more beer over his melting ice. "He'll find out soon enough."

Chapter 23

WITH TWO OF MY recent alter egos taking a well-deserved break I decided to kick back and relax.

I wanted to congratulate them both for their terrific performances and how they ran off the irritating foreigners. Crazy Jack and Chicken Eddie were two hell of a guys and I would really like to hang with them. Maybe have a few beers with my new buddies and just shoot the shit, you know, like regular guys do.

I was drinking my iced beer like a native and ordered a second. After a while I was getting a bit of a buzz from the strong brew and went to the bathroom to take a leak. There I saw Bradley the Brit squatting in a door-less stall still looking for some shit paper.

"I say there old chap. Would you be so kind as to hand me some toilet tissue?" the snooty bastard asked me.

"Sorry bub, all I have are napkins," I told him as I left the restroom.

What a fucking pathetic sight!

The restaurant was quickly filling up as the lunch crowd moved in. Businessmen with their clients, university students from several of the local colleges, a family or two with their young children, a few more foreigners. Just about every table was occupied, the cooks and servers were busy, and the flies were loving it.

I held steady at my solo table watching the mass of people going back and forth. The young ladies were out in large groups prancing along in their stylish school uniforms of knee length black skirts and tight white blouses. They looked like studious playgirls.

Reminded me of one of those adult movies, *Sophomore Spring Break, Part Two,* I rented last summer when my lovely wife was out with her girlfriends.

What a parade!

Maybe I could get a job teaching English at one of the local community schools. I could instruct the young girls on proper Bostonian English and help them privately after school with their studies. Oh, what I could teach these innocent lasses. But somehow I'd have to sneak out of the house nearly everyday to perform such a noble duty. My fabulous wife would probably wonder where the hell I was all day and why I was skipping my daily afternoon naps.

The street view was like a constant runway of gorgeous models showing off their assets to the staring eyes of at least twenty old foreign guys squinting through the plate glass windows. I felt as if I was in a theater watching a daytime fashion show and deciding which one to put my bid on. The cookie jar was full.

I placed my digital camera on the table facing the street.

Through the window I kept clicking off shots of the beautiful Thai females as they strolled by unaware they were being digitized for posterity. And of course, for my buddy Hank.

Hey pal, I look out for my friends!

I almost felt like a stalker with the stealth Sony. I swear, if I had a baht for every cutie walking pass me I would be a very wealthy man inside of an hour. I thought about putting together that picture calendar, each day splashed with a photo of one of these natural beauties.

Hell, maybe I really will do that. My precious wife has always encouraged me to develop a hobby. I was in my element thoroughly enjoying the show even if the beer was watered down and not quite cold enough.

I couldn't help but notice a huge white dude sitting at the far side of the joint. He was one ugly motherfucker, probably close to three hundred pounds, or 136.3 kilos, depending on who was looking at him. His barrel belly appeared to have swallowed an entire keg of beer, including the keg. He had on one those wide striped don't-I-look-stupid suspenders over his tank top shirt that failed to hide any of his thickness or ape-like body hair.

He was one hairy bastard. The Bigfoot of Thailand. Sort of looked like an extreme Rogaine experiment gone wrong. Clumps of bushy armpit hair protruded out over the sides of his chest like muskrats peering around corners.

I wanted to say, "Hey you fucking hairy goon, why don't you go get one of those full body wax jobs and join the human race." But I kept my opinion to myself since he was such a huge bastard, and because I really don't like to judge people.

He was a disgusting human being and could have easily earned a part in one of those *Planet of the Apes* movies, sans monkey makeup. I wanted to turn away, but I couldn't. It was like when you try to turn your eyes from the gruesome scene of a bloody accident on the highway or a deformed performing carnival freak, but you just can't stop yourself from staring. The worse thing about him, however, was that he was drinking warm Singha straight from the bottle.

That was a sure sign that he was fucked up!

With the side view I had he looked like a brown bear all covered with tuffs of fur growing from every part of his skin. From a distance I'd bet he was from Bulgaria or one of those places where they looked like that.

I felt sorry for the small Thai lady sitting with him. She forced a weak smile whenever he put his bottle down and said something to her, nuzzling her ear with his bearded snout. I could see her cringe whenever the gorilla stoked her strapless back with his hairy paw in a simian-like attempt at fondling her abundant breasts.

She wasn't the best looker in town but nevertheless she was probably thinking, "How in the hell did I end up with this beast? No more blind dates for me. I'm gonna kill my boyfriend for setting this gig up. And here I am pretending he's handsome and fun to be with when he looks like that Sasquatch dude from America and smells like dead fish. He gets on top of me one more time I'm dead. All this for ten lousy bucks? I need to get out of here."

I felt her pain and knew what she was thinking and totally agreed with the poor girl. Hell, I'd give her ten bucks just to save her life, because that's the kind of guy I am. But I'm down to my last ten dollars and change myself sweetie, so you're on your own. Hey, go to the bathroom. There's someone in there who could use your help and is not as gross looking. Oh, and take a roll of napkins with you.

Good luck kid!

After snapping tons of secret pictures I was about to leave, having seen enough of the window show and the side attractions inside, when a gentleman wearing what appeared to be jungle safari clothes stepped in and sat at the cleared table beside me. The first thing I noticed was his khaki cargo pants.

Ah, a comrade!

"G'day mate!" he addressed me with a big tanned smile. "Another scorcher out there, by critchy."

"Hello," I said, having already chosen my next Blue Beard character. This was getting easier.

He ordered a tall Aussie beer from the counter girl, but through head shakes and hand signals discovered they didn't carry it. Then he asked for a cold Dinko but again came the shoulder shrugs and hands in the air.

"Crimy, what kind 'o god forsaken pub it this?" he said to no one in particular.

It was obvious he didn't know a word of Thai and I thought about helping him out, you know, with my feel for the language and all, but then I figured he'd have to learn on his own.

Just like I did!

He looked around and saw I was drinking some sort of beer from a water glass filled with ice cubes and shook his head in disbelief. Then, eyeing the rest of the odd balls in the place, he saw the big furry guy filling his gullet.

"Oh, chickie," he called the girl again. "I'll have what that bear over there is drinking." He pointed to the large ball of hair still waiting for his girlfriend to come back from the toilet.

"Make it two, sweets. I'll be here for a bit. It's fuckin' hot out there. Hotter than a week old skinned gater in the back country."

He seemed like a nice enough fellow, plus I've heard the Australians where a bunch of fun and rowdy blokes, like the great crocodile hunter Steve Irwin, god bless his soul, and Crocodile Dundee. Oh yeah, and there's Mad Max, my favorite, who later on became Mel Gibson the movie star.

I extended my hand over the table.

"Rich Diamond here, from the good old U. S. of A."

"Name's Jaimie, mate. Jaimie Crock they call me. On account that I hunt crocks and other critters in the wild back in the far country. Mumbo snakes, spiked lizards, razor boars, and the dangerous Aussie frog. Spit your fuckin' eye out from ten meters away, it will. But the crocks, mate, they're the worse. Mean hungry bastards they are. Once got caught by a bull crock. Must have been twelve meters long from head to tail. I got too close to the river's edge and he pulled me under by my leg. Nearly tore it off, he did. Twisted and rolled until the son-of-a-bitch thought he finished me off. That is until I grabbed hold of his upper jaw and yanked it all the way to the spines on its back and broke his fuckin' grip."

"Sounds dangerous," Diamond said, not believing a friggin' word out of the Aussie's mouth.

"Not if you know what you're doing. A Yank, aye? Good blokes, you Yanks. Always there when you're needed. Never get the damn credit you deserve. What the bloody hell you doing here mate?" he asked, already finishing his first bottle of warm beer.

"Looking for gold my friend. I'm a precious metals and gems investor. Gold, silver, valuable stones. Diamonds, of course," Rich answered with a hardy chuckle.

"That so?" The Crockman answered. "We got some of the finest opal fields down my way, mate. World known prettiest fire opal stones ever come out of the ground. Back home a guy can walk out his door to take a whiz and sure enough he'll spray off color. Polished chunks of raw opal brighter than the noon sun. Blind your fuckin' eyes out if you look straight at 'em. You can scoop up handfuls of the Australian beauties just about anywhere you look. Why I've seen farmers fill up their wheelbarrows with opal rock just trying to clear their fields for planting."

Rich Diamond knew right off he had met his match. This was fun shit. Jaimie Crock. Yeah, right. More like Jaimie Crock Full of Shit.

But Rich liked this guy. There was sort of a kindred spirit about him. Two bull-shitters trying to out bullshit the other. Story tellers passing tall tales, trying to get one up on the other. After all, it was legendary that Australians had a natural instinct to lie, connive, rape, pillage, and steal.

It was in their blood!

Chapter 24

IT'S A WELL-KNOWN DOCUMENTED fact that the people living Down Under are nothing but a bunch of convicts, undeniable traits of their devious and despicable behavior passed down from generation to generation.

Not that they're bad people, they just have convict genes running through every one of them. Can't be faulted for that. It's just a part of their hereditary make up.

Like red hair or freckles or webbed feet!

Rich Diamond knew the historical facts about the land and its people, just as he knew everything there was to know about precious stones. You see, way back in the 1800s when the British Empire was run by kings who took no shit from their subjects, the Royal Court got rid of most of the lowlifes who hung around the island state stealing things, jumping other guys' old ladies, and causing trouble in general.

The king came up with a clever solution to handle the increasing number of trouble makers. All the dungeons were full, the prisons were over crowded, Ireland was already occupied by tribes of no good drunks, the Scots were just plain anti-social, and just about every Department of Corrections motel had either been booked solid for the next fifty years or were being converted into a chain of Comfort Inns for the tourists.

They had to do something with the growing number of cons.

So, having conquered or stolen many parts of the known world in the name of the Throne, the Brits decided to convert one of their largest recently acquired territories into a huge penal colony for all the guilty, drunken rabble rousers locked up back in Camelot.

Australia seemed to be the perfect island resort they were looking for since it was very large and surrounded by water so none of the inmates could swim back to the British Isles. It was also relatively cheap to ship the undesirables there since it was only a one-way trip, non-refundable.

Any son-of-a-British-bitch who looked at the king cock-eyed, or merely spread rumors that the leader of the empire was banging someone other than the queen—which who could blame him if you ever saw the pig-ugly queens back then—was immediately put in leg irons and handed a boarding pass to the Great Aussie Isle of Leisure.

The Crown and its PR people made the place sound terrific!

The state had put out a super promotional campaign extolling the wonders of the Outback. The exotic plant life, the unique variety of animals and creatures, like giant rabbits with pockets in their bellies, and friendly lizards that lived in the clear cool waterways throughout the land. They described the vast warm stretches of sand like inland beaches for that endless summer vacation and the cute wild dingo dogs that just loved to play with the curious newcomers.

Australia sounded like heaven on earth with an all expenses paid trip by ocean liner, a warm getaway far from the gloomy, miserable, wet homeland empire. It got to the point where all the prisons were being emptied and their residents lined up for the trip of a life time.

Hordes of no good scoundrels crowded the docks hoping for an open berth with a view on the next voyage. It got so bad that honest and worthy citizens, becoming sick and tired of the gloomy, miserable, wet homeland climate, began breaking the law just to get a free seat to paradise.

The Royal family even offered a comprehensive dental plan to any naturalized citizen, kind of like the one that we're ready to have back in the States if the Democrats have their way. How could the people turn down such a tempting offer? I know you think I'm making this shit up, but it's all true. Every last word. I read the whole thing in a history book back in college, "True Myths of the British Empire."

Yep, fleets of His Royal Majesty ships headed into Australian ports loaded with merrymakers and singles looking for more than just a good time. The lucky tourists would be shuffled off board onto shuttle boats taking them to their new home. Reveling in their good fortune the passengers yelled and shouted at the vast crowds of welcomers on shore who were throwing coconuts and sticks and boomerangs at their arriving cousins.

The inmates on land were also screaming and shouting and waving hysterically. "Go back! Go back you stupid son-of-a-bitches!" they yelled. "It's a trap. They lied to you. They lied to all of us, the royal bastards. Turn around, mates. It's not a paradise, it's a fuckin' prison, by cricky!"

The hooting and hollering was so loud neither side could hear what the other was saying. Revelry filled the warm, humid air. It was a festive party atmosphere.

The new inmates, loaded down with their snorkels and beach-blankets, their coolers and sunscreen lotions, their fold out beach chairs and colorful umbrellas, were dumped off just short of the beaches. The shuttle boats quickly turned about and headed back to the waiting ships before the duped vacationers figured out that the whole thing was a fucking scam.

So that's the honest to god's truth about Australia and its indigenous population of seasoned criminals and misfits. Maybe that's why we Americans like the blokes so much.

"Yep," Rich Diamond continued talking to the Aussie. "Come to check out the opals they dig out up north near the Burma border. Heard they're as big as pigeon eggs. Come out of the earth already shaped and polished to a high fire just waiting to be set. The miners have to wear asbestos gloves on account the stones are so full of natural sun fire they'll burn right through their hands."

"That so?" the croc hunter said, a strong sense of suspicion showing on his sun-drenched face. These damn Americans are a bunch of liars and revolutionaries, he reminded himself. Always getting themselves into some sort of confrontation and then asking us for help. Need to be bailed out all the time. Them arrogant, rich bastards think they're the chosen ones. That's what they think. Nothing but a whole country of drug dealing, business cheating, corrupt no-good convicts. That's what they all are.

The American kept talking.

"The rubies they harvest down south grow on trees so I'm told, like spring leaves hanging from the branches. Old growth teak trees sprout right through the precious veins and carry the deepest red stones you'll ever see up with them as they grow and spread. Why, it's like picking ripe plump cherries from the branches."

"Sounds right peculiar to me," Jaimie remarked.

Fuckin' lying Yanks!

"Come to see the gold too," Diamond said. "There's too much of it over here. Every one wears gold, even the poor people. They sell it on every street corner. Why, it's so abundant the fishermen use it to weigh down their lines. They paste hundred percent pure gold flakes on their national statues and holy sites. Even babies wear it around their ankles, their arms, necks and ears. I want to smuggle…I mean buy some of this Thai gold and take it back home."

"Damn right," Jaimie Crock said, tilting his third bottle of Singha toward the American precious metals investor in his cargo pants and white Converse sneakers. "I haven't seen this much gold since old Leroy's mouth was sewn up and laid to rest," he cracked.

It was getting time to move on. There was lots more to see and do in Korat. Rich paid his tab and said so long to the Crockman, two lying sons-of-a-bitches sharing bogus tales and neither believing a damn word of the other.

It wasn't much different than Wednesday night at the American Legion.

I stepped out of the restaurant followed by my entourage of interesting characters as the Aussie was rubbing sun tan lotion on his face and forearms. He then opened his brightly colored beach umbrella before going out into the sun. Two tall foreigners, both with black eye patches strapped to their faces, moved in and took over my abandoned table.

Dumb sons-of-a-bitches!

Chapter 25

I WANTED TO HEAD to the other side of town where there was more shopping and interesting places to see. If I remembered correctly from the time I had visited with my dear and loving wife the week before, I had to catch a certain bus. But instead, I decided to walk along the main boulevard and mingle more with the natives.

Before I even left the front of the restaurant I encountered a strange little man who shuffled along the sidewalk next to me. He had a crooked smile with crooked teeth and wore old baggy clothes that seemed too heavy for the stifling hot weather. He didn't appear to be functioning at full gear, if you know what I mean, a few sips short of a full bottle of beer.

The odd fellow looked like he was jobless and homeless. He reminded me of that fair weather loser who stands at the entrance road near the corner of Wal-Mart with a hand-painted sign that reads, "Homeless and jobless. Will work for beer. God bless you." At least he was honest about it. This poor fellow following me even had his worn out flip-flops on the wrong feet.

Either that or his feet were really fucked up!

I thought of Hank's brother crushing cans. At least he had a job.

So I tried to stay well in front of this miscreant, figuring he was another pesky, starving, down on his luck peasant hoping to score a few baht from a kindly gentleman. He spoke some gibberish to me and I quickly said "No!" loud enough so he could understand me and I moved on. Then it occurred to me that he might be a pickpocket or something like that, trying to befriend me while all the time planning on stealing my money or camera.

Maybe my sneakers!

Even with his two feet going in different directions he managed to stick with me.

"Go get a fucking job. Go crush cans or something," I told him with a smile while trying to maintain a safe distance from him. He smelled worse than that shit load of dead, dried fish I kept running into.

Finally I stopped and turned toward him and said, "Hey you lowlife bastard. You think you're going to steal from me. No fucking way my friend. I know your type. Sweet smile, trying to bond with me, make me drop my guard. I ain't falling for it buster. I've been around."

The guy, who must have been close to eighty, stared back at me for the longest time as if he was at the end of his rope.

He probably was thinking, "Hey you dip shit foreigner. I don't understand a fucking word you're saying. I don't need your cheap shit. Look at the way you're dressed. You ought to be ashamed of yourself. Cargo shorts, a shirt with a big elephant on it, some cheap ass Converse sneakers. All you need now is a camera hanging around your neck to let us know you're a lousy tourist. And look at those god awful white legs of yours. Cover those blinding things up before someone gets into an accident from the damn glare. Representing your country that way. Bunch of arrogant Americans. You all think you're the chosen ones, don't you?"

His sad eyes made me feel a bit guilty.

Here I was in my good clothes, some cash in my pocket, in good health, both feet going straight. I was being selfish. He was a human being asking for help, a bowl of rice maybe, perhaps some soup to restore his strength and give him back a little of his lost dignity.

Is that asking for too much? I thought.

I pulled out a twenty-baht note from one of my pockets and handed it to the good man, hoping that the small offering would get him through another day until some other generous soul came upon him. He took the money with both hands displaying a tattered face of genuine gratitude as if he had been saved by the most glorious philanthropist there ever was. I felt at peace deep inside having shared my good fortune, reconfirming one more time what a great and caring man I was.

The beggar left me and hobbled away toward a row of street vendors selling simple foods and drinks. He pocketed the generous gift and thought to himself. "What a goddamn fucking cheapskate American, stiffing me with a lousy twenty. What the fuck does he expect me to buy with that? A friggin' bowl of rice or soup? I need twice this to buy a beer. Ten times at least to get laid. Big shit rich foreigner has nearly ten bucks in his pocket and drops some change on me. That should buy you a ticket to your heaven, asshole."

I walked further down the road knowing I had done a good deed for the day. The old man crossed the busy street behind me, thinking to himself that he must find a better section of sidewalk to work, as he slipped on my brand new Hollywood sunglasses.

It was getting hotter, the blazing sun high in the sky, and my stomach was still feeling a bit upset. I decided to stop at one of those hole-in-the-wall kitchens to eat something before I reached downtown. The lunchtime traffic was louder and heavier than before and people were crowding the open diners.

I loved watching the motorbikes pass by with young Thai ladies wearing short skirts sitting side saddle on the back seats as if it was no big deal. They sat there glued to the bikes while they were driven in and around traffic, feet dangling an inch or two above the speeding pavement. It was as if they were Velcroed to their seats without the slightest concern of falling off. Not to mention it was a very sexy looking ride.

Maybe I should get me one of those motorbikes, I thought.

On the sidewalk people were selling small birds in straw cages to be released as a sign of forthcoming good luck. Yeah, good luck for the vendor. Forty baht and five minutes later the friggin' homing pigeons come right back to their roost waiting for another sucker. I have plenty of good luck going on in my life pal.

Puppies in boxes begged the passing pedestrians with their cute crying eyes to be picked up and taken home before the Korean meat wagon came along. Oh, sorry. They don't do that anymore. Ah…ha!

There were trinkets and shiny souvenirs, carved wooden elephants, rolls of Thai silk cloth, and silk scarves and dresses, imitation Gucci and Dior purses, all fifteen percent off. Even more of a discount for the foreigners as I soon found out if you showed a twinge of interest.

"Hey handsome man," one vendor turned to me. "Come in my store. Almost free for you. I give you special deal." The closer I got to my final destination the better the merchants' English became. There were hundreds of street vendors selling shoes and makeup and hats and sunglasses. I stopped to check out Safari hats, but decided to save my money for other things down the road.

Then I remembered!

"Hey, where the fuck are my sunglasses?" I yelled out after discovering my empty shirt pocket.

"Son-of-a-bitch! Fucking Aussie convict!" I knew I shouldn't have trusted that lying island bastard.

I kept walking through the crowd, pissed off at my loss.

There were cell phones. Thousands, tens of thousands, millions. Everywhere I looked people were buying and selling cell phones. Everyone I saw carried a cell phone. Bus drivers were on their phones. School kids had them in little pouches. Vendors talked into theirs as they sold their merchandise. Kitchen cooks spoke into them while they stir fried. Shoppers worked their way through the massive throngs of bargain hunters, most all of them with a phone stuck to their ears.

What the hell did these people have to talk about all day?

The women in their tight dresses and even tighter blouses carried on conversations while they wiggled along. Motorcycle riders used their cells as they weaved in and of traffic. On the ride into town I even saw a farmer in the middle of a rice field mouthing something into his phone. What the hell did he need a phone for? Was he ordering Chinese take-out? Checking on the weather? Talking to his girlfriend?

It was obvious in some ways people in this third world country were way ahead of us more advanced nations.

I pulled into a dark little place to eat. I guess you could call it a restaurant. There was a dilapidated sign hanging outside that looked like it read, 'Soup Barn.' There was a propane gas cook-top, a couple of pots boiling away, some tables and small plastic chairs. A typical street-side diner offering the basics for lunch.

I pointed at something simmering in one of the pots and the lady knew what I wanted to order. I sat down and in a matter of minutes my lunch in a bowl was set in front of me. From the condiment server on the table I swatted away the flock of flies and scooped up a little of this and a little of that. Sugar, hot pepper flakes, vinegar, crushed peanuts, smelly fish sauce, all standard Thai spices, and sprinkled the items into my bowl.

The soup smelled good. It had a bit of a zing to it, but all Thai food tasted better with some spiciness. I picked up a pair of fairly clean chopsticks so as not to look too out of place with the other diners. The noodles were long slippery suckers making it a challenge to grab with two fucking pieces of wood. It was like trying to catch a fish with oversized slick canoe oars.

"Hey, people, that's why we have forks, you know. What the fuck, over. Yeah right, you try eating spaghetti with candlesticks," I mumbled away to no one in particular.

I was about to sharpen the ends of the sticks against the concrete table so I could stab the stringy pasta bastards and skewer the few tiny chunks of grisly beef-like meat, but decided it wasn't cool to destroy the silverware.

The peppers were getting hotter and hotter with each additional swallow. I started to suck in air to cool off my burning tongue. My forehead began to sweat in a futile attempt to release the heat. My entire body was turning into a raging fireball. I asked for a bottle of warm water. What else! That's when I saw something kind of bobbing in my half-eaten bowl of spicy soup.

I remembered another Thai phrase I had taught myself.

"What the fuck is that?" I screamed as loud as my seared mouth would allow. The old lady cook took her sweet fucking time coming over to my table, looked at my food, and said something that sounded like 'cow's heart,' which is exactly what it looked like. The big blob of blood brown squishy guts surfaced among my noodles like a bludgeoned cow taking a bath in a dirty watering hole.

There was no friggin' way I could eat this crap. I gulped down my water, paid the old sadistic broad her thirty baht, and got the hell out of there, making sure to never recommend that joint to any of my friends.

The cook calmly cleared the table, dumped my leftovers back into the big pot and thought to herself, "Another fucking food critic from America. What do they think this is, Jack in the Box? Hey, you asked for the heart soup, dumb shit. Who do they think they are, the chosen ones?"

My mouth was still burning and my tongue was numb from the pain, like when the dentist's needle slips and injects novocain into my tongue instead of the gum. I was starting to talk funny and drool leaked from my swollen lips like a sloppy retard. Oh..sorry! Like an unfortunate mentally challenged citizen. Finally the blistering sensation went away and a sense of feeling returned to my face.

I turned toward my intended destination when I heard a loud, rumbling, clanking noise on the opposite side of the street that caught my attention. A large tow truck was hauling a disabled city bus. It looked kind of familiar. Blue and white and barely held together. Yep. It was the bus I had ridden into town on, finally going to the bone yard where it belonged.

As it passed closer I saw what had killed it. There was a huge gapping hole on the outside, about halfway down its beat up body. It looked as if a giant can opener had been used to pry open its rusted tin siding. Like an explosion from within had torn through it leaving nothing but sharp jagged edges mushrooming out. Three complete bench seats had been yanked out of the coach in a valiant attempt to save poor Jabba's life.

Hello!

Didn't I warn somebody the fat bitch was going to get stuck?

Chapter 26

The afternoon heat was becoming a bit too much for me to keep walking on the sunny side of the street.

My mouth still had remnants of pepper bits that kept popping off bursts of flaming spurts of fire. My stomach began to growl uncontrollably and percolate more than before. What made matters even more urgent, the soup d'jour was trying to work its way through the winding wasteland tunnel.

Okay. I had to take a wicked shit, and it wasn't going to wait very long.

That was for damn sure!

I was in unknown territory, strange land that I'd never stepped foot in before. I was in a desperate search for a nice, modern, clean restroom with a private stall and a locking door, and was far from any innocent bystanders' ear shot. A sense of panic began to overtake my normally calm and rational manner. Each consecutive step I took produced more painful cramps, an ugly sloshing churning sound, a sense of time rapidly running short.

For some reason most of the little eating places on the street didn't have bathrooms. How'd they get away with that? What about hand-washing? Don't they have posters for that? Where the hell is a Shell gas station when you really need one? Now my stomach was getting ready to heave. Both ends were ready to open up.

Up ahead I saw what looked like a public toilet on a corner near a bus station. I knew it was a rest room because it had a sign that read 'Public Toilet.' I raced toward it, tightening my butt cheeks with only one thing in mind.

I hoped they had some toilet paper!

Have you ever noticed that the closer you get to a shitter the worse you have to go? I've often wondered if it's sheer anticipation? Or could it be something deeper, a phenomena yet unexplained by science. Anyway, I was just about in tears ready to burst a gasket as I entered the restroom.

To my painful surprise there was a bent over old man sitting at a makeshift table in front of the inner doors leading to both the men's and women's sides. A handmade sign sat on his table and he had a plastic basket with a bunch of loose change in it. I've heard of this devious tactic set up in public toilets, though this was my first personal encounter with it.

The sign was crudely scribbled in both Thai and English. It indicated a charge for use of the restrooms.

OMG!

Who in the fuck thought this one up? Some entrepreneurial liberal who needed more government funds so they could build a summer retreat? Maybe the city needed the cash to fix the goddamn sidewalks.

A shit tax!

It was simply undignified charging to use the bathroom. What if you had no money, only large bills, no time for change? What then? Where is the humanity in such a practice?

The first thought I had was that the money man was a fake. Instead of trying to make an honest baht cooking and selling food or collecting aluminum cans, maybe he incorporated his own little enterprise by posing as a bonafide tax collector of sorts and was freelancing his way to riches by charging on the waste management side. But I guess I really didn't have the privilege of arguing at a time like this. Sometimes you just have to pay the piper when you've got to go.

I reached into my zippered pocket to fumble for change. The sign read, "1 baht," but written in very small script beneath it was added, "forigners—5 baht."

Now I was really pissed!

Five baht to take a shit. Just when I was getting to like this country they overcharge me to take a dump. I wanted to file a complaint with the Better Business Bureau or the Mayor, or the local Chamber of Commerce, anyone in charge. But I figured it wouldn't do me any good because they were probably all in on the elaborate scheme enjoying their kickbacks from the devious scam.

The smallest denomination I had was a fifty baht note, which is about a buck and a half in the real world. I handed the money to the attendant and he shook his head. Maybe he was taking pity on me feeling the obvious pain running through me. Maybe he was going to let me pass this time, for the sake of good diplomacy.

Perhaps he was compassionate about my situation and today was his day to perform a good deed. Maybe he wasn't going to charge me realizing I may have been one of those brave soldiers who helped save his country from the Communist domino theory decades ago.

Not on my life!

The capitalist bastard put his hands up as if to say, " Hey buddy. You're fucked. I can't change that. Go break it somewhere else then come back."

My options were limited. I was either going to explode right there in front of him and ruin my cargo pants, deck him with one swift jab to the neck and step over his limp body, or pay him the whole fifty.

The glassy look in his eyes let me know he recognized my dilemma. It was his lucky day. He gave me that smile they all do when you're about to be ripped off. So I threw the money down and ran for the commode.

"Keep the fucking change pal, may you burn in hell!"

I just hoped he was the same guy who cleaned up the johns. "You'll have forty-five baht worth of crap to clean up, you miserable bastard. Mess with me will you?"

I rushed into what looked like a stall. The place was fucking gross. I mean, have you ever gone into the restrooms at New Jersey's Newark

International Airport? Well, this Thai public toilet wasn't as bad as that but it was pretty darn gross.

"Now what the fuck?" I said, looking at the weird porcelain toilet.

It sure as hell was no American Standard I ever encountered.

Then I remembered from way back during the war when they had these kind of latrines. Instead of a comfortable let-me-sit-down-for-fifteen-minutes-to-thumb-through-my-*Reader's Digest* sort of toilet, it was one of those squatters. For only one baht—five for foreigners, if you have the correct friggin' change—you put your feet in the impressed ceramic footprints, squat down like you're fishing for sunfish, and let 'er rip. It's not very conducive for reading, but with a straight uninterrupted, no curves shot, it sure does the trick.

I got into position hoping not to slip in. Counting the broken tiles on the floor, on the ceiling, and on the walls I promised myself never to eat that hot Thai pepper again, otherwise I'd be sitting on a donut cushion from now on and be restricted to eating hospital Jello.

There was some graffiti on the stall divider. Those kids, I thought. I saw a telephone number and could read some of the message just below it. Of course I couldn't read the squiggly words but I'm sure it was the same advertisement we see in the States. Something like, "For a fun good time, prease call me for yo best joy. 100 baht special."

It was signed, 'ICE.'

That fuckin' guy gets around!

After I finally finished my business I felt light-headed, a little faint, just like I get after a quick romp in the sack. It was like having just had a colonic cleansing from the tonsils down. I counted one hundred ninety three tiles and was glad to be done in there. Just for kicks I took my pen and scratched out Ice's phone number on the wall and wrote my sister-in-law's cell number. She's been looking for a date for some time, so, who knows. Plus she could use the extra cash.

I looked around the miniature stall after having flushed with about a hundred plastic cup scoops of water from a large tub. Now what?

To my dismay there was no toilet paper!

No roll of napkins, no tissues, no protective seat covers, no *Korat Times*, no Sears and Roebucks catalog. I wasn't even wearing a T-shirt that, let me tell you, would have come in real handy at such a time. Plus I was sans...you know what.

I was in deep shit, in more ways than one.

I started calling out.

"Help! Help me! I need some shit paper in here!"

My words echoed off empty walls. Either nobody heard me or didn't understand me. So I called out louder. I screamed to the old man stealing money at the entranceway.

"Hey mister. Kind friend. I could use some TP in here."

After several minutes of pleading there was still no answer. I heard a few gentlemen enter the restroom and immediately leave, coughing their little brains out. Recycled Thai pepper does that.

"Hey mister!" I yelled once again to the nice attendant. "How much for a roll of napkins?" I asked, figuring out that's exactly what he was waiting to hear.

I could almost hear him saying, "Ha, ha, you dumb shit foreigner. Should have brought your own. One hundred baht, ha, ha. One hundred baht!"

But it wasn't him saying it. It was me thinking it because I would have gladly forked over the money to get out of there. I finally realized the bitch had booked, taking his charade on the road having most likely made his quota at this station.

Then I remembered my paperback book. The one I slipped into the large lower pocket of my cargo pants. I pulled it out and read the title cover again, *The Clinton Legacy and Other Lies.*

I was saved!

It was actually a fascinating book. Over the past week I had read through the first twenty pages and learned some great tips on how to pick up young female interns, whatever those are. I also learned the true meaning of what 'is' is. I was looking forward to reading other schemes and lies but now was not the time.

It took every page of the first three and a half chapters to take care of my business. Like they say, "It ain't done 'til the paperwork's complete." I put the remainder of the book back in my pocket and stood up, a bit wheezy but a new man ready to continue my journey.

I knew that book would come in handy one day.

Now, if I could only get my hands on that bastard of a toll collector.

Chapter 27

It was nearly two o'clock by now. I was on the lookout for bus number eight. Well, it wasn't really a regular hundred passenger, chicken carrying, twenty-mile per hour, rattling blue and white tin can bus. It was a pick-up truck. One of those small Nissan four-bangers we use back home to haul two people and four bags of potting soil from the plant nursery.

Over here, rigged up with a full line of extra accessories they're called buses. Benches line each side of the truck bed to accommodate at least twelve seated customers. There's a nice awning and railing to keep the passengers from falling out. With the tailgate removed additional standing space and steps extend to accommodate late comers who rely on thin metal hand-holds to stay with their ride.

There's a whole fleet of these vehicles, called eight-baht buses because they all charge only eight-baht to their particular destinations. Numbered one through twenty, each unit loops through the large city along their designated routes and hundreds of them are continuously circling the streets. It's a fun and cheap way to travel.

The eight-baht buses are clearly marked and I was waiting for my number to show up. Looking around I happened to notice a massage parlor business squeezed between a street restaurant and a very busy cell phone store. There are lots of massage joints around, most of them advertising in their windows their foot massage specialty, aka 'the hook.'

I think that's a code word for, 'anything goes for the right price,' but the big promos are basic, no frills, foot massages, sort of like a loss leader to get the customers in the door.

Last time in town with my wonderful wife she told me to get a massage while she shopped in the shoe stores nearby. I knew it was her way of testing me.

Because no wife in her right mind who totally trusts her husband—who I swear to god has never in all our years together has ever strayed from our sacred marital vows, in spite of the numerous temptations, the female advances, and the company picnics—would allow her man to get a massage on the streets of Thailand without wondering for the rest of her natural life if he had asked for the super duper special.

Men should never, ever knowingly be put in such a situation because there is a point of no return when evil forces can take over a naturally loving, conservative, stay-at-home, don't-want-no-trouble, never-done-that-kind-of-thing guy. It's like having the fox guard the chicken coop. Like telling the kids to keep away from the cookie jar. Like asking a beer drinker to cut his consumption from a case to a lousy six-pack a day.

These things just can not be done without life threatening risks!

There are also other factors to contend with too. Like Big Slick in my case, or whatever else he is called by the millions of owners and trainers out there. My advice to all women is, "Please don't put us in those tempting environments. The blame can only rest with you. We can not be held responsible."

Ah...but maybe if you sign a disclaimer... Or maybe a prenuptial agreement.

Just kidding, honey!

I was drawn to the massage shop window like a moth to a flame, ready to get burnt by the sweet glow of the wicked temptresses waiting inside, as spiders wait for their trapped and writhing prey caught in a fine silkened net. My feet unconsciously took me closer to the front door.

I read the English menu painted on the glass.

'Traditional Thai Foot Massage—100 Baht.' Other services included, 'Classical Thai Body Massage—250 Baht.' The list went on, 'Body Oil Massage—400 Baht,' 'Body Oil & Cream Massage—450 Baht,' 'Full Body Massage & Sauna Treatment—600 Baht.'

They had an enticing selection. The closest I've ever gotten to a body massage was when my wife pulled my finger and I accidentally dropped a silent, but deadly one. Oh, and there was that time when I got a fish hook lodged in my back and my nursely wife cut it out and scratched my back.

Finally at the bottom of the list, surrounded by big red hearts and sparkling stars, was 'The Super Duper Special!!—1000 Baht.'

I checked my pockets and determined I had enough to spare for the cheapest Traditional Thai Foot Massage, as long as the young girls didn't try any funny business and attempt to up sell me with the old bait and switch technique like the car dealers use back home.

The foot massage is actually a popular form of relaxation for many Thai citizens, dating back to ancient times. It has become even more prominent and accepted in modern days as people here tend to walk a lot in the hot sticky climate and can appreciate a little personal pampering on a frequent basis.

There's one guy I met, an older, retired Army Colonel living in Korat, who told me he religiously gets his creaky body pampered at least once a day, sometimes twice on paydays, ever since his wife left him. He mentioned it was cheaper too than being married.

I cautiously opened the door and stepped into the small shop. A little bell rang above the door announcing my entry. The place smelled of lotus flowers and body oils, enhancing its oriental atmosphere. All the pretty girls in a row didn't hurt much neither. A mile of smiles greeted me like I was the King of Siam. What a nice little harem this could be, the naughty side of me thought.

One for each day and two on Sunday.

I heard music coming through speakers and recognized it as Barry Manilow's, "Copa Cabana." What the hell? I immediately thought the worst. This must be a homosexual massage parlor. Then I instantly turned around to leave the twisted shop of pleasure.

Some things just aren't worth it!

A beautiful little princess with perfect white teeth moved away from her empty massage chair and gently grabbed my arm. She said in passable English, "Yo come in prease, make happy joy."

Well, how in the world could I possibly refuse such a sweet invitation? I could use some happy joy, thank you very much. I tuned out the gay music and let my girl draw me in closer.

There were eight massage stations crammed in the narrow shop. Four were occupied by people being rubbed and caressed. Two Thai businessmen, who apparently fucking off from work, were getting their feet mangled and squeezed by the girls. One Thai lady was fast asleep as her legs were being tortured and relaxed. Another patron, some fat white dude, was lying on his round stomach as a petite masseuse attacked his thick calves like a baker kneading a blob of dough.

Somewhere in a back room I heard grunting and groaning which reminded me of the time my wife and I, trying to save a few bucks for overnight accommodations, mistakenly booked a room at a romp 'n roll hotel in the sleazy part of Vegas off Fremont Street. The guy in the back room was obviously getting the works with the super special.

Lucky bastard!

I was ready to up sell myself to the deluxe treatment but realized I didn't have enough cash to buy that much pleasure, so I settled on the cheapskate basic foot massage with no extras.

My private foot masseuse was a pretty little thing with long black hair, a radiant face, and that great Thai smile I've been telling you about all along. She and the other girls wore loose light green smocks that must have been house uniforms and had 'spank me' written all over them. I knew I shouldn't be there and was prepared to enter the soulless depths of hell, if not for my actions, at least for my thoughts.

The chair was extremely comfortable and I lied down as instructed. My girl sat across from me on one of those small stools that shoe salesmen use when trying your new shoes on. She unlaced my sneakers and tenderly removed my perspiration stained white sports socks.

Just for kicks a few years ago I ordered a complete set of personal running wear—sweat shirt, sweat pants, and running socks. It was fun in a bizarre sort of way. Each item had my name embroidered on them. Even the socks. My right sock said 'Bob's sock,' while my left sock said 'Bob's other sock,' in big, bold red lettering. As if I was a damn idiot and couldn't figure it out myself. Anyway, I don't think my foot girl actually got the humor in it.

I realized it was the first time in my life anyone had ever taken my socks off, except my mother of course. And that one time when me and a dear sweet friend were fooling around one evening on the wet sands of Hampton Beach back in my high school days before the cops chased us off.

I thought maybe my feet might smell like fermented plastic, as they sometimes do being cooped up all day in my bargain sneakers. It didn't seem to faze my masseuse any, having obviously encountered similar sweaty feet on a daily basis. The girls on either side of me, however, still waiting for customers, quickly left their stations, probably remembering it was their break time.

My bony, pale white feet were lifted and softly lowered into a bucket of steaming hot water with some cleansing solution dissolving in it. Instantly the near boiling water began to bubble up and fizz like a giant Alka-Seltzer. I grimaced and took the pain like a man, feeling my footsies being cooked like a New England boiled dinner.

Green slime rose to the steamy surface and globs of something disgusting looking stuck to the side of the pail as the water turned into a murky gray stew like the swamp water we used to play in as kids. I thought my feet were being acidized and wondered if there was anything left at the ends of my ankles.

Now I know how poor lobsters feel at the summer clam bake.

My girl smiled at me like this was common. She then removed my reddened stumps from the pool of scum and gently wiped down my feet with a soft towel and transferred them into a fresh bath of warm soapy water. Once my feet had stopped cooking it felt fabulous.

I knew she was trying to butter me up but I insisted she only do my feet. She nodded, knowing what I wanted, and started scrubbing down the old dogs with a foaming substance and stiff brush that was firm enough to scrub oil stains off the garage floor.

Behind that pretty smile of hers I suspected she was saying, "Here I am washing another smelly foreigner whose fucking raunchy feet would kill a water buffalo. There he is, sitting like the King of Siam, getting his filthy feet cleaned and rubbed down for a lousy hundred baht. Cheap fucking bastard. He probably thinks I want him too. The chosen ones they think they are. Damn it, I need to make some real money. Need a couple of sauna jobs today, maybe one or two super dooper specials to pay the rent. I should have listened to my mother and opened up a laundromat."

After my tender feet were dried the girl started to rub and squeeze and massage every bone in each foot. It hurt like a bitch but I just puckered up my butt cheeks and smiled back at her while she continued hurting me. I was glad I had cut most of my toenails last month so I had nothing to be embarrassed about.

She kept rubbing and creaming, rubbing and creaming, and the experience had turned into a very enjoyable one. I think she was fascinated with the fair hair on my legs, especially where it had worn thin from my high socks. White skin really turns these girls on. It must have been the highlight of her day to be handling a real man, I thought.

Maybe I could convince her into throwing in a few frebbies.

Oh hell! That hurts!

Chapter 28

My private masseuse kept moving her strong but sensuous hands up my ankles, over my calves, and around my knees, all the while pressing and pushing and caressing. Pressing and pushing and caressing.

The pressure hurt like a son-of-a-bitch. Do you have any idea how many nerve sensors there are in the foot? Well, neither do I, but there's a shit load and she found every one of them and prodded each one with a round wooden dowel until I was on the verge of tears.

I wanted her to stop but it hurt so good!

Every time she stroked my legs with her firm, slender fingers her little tight body moved with the smooth rhythm of her arms and I noticed some mammary jingling through her open uniform top. I kept staring at her credentials bouncing ever so slightly and was working up the courage to go for the whole shebang.

"This is just the basic foot massage I wanted, right?" I asked. Her smile got bigger, or maybe I just imagined it. My smile grew larger too and I definitely wasn't imagining that. I heard some more grunts coming from out back and thought maybe, if I was lucky or turned on the good old boy charm, I could get a good-guy discount on the special they advertised.

A whole hour of this sort of treatment was going to ruin me. A simple one-minute back scratch from my wonderful wife after a fishing accident was never going to do it for me again. My nerves were being excited, my muscles exonerated, my stiff joints liberated. I was being spoiled at the luxurious fingertips of a nymph-like goddess. I was becoming addicted to the infamous Thai foot massage. I was beginning to really, really like living in Thailand.

She poured some hot lotion on my tender thighs and rubbed it into the depths of my neglected pores. With all this creaming going on I hoped I wasn't being overcharged. Each time her warm but firm hands swooped up my leg, soothing my tense muscles, her fingers inched further up beyond the knobs of my knees.

Within twenty minutes of creaming and rubbing my skin just below the bottom of my cargo pants, my well-trained masseuse had begun to turn on her natural feminine charm.

The clever bitch was working me and I began loving every minute of her seductive dance. "Take me you cute little thing, I'm yours," I wanted to say. But I'm a man of self-control, of personal restraint, of taming my natural impulses. I then lifted her hand and moved it back to my inner thigh.

Then she broke through the point of no return and entered the private zone. You know, the tender and ticklish part of a man's inner femoral region wonderfully touched and fondled by strange female hands with long, searching fingernails. Her teeth looked much whiter, her smock much shorter, and her expert hands much, much friendlier. I was being violated right in front of my own eyes and swore at my trusting wife for putting me in this chair.

My young masseuse stared at me with her big dark kitten eyes as if she wanted to marry me and bear my children. As if she wanted to be my personal masseuse for the rest of her life back in America. As if such an arrangement could actually work without my jealous wife knowing about it.

Not!

But I knew her ploy.

They all wanted to hook a big, handsome, well-off man from the States. That was their game plan. Make a rich American fall in love with them. Then comes the big house with a white picket fence, two cars in the garage, a swimming pool in the backyard, unlimited bowls of rice, a personal checking account, and a Sears MasterCard. Later her entire family would get their green cards, and before you know it half the friggin' country was living in your family room. The girls even came to work every day with a suitcase already packed with their personal items should they find Mister Right during their work shift.

Just in case!

I let her have her way with me. Let her think of her often dreamed of fancies far, far away. I let her fall in love with her own delusional fantasies wishing to be part of the great American experience. I let her secretly hope her gentle ways would convince a man such as myself to carry her off to a life of luxuries.

"Bullshit, babe! Ain't gonna happen today. Although I personally kind of like the idea, my loving wife would never allow it," I quietly squealed to myself.

"Keep rubbing."

In a brazen attempt to make her nonverbal attack more convincing, and with time running short, her nimble fingers had broken the forbidden seal by entering the twilight zone, the edge of man's most prized possession, the hidden secret so few have come to know.

I had this crazy thought about stuffing her in one of my suitcases, along with two of her friends. But my luggage was already over packed with souvenirs and knick-knacks and throw pillows. Plus, I'm pretty sure my darling wife would start asking questions as to why we all of a sudden had three cute little Thai girls living in our home massaging their master and doing other household chores.

I asked if I could take a picture of her with my Sony. She was thrilled to pose in her working position, hoping that perhaps her portrait would soon sit on the fireplace mantel of a spacious home in the suburbs.

Then the bad thing happened.

Big Slick was awakened!

I saw an old guy walk out of the back room, supported under both arms by two sweaty little girls in their disheveled work uniforms. His legs were all rubbery, his aged face as blush red as a beet, his thinning white hair a frazzle of tangled turf. He was wearing his buttoned down sweater unbuttoned and wore untied dorky looking sneakers.

The man had no shame but he had the biggest friggin' smile from ear to ear I have ever seen plastered on a guy's wrinkled mug. I heard him mumbling something that sounded like, "Holy Mary, mother of God. It's a beautiful day in the neighborhood."

Must have been a religious man.

"See yo tomorrow again, Mister Wogers," one of the masseuses said as he limped out the door and lied down exhausted on the curb for awhile.

"Have a preasure day," the other girl said.

I had always thought he was a little light in the loafers, if you know what I mean, like that gay singer Manilow. I thought the old geezer had died when his show went off the air, but instead he was hiding out in Korat getting his rocks busted every day. Retirement served him quite well.

The fucking horny rascal!

He looked at me with a long, unsure gaze in his bloodshot eyes, as if he didn't know where he was, or for that matter, who he was. And to tell you the truth I don't think it really bothered him a damn bit. Over here I wouldn't be surprised if I saw Captain-fucking-Kangaroo pimping out Farmer Green Jeans.

"Mr. Rogers!" I said to him before the door closed. "You fucking rock, man!"

Slick was liking the attention directed at him from our masseuse. He was a hog for the spotlight from the word go. He had let earlier opportunities slip past him. My girlfriend on the bus ride, the woman selling fish, even the queer boy. He had allowed the big, goofy white guy decide what was right and what was wrong. He had been a whipping post long enough and vowed this time to get his way.

Looking down his loose pants he could see right down her dress. He so wanted to fondle her but he had no hands. He could smell her feminine desire. He could feel her gentle touch nearly embracing his manhood, asking to be hugged, cherished, stroked and loved.

Oh my fucking god, was he so friggin' ready!

Big Slick saw the sweet little girl's brilliant smile. She was smiling directly at him, calling him, enticing him to reach out for her worldly pleasures. She was ruthlessly mouthing sweet nothings into his tiny little ears. He smiled back, a bit of drool slipping out the corner of his mouth. He looked at her most gorgeous eyes, knowing he had finally gotten the green light from the dumb ass he was attached to.

"It's about fucking time!" he swore out loud. "Finally, you let me make my move," he thought, in his heated frenzy. He winked at the beauty and was sure she winked back. He was hers. God, was he ever ready. In the final instance he lunged for his love, lurched from the base of his spine toward everlasting Nirvana.

Then, an alarm clock rang from behind my chair. My girl got up from her knees, wrapped up the used towels, gathered her creams, patted me on my legs, and motioned for me to leave.

My time was up!

"Next," is all she said, as she smiled a "Sawadee" to me.

I had two of the girls help me up and walked with wobbly legs to pay the counter girl. I left a hefty fifty baht tip for the best damn foot massage I've ever had, and for the best sex I never had. I exited the shop of pleasures and sat on the curb next to the old guy who apparently had passed out from his deluxe massage, then I put on my damp socks and stinking sneakers.

Big Slick and me were shocked, disappointed. Speechless. Both our jaws went limp in disbelief.

"What the fuck just happened?" Slick asked.

"I don't know. Guess we were cut short," I answered.

"Well, that fucking sucks!"

"I know."

"You should have brought more money!" he admonished me.

"I know."

"You should have stolen some money!"

"I know. Shut the hell up."

"You are one dumb son-of-a-bitch!" he added.

"Yes, I know," was all I could say.

Chapter 29

I MEANDERED DOWN THE walkway slowly recuperating from the strenuous ordeal I had just survived. My feet were tender and sore, my legs as limp as spaghetti, my Johnson as hard as a rock. I was looking for bus number eight again. I guess I was. It really didn't matter to me right now.

Oh yeah. I needed to keep moving on.

The eight baht special was about the best damn bargain you could find anywhere in town, except for the 100 baht traditional Thai foot massage, with a bunch of extras thrown in, of course. What else nowadays could you buy for only a quarter? A lousy pack of gum? I had the feeling this truck ride was going to be a lot better than chewing some gum.

Dozens of buses whizzed by me, people singing and whistling. More happy Thai people. Thin tanned arms and legs flying every which way. The city folk were having a grand old time being shuttled around like balls in a pinball machine. Then I saw my mini-bus lumber around the corner, being chased by a swirling cloud of smoky exhaust. My lucky eight ball.

To say it was over loaded would be an extreme understatement. That would be like me saying my Uncle Joe passed fluffies. It was filled to the rafters with passengers, all seeming quite content in their cramped quarters, glad at least to have a ride.

The only ones making any noise were the dozen school kids hanging out the back, a few desperately holding onto their friends' backpacks to stay with the traveling pickup truck. Just like kids throughout the world they appeared to be enjoying the cruise as if it were a twenty-five cents roller coaster ride down in Coney Island.

The driver pulled up and yelled something to me like, "Get in Joe," ready to take on at least one more fare.

Hell, his rear tires were running on the rims and his front end barely touched the pavement, making it necessary to use the kids dragging in the back as his rudder whenever he came to a turn. I lost count at twenty-nine persons in the back of that four-cylinder bus. It was like trying to count jelly beans in one of those large glass jars where the winner gets a free movie ticket or something.

"Hey, you little fuckers, stop moving! I'm trying to get a count here."

Ha, ha! Just having some fun with my Thai friends. Not wanting to be the one to break the camel's back, nor looking forward to hanging on by my pinkies and tippee toes, I waved the driver off and waited for the next number eight.

There was a Buddhist temple across the street. There are quite a few temples throughout Thailand, and Korat had its fair share. They range from the simplest of wooden buildings draped daily with fresh wreaths of flowers built along the roadways, to the gargantuan configuration of temples and houses of prayer that can embrace thousands of worshippers at one time. In size and grandeur any one of them would rival, if not surpass, the celebrated cathedrals of the Western world.

The towering structures, with their high peaked roofs and extravagantly decorated exteriors, are graced with ornately hand carved wood scrollings. Delicately painted inlaids come to life with brilliant mixes of reds and yellows and greens, deeper colors of which I've never seen before.

Portions of the temples are layered with precious gold, sparkling in the tropical daylight and shimmering in the dark of night. Massive granite steps and polished tile floors are the altars of the true believers.

Bells and candles and incense are the instruments used to give reverence.

These temples, symbols of Thai beliefs and philosophy of life, monuments to their ancestry and heritage, are honored and respected by every citizen. Pedestrians bow and put their hands together in a brief and silent prayer to their temples. Passengers in buses and tuk-tuks and samlars also briefly bow and honor the temple as they pass by.

Even the drivers solemnly but quickly show their deepest respect by doing the same while en route. Bus drivers and private drivers softly tap their horns so their Buddha knows they are there giving homage. I've seen this before. Words can not describe the overwhelming sense of true spiritualism intertwined in these peoples' lives.

I was humbled to see an entire country of citizens, whether rich or poor, young or old, in a rush or simply strolling along, take a valuable moment out of their day to acknowledge their place of worship and their god. They know what respect is and carry it with them through every step of their lives. It's an ingrained feature of who they are, an indistinguishable characteristic that makes them unlike any other peoples I have ever met.

Maybe that was one of the reasons they all seemed so happy. Maybe that's the reason they smiled so much.

Maybe that was a part of something I could never comprehend.

Monks live in these temples. Men with shaved heads wrapped in simple orange robes and wearing thin sandals, carrying small orange cloth satchels with their few belongings. Women priests wear similar garb, but robes of light white cloth.

All have forsaken their worldly possessions and old selves to conduct the business of religion and goodwill. Their mission is to learn and to teach Buddhist studies, to discover the strengths and weaknesses of man, to find the way to enlightenment. I see them travel the streets, ride the buses, eat in the small sidewalk restaurants, shop in the open markets, and every one seems to have a sense of contentment about them.

The monks are visible everywhere and are an integral part of the landscape and its people. They eat but one time a day, always before noon, all food donated to their temples by followers each day of the year.

Everyone gives to the temples. There is a constant and abundant flow of money, food, honor and respect. I saw the poorest of the poor bow down in front of a temple altar and donate her last twenty baht for the monks and their own salvation. I saw well-dressed believers weep while praying to their god, their hands clasped together touching their heads honoring what they have faith in.

Here everyone gladly gives.

I could not imagine what such a strong belief system is like. I last donated a few bucks at church some forty years ago and since have declared myself a retired Catholic, having lost faith in more than my religion. Even there I had no heroes. Perhaps the Thai people, with all their backwoods ways, their simple contentment in the face of poverty, their slow pace of life, their belief in something larger then themselves, could teach lazy, fat slobs like me a thing or two.

Many of the monks are not lifelong clerics but instead are average citizens, from farmers to soldiers to business owners to students. It is tradition that every male spend time as a monk, for perhaps as little as a few months.

It is there, in the temples, dressed and living as holy men, they learn of their religion, their god, their culture and traditions. It is there where they acknowledge who they are as a person and a people. It is there where their beliefs and convictions are solidified, their duties and obligations are revealed, their purpose identified.

There is absolutely no way in the world if you spend any time amongst these hard working, energetic, spiritually content people that you could not learn to respect and like them.

I fully realized my simple sense of shallowness was overwhelmed by their unspoken humility.

But hell, I'm an American and that's what we do.

Chapter 30

A LOUD TRUCK HORN woke me from my daydreaming. My pick-up bus pulled up and I was glad to see there was plenty of room in the back. I climbed on board and sat on the narrow vinyl bench. There was only a handful of people boarding on with me.

Of course the first ones I noticed were two fine looking young ladies in their university uniforms with two pair of wonderfully attractive legs. I sat across from them, my big bony knees almost touching theirs.

I was slightly uncomfortable, but to tell you the truth I was getting used to the feeling. I felt like I was in an elevator, not wanting to stare, pretending to read the advertising posters plastered inside the lid of the bus, which of course were in Thai so they did me no good anyway, except for saving me from my evil thoughts.

I casually smiled at one of the lovelies and her cute face flashed a slight curve of a smile back to me as she turned to look at the posters. She sort of reminded me of my new girlfriend. Just another beautiful Thai young lady.

She was probably thinking to herself, "What does this old guy want? He keeps looking at my legs. They're not that ugly, are they? Be a lady and keep them tightly closed. I've heard stories about these rich foreigners. They come over here all the time looking for women. Young girls mostly. He is kind of cute though, like one of those famous

American movie stars. But he's wearing a wedding ring. Ah…that's too bad. I'd like a big house someday."

If I was Hank, I'd probably take that as a sure sign she wanted me and I'd jump her right there in the back seat of my eight baht bus and have my way with her until I reached my destination. But I'm not Hank. I'm much better than that bastard of a pig. I can control myself, but not what I'm thinking.

I wonder how the Red Sox are doing?

An older woman climbed in and sat beside me. I "Sawadeed" her, because that's what I do, and thought perhaps it would make a good impression on the college girls with the legs across from me. See, I'm not so bad. Sure, I'd really like to do you right here and right now, but as you can see, I do have manners. I speak Thai too.

My haggard old seatmate didn't smile. She just kept her eyes on the floor of the bus, twitching her nose, most likely from the scent of the oils and creams rubbed on my feet and legs not long ago.

"I just had a foot massage," I said to her, with a big goofy smile, as if she should be happy for me. She didn't bother to respond.

I could tell her feeble mind was thinking about something else by the way her shifty eyes were darting back and forth, never leaving the floorboards. Just another crazy old senile senior citizen, I thought. Sort of like the seniors in the Boston subways trying to find their way home on the red line. Or was that the green line?

"I once dated a young, horny GI. It was back in the '70s when everything was wild and I had a body to die for," she was silently mumbling to herself. "He didn't know when to stop. I think he was a little crazy because whenever we were doing it he kept yelling out some other guy's name, like 'Slick stop that!' or 'Don't get caught doing that Slick.' He was a looney tune but sure was good in the sack."

She stopped for a minute and licked her tongue over her wrinkled lips and single front tooth.

The woman continued to dream about her past. "Had all my teeth back then too. Couldn't keep the men off of me. Those were the good old days. Except for when he left me, the no good son-of- a-bitch," she continued to mutter in Thai.

"Sure, at first he was charming and nice, giving me the time of my life, buying me candy and cigarettes and apples. As I recall his name was Boob, or Bob, or something like that. This fella' next to me sort of reminds me of him. Every night he said he loved me. Promised to come back and get me after the war. Then he went home to his fat blonde wife in America, or so I heard. They're all liars, they are. Act like the chosen ones, for god's sake."

I slid down toward the end of the bench hoping my old squeeze Suzie Q wouldn't recognize me. I wish I had my fucking sunglasses.

I looked over at one of the cuties with the legs and raised my eyebrows like the devil I used to be. I could have flared my nostrils and wiggled my ears and really cracked her up, but decided that was too silly. She giggled to herself, having understood what the old bag near me was saying in her native language. I giggled a little bit too, to show the young girls my sensitive and fun side, then shifted my focus on the traffic behind us.

I was enjoying the ride as the driver sped down the main boulevard like he owned the whole damn street. People were waving at him as he cut them off trying to catch up to the earlier number eight. He must have lots of friends around here, I thought, as other drivers and motorcycle riders continued to throw their hands up at him. I waved back at a few of them myself being the friendly visitor that I am.

All along I kept catching another male passenger sticking his head in from the back. He was holding onto the rear hand rails and kept glaring at me like I had taken something from him, like something was wrong. He kept shooting the stink eye at me.

This guy was beginning to bug me.

"Hey man, don't worry. I'll pay when I get off," I said in a calm tone, not wanting to rile him, but strong enough to let him know I knew the routine. He was a tough looking hombre, probably about forty, or maybe he was twenty. It's impossible to tell here. He had a large scar on one arm and tattoos on the other.

One design looked like it said, "Mama," but I think that meant 'Mad Dog' in Thai and thought it best not to ask. Even though he was small and wiry I didn't really want to take him down here in the streets, especially since my legs were still a little weak from that fabulous massage.

He saw me eyeing the young girls and was thinking to himself, "You fucking foreigners come over here with your fancy talk, your nice little gifts, your money, your fake promises. You take all of our beautiful women for your own selfish, hedonistic pleasure and leave us the scraps."

He didn't look very happy. No smiles here.

I could sense he wasn't having good thoughts toward me. I have a cunning feel for people's body language, and this guy wasn't registering too high on the nice guy scale. I just sat back and let him continue his inner rampage. It's always best to let people vent before you react.

"You guys flash all that cash of yours and have your way with our women, leaving just the leftovers and ugly ones for us poor working Thai stiffs. That ain't right man," he suddenly finished, when I thought he had more to say. Luckily there were no weapons visible, though I did have my cell phone should I have to call 911, or was it 119?

I can only take so much shit when it comes to being accused of things I haven't done yet, or been caught at. So I couldn't hold it back any longer. You don't want to see me get angry, I thought to myself, hoping he'd see where I was going with this. But out of respect for the young girls across from me I thought it best to try to reason with this pissed off, womenless Thai working jerk off.

"Listen pal," I stood up in the bus, my neck bent at the short ceiling. "You guys had better take care of your own shit at home first, if you know what I mean. Women like to be treated with respect. They like being appreciated and swooned over. They like to be complimented. Otherwise, pal, you're out on your ass. So don't blame me or my buddies. This is your house. You handle it."

I really don't think he understood a single agitated word I threw his way but it appeared he got the drift of my friendly, though, harsh advice.

The two young females with the gorgeous legs said something like, "You go man. You tell him." They seemed all excited that I was standing up for their rights too. The cuties giggled some more and thought, "Maybe this dude would like to take us both home with him. We like the way he thinks."

I knew they were on my side so I took out my handy digital camera and motioned toward the girls that I wanted to take their picture. The two squeezed together, showing off their big smiles and fantastic legs. I wide-angled the shot and got every bit of them. Then I retrieved the photo in the viewfinder and showed it to the lovely students. That always gets them to laugh and giggle.

Me too!

It also gets them to see what a nice gentleman I am.

Ah...ha! Another great pic for the calender. The Gemini twins, perhaps.

The old lady on the seat just shook her head, knowing everything I said was a damn lie. She squinted her eyes and looked at my face as if she was searching for a long lost friend.

As the bus came to our stop I felt bad regarding my mean words aimed at the Thai gentleman. My outburst was uncalled for. I should learn to be more patient, to take my time before exploding, to count to ten in Thai before I vent my outrage, to look at the good side.

Trying to make amends I smiled at him and said, "Here, you can have this one," pointing to the bent over old hag exiting the bus. "She used to go by the name of Suzy Q. Give you one hell of a time pal. Just give her an apple and she's yours."

Fuck him if he couldn't take a joke!

After offering my generous gift to the disgruntled whiner everyone disembarked from the bus and dutifully paid their fare to the driver's helper in the front seat. I followed the gorgeous legs disembarking in front of me. I was so mesmerized by their sleek steady movement I almost forgot where the hell I was going.

But for the moment I really didn't care!

Chapter 31

We were dumped off right in the middle of a sprawling sidewalk food court. Every bus, taxi, tuk-tuk, samlor, and eight-baht pick-up truck stopped at this spot. Guess everyone else was following me. There were grills and woks and pots and pans all cooking something different, most of which looked spicy as all hell and smelled eye blistering strong.

It smelled so good!

After my last run in with the cow's bloody heart slop at the Soup Barn, though, I promised myself to stay clear of anything that might kill me. Besides, I was actually hoping to find some more familiar food to eat. Something cooked on a greasy grill, something loaded with salt and artificial flavors, something packed with artery hardening cholesterol, heart attack inducing fat and deliciousness. In other words, something more American like a chili dog or a quarter pounder with cheese or even a double bacon burger with the works.

I knew exactly where to satisfy my inner cravings.

I looked across the congested eight-lane boulevard and finally saw the true destination of my day-long adventurous journey. The traffic noise was muffled by the roar of a majestic man-made waterfall in front of central Thailand's largest indoor shopping structure. Cascading sheets of tinted blue water spilled over the crest of a forty-foot tall artificial mountain. The endless waves of water replenished a huge fish-filled curved pond running more than a hundred feet along the tiled course of a marble inlaid sidewalk.

The walled pool, decorated with tiled panels of Thai historical scenes and vast temples and celebrated national figures, funneled thousands of patrons through the grandiose entrance of the most fabulous shopping in all of Korat. In short, it was an astonishing retail resort. A haven for the distinguished and even simple palate. A gateway to the goods of the world's merchants. A fully self-contained city within a city.

It's also a terrific location to check out the most beautiful women alive strutting their stuff.

Now we're talking!

I was standing in front of what was simply named, The Mall.

I know you don't believe me, but in all the time we've known each other have I ever lied to you yet? Nobody around here speaks English, not that much anyway, but they really do call this place, The Mall. How internationally metropolitan.

Last week my frugal wife, her two sisters, and me came here to browse the stores and outlets. The women call it 'browsing.' That way it doesn't sound so fucking lethal and absolutely boring. Like four friggin' hours of looking at stuff we don't need and trying on things we don't want is an enjoyable time away from the TV set. How fun is that? I call it a waste of half a day of valuable drinking and napping time.

I was so sick and tired of 'browsing' I wanted to drop a wicked smelly fart right there in the middle of the young women's lingerie department and get it over with. Come on spicy chicken, don't let me down now. But my ever-observant wife, seeing that pre-flatulent strain in my eyes, gave me the evil look. You know, the one that says, "You better not even dare think about doing it, mister."

So I snuck over to the electronics section while the girls were trying on new bras and blessed a few of the male clerks with a little spice of life. Needless to say, I'll never be buying any DVDs from those guys.

As an aside, I have to tell you my wife is a shop-aholic. A true addict if you want to know the truth. She'll spend all day in one store touching every fucking piece of material, every damn dress on the racks, every friggin' blouse on the display tables, just to see what they feel like.

Hell, her and the girls can walk twenty miles shopping for nothing and never get tired from their all-day trek. This, from a woman who sends me out to get the friggin' mail because the mailbox is too far. The same woman who will drive around the parking lot ten times to get a parking slot one space closer to the front door.

You've got to love them!

I swear, my wonderful wife is an accomplished, professional shopper. Hey, that's what she does. Back home she goes to three or four different stores everyday. I mean every single day. Hell, there's not a single level spot in our house that's not filled with knick-knacks and photos and of course, scented candles. I mean, how many candles does a house really need? I never knew they made so much shit to keep the women busy.

We should have never become so friendly with China.

When we run out of tabletops and shelves and other level surfaces to put her crap on, she buys more tables and shelves. One day, when we're both gone, the kids will have one hell of an estate sale. It will be like a junk museum going out of business with the fast-talking auctioneer selling every piece of crap accumulated over the years for pennies on the penny.

The retail stores will no doubt fly their flags at half mast on that day.

I actually get calls like this from the local major discount stores. No shit!

"Hello, Mr. Swift?"

"Yes," I answer every time, knowing who it is by the hour hand on the clock.

"This is Mr. Snoodgrass, the manager of Big Lots here in town."

"Yes," I answer half-heartedly. "I was expecting your call."

"Well, I'm calling to see if your lovely wife is okay. I mean, it's after noon and we haven't seen her yet today. I hope everything is fine."

"Thanks for your concern. She's fine, just running a bit later than usual with her shopping girlfriends," I explain.

"I'm very glad to hear that Mr. Swift. We were getting worried here," he comments with a sigh of relief in his cracking voice.

"She'll be there soon, I'm sure. Thanks for calling. Good-bye."

And the calls from Wal-Mart, and Marshalls, and Ross, and the Dollar General continue throughout the day. These guys are like old friends to me. I wonder if they like beer? Well, at least my darling wife has a hobby.

Hell, I'm a man, and when I need something I run into the nearest 7/11, get my beer, maybe a pack of rubbers, and I'm out of there lickity split. Takes me three minutes, tops. I don't have to go touching every piece of SlimJim jerky or Sara Lee cake snack to satisfy my thirst.

Guess that's why we're different!

Men and women, I mean.

Men are the hunters and women are the gatherers. The male kills the meat, brings home the bacon, as it were, while the women pick the berries and collect the friggin' knick-knacks. That's what makes us different. Must be the Venus and Mars thing, whatever the fuck that's supposed to mean.

Anyway, the magnificent building in front of me covers several city blocks. It houses thousands of retail outlets, from the cheapo shit to the very expensive you'll-never-see-that-kind-of-stuff-in-my-house luxury items. There are furniture stores and banks, learning centers and souvenir shops. There are at least a hundred, perhaps more, places to eat, from the small kiosks selling prepared foods to the gigantic food court that I'm sure is bigger then twenty Arby's put together. Then there're the dozens upon dozens of real sit-down restaurants, some of which are very familiar.

If you can believe it, ATM machines are in every other corner too, for the short-on-cash customers. Damn, I don't even have an ATM card or debit card. My prudent wife handles that kind of stuff. So much for being in a backward country.

I'll bet you if this building had a hotel in it, which it just might, a person would never have to leave. It could be his entire world all contained within the walls of this mega-center. Did I tell you it had a giant bowling alley, a Home Depot—yep, a friggin' massive movie theatre, an expo center, and more? There's a kiddie play center, which is larger than any carnival traveling the summer circuit. Oh, I almost forgot. There's also a pool area with slides and tubes and several pools and spas and private cabanas, all of which would dwarf any Water World.

Downstairs is a bargain basement selection of whatever you need. Kind of like a low rent indoor swap meet. On my previous 'browsing' excursion I also noticed there were a bunch of small themed bars for the thirsty tourists and tired businessmen who had enough of shopping and merchandise touching.

Except some of the 'merchandise' down there wore very skimpy, and sometimes see-through, uniforms while servicing their customers in the dimly lit watering holes.

When with my fabulous wife I couldn't go down stairs without her knowing it, you know, because of that radar thing most wives have where they can pinpoint the exact location of their wayward husbands. Their GPS-like talent is so accurate they can determine what floor, what quadrant, which corner, which bar, even what stool their guy is sitting on. I believe she could also name the friggin' brew I was sipping and the cutie I was talking to.

NASA should be so good!

I hope to god her radar can't travel the twenty-five or so kilometer distance between us, because one of the first things I intend on doing is to fraternize with the help. I might get lucky enough to feel up some of the merchandise, if you know what I mean. That is if I have any money left.

Beep…beep...beep.

Just kidding honey!

Chapter 32

I SQUIRMED MY WAY through the pedestrians past the smoky street banquet and slowly climbed the steep metal stairs leading up to the overpass on the second story level of The Mall.

No doubt it was the safest way to cross the street. No crazy tuk-tuk drivers going for my big toes in search of holy blessings. No falling apart tin can bus piloted by a sadistic bastard picking up anything that moves if they're willing to pay the piper. No dodging two-wheeled push carts selling god-awful hotdogs on a stick.

The raised walkway offered a terrific view of the surrounding buildings, people, and traffic. It was a majestic city, some parts new, some old. I'd venture to say that most Americans would be surprised at the modern and somewhat sophisticated ways of so-called third world countries, particularly here in Thailand.

We conjure up images of thatched roof shanties, backward technology, bare-footed natives, devastating hunger, impoverished people surviving one step ahead of agonizing death. Well, they have all that here, but more. We're easily swayed to these sorts of images by watching too much television and, in our own ignorant ways, believing everything we see.

I saw something I didn't like up ahead, just before the entrance door to The Mall. A middle-aged woman in ragged clothes was sitting on the concrete walk holding an infant child in her arms. The baby had abnormally short arms and was having a hard time playing with an empty plastic Coke bottle. The child had a crooked and frustrated smile on her young face disfigured by a pronounced cleft lip.

The first thing that comes to my mind whenever I see something wrong like this is, "Why does God let such things happen?" Funny to hear a guy like me say that. Huh?

Sometimes I wonder about things like that.

Like when my Uncle Chip, after thirty years of teaching, suddenly was diagnosed with a massive brain tumor just one month after he retired. Or when my younger brother Eddie, who I hadn't seen in seventeen years died in a coma, never knowing I was finally by his side when the life-supporting machines were shut off. Or when I had to take our long time pet cat Sammy to the vet's office realizing that stupid cat wasn't coming home again.

I think maybe my dad was right about life not being fair.

The poor mother on the elevated walkway held out a three-fingered hand begging for a few baht. No social security plans here. No government handouts for the truly needy. No Salvation Army food lines or St. Vincent de Paul's voucher programs for the castaways. Most passersby simply passed her by, barely noticing the tragic duo, self absorbed in their own petty need to shop.

Cheap bastards!

The scene wasn't like back home where lazy ass bums with two good hands, two healthy feet, and a strong back simply loiter on a busy corner in front of Target in search of a free ride off the goodwill of generous people.

I once offered a street corner derelict twenty bucks to cut the grass in my backyard. It was about a two-hour job and I figured it was a fair wage for a job done well. The grubby bastard eyed the cash in my fist as if his wayward ship had come in and he could cut his shift short to hit the old bottle. But he still had the balls to say, "I can't do that kind of work mister. I have a bad back."

Oh yeah, he still wanted the money. The only thing he wanted was a free handout for doing nothing except waste his sorry life on the curb. I put the bill back in my pocket and told the no good son-of-a-bitch,

"Hey, my back hurts too pal from working over the past forty years. But for twenty bucks I'll cut the goddamn thing myself."

Not being a bleeding-heart liberal giving away free cheese to the undeserving, I say let the no good slothful miserable excuse of a man starve to death. Let him get a job if he's that friggin' hungry. I have absolutely no tolerance for ungrateful, lazy bastards like that. And I'm not sorry about it one damn bit.

That's just how I am!

I reached into my pocket and gave the lady on the floor a twenty-baht note. It wasn't much, and maybe I was being ripped off by the oldest scam in the book, but I could afford it and I truly thought it was the right thing to do. Clasping the money she put her wretched hands together and gratefully bowed her thanks to me. She said something in Thai, which I partly understood as, "Thank you kind sir." I didn't even expect her to cut my grass. I felt good and bad at the same time.

I felt pretty damn fortunate.

A young man in full get-up opened the double door for me as I entered The Mall. In his uniform he looked like the doorman at The Ritz-Carlton. He sharply threw me a military salute with his white-gloved hand along with a hardy "Sawadee." I returned his salute and smile, then thanked him in Thai. He was a good guy, working the door all day, glad to be there and not complaining that his back hurts.

What a nice, clean, open, well-lit, good-smelling place this was. It reminded me of those very upscale establishments in the rich part of downtown Boston that we visited a long time ago. Places we couldn't afford to shop in but they were something to see. Having never stepped foot on this level I was amazed at what I saw. It was nothing like shopping from the street vendors, though they do have a sort of charm of their own way even if they don't have the glitz.

I looked down the long crowded hallway and saw something absolutely amazing. Past the jewelry stores, the cell phone shops, the souvenir stands. Beyond the clothing racks, the sit down restaurants, the ATMs, the candle stores, I saw the most beautiful sight. It made me instantly feel at home, comfortable, safe, amongst friends. I was no longer in a strange universe. The familiar scent drew me to a place where I had grown up.

I walked faster to the one spot I knew so well.

There sat an old buddy of mine. A friendly face. Someone I could relate to. Ronald McDonald was resting on his plastic bench outside of the fabulous Golden Arches. "Yes!" I shouted to myself. "Eureka. I've found it." Home of the Big Mac. I could live here forever and be fulfilled. My cravings satisfied. My being made whole again.

I remembered when I was sixteen and had my first car. It was a two-tone Ford Fairlane with ripped plastic vinyl seats and a ton of Bond-O holding the rusted out fenders together. It looked like a piece of shit, but it was my piece of shit. On Saturday nights my buddies and me would hop in the jalopy and drive three towns over to one of the few McDonalds restaurants around.

The whole parking lot would be filled with muscle cars, chopped down roadsters, and clunkers like mine, in the take-out only joint. We'd eat our twenty-five cents grease burgers, admire the popular guys' supped up cars in the lot, talk about girls, especially the easy ones in high school, and shoot the shit. It was our way of having fun. That's when I fell in love with MickeyDees. There's no way you can go wrong with a big sloppy cheeseburger, large greasy fries, and a tall chocolate milkshake.

I walked into the restaurant, which looked like any other McDonalds in the States, only much nicer and a hell of a lot cleaner. The place was packed with another generation of young people, all Thai, hooked on the fatty, cholesterol filled, heart attack on a sesame seed bun. I couldn't wait to put in my order.

I hadn't eaten anything in hours, not counting the bowl of cow's guts soup, which in my book wasn't really food. I was starving for something fat and oily. I was about to have a Big Mac attack by the time I moved up to the counter. I couldn't read the foreign menu on the wall but the pictures helped. To make it easier for myself and the pretty attendant waiting on me, I pointed at the Number Two meal with a hot apple pie thrown in. It cost me almost three bucks, a big chunk of my cash, but it was well worth it.

You can not put a price on a dream.

I found an empty table next to a group of students doing their homework while they ate and laughed, and in general were having a good time. They were mildly studious and quiet and courteous. They weren't throwing drinks around, or yelling obscenities, or picking their nose rings, or causing a ruckus. It was a different world from the McDonalds back home when the friggin' high school kids, who can barely read, skip classes and take over the joint trying to intimidate the older guys waiting for their senior coffee.

The quarter-pounder with cheese and hot salty French fries hit the spot. Too bad they don't sell beer here too. Burgers and a beer. How much better could it get? The food was exactly what I was used to eating every Monday, Wednesday, and Friday for lunch. I wondered if they had egg McMuffins for breakfast. Maybe those McPancake plates with the little syrup thingies.

A happy man, I picked up my bag of baseball caps, tossed the food wrappers into a container, and carried my half-empty shake into The Mall.

Without warning a herd of beautiful women rushed past me from every angle. It was quite a sight to watch so many gorgeous legs flashing by as the female wave stampeded toward a corner store. They were moving so quickly my stealth Sony digital camera was too slow to catch their high-speed motion. A high-pitched cackling noise followed the flock of chickies at the speed of sound. .

Stunned, I didn't know exactly what was happening but I suspected what it might be. I've seen similar phenomena before on the rare occasions when I used to go shopping with my dear wife. It was something no man alive would ever want to get caught up in. It was an uncontrollable, infectious drive brought on by extraordinary levels of estrogen and the irresistible smell of a half-off sale.

Drinking the remainder of my chocolate milkshake I tried to step back. Then another swarm of ladies slammed into me like a level three hurricane and lifted me off my feet as they headed in a feverish mass toward the gathering commotion. I was being carried along by a hundred or so lovely ladies, as if I were a star quarterback being swept off the gridiron by my winning teammates. I honestly can say that such a man handling was not an unpleasant experience.

The frenzied mob of females had the look of crazed animals in their mascaraed eyes anticipating the battle ahead and the blood-curdling thrill of the kill.

Their relentless drive toward the ultimate shopping experience was as persistent as Marco Polo's search for the hidden trade routes of the

Far East. Colombus' quest to discover the New World was not nearly as determined as this crowd of feminine treasure seekers. I would venture to say that even Genghis Khan, afraid of having his hordes of Mongols massacred, would have stepped aside and steered clear of such an army of fearless shoppers.

Yes, my friends. It was a shoe sale!

A friggin' shoe sale, which we all know, no women in the world can resist and not a man alive can understand. I was in the midst of a gang of skirts and silk blouses and soft body parts, a hapless piece of manly luggage happily caught up in the vicious assault. As my group neared the tables filled with thousands of shoes, all marked fifty percent off, I was violently tossed to the floor like a sack of rotten rice.

I was stepped on and kicked hard and run over and trounced upon. I was gouged and scratched and beaten and pummeled. I didn't know whether I should protect my face or my nuts. But of course I saved my most cherished possessions and covered Big Slick and the boys who, if you remember, had very little protection.

"Hey, you can have them all. I don't want any shoes today," I yelled in a feeble attempt to save my own skin.

The riot escalated into a full-blown merciless war. It was everyone for himself or herself. Darwin was right. It was survival of the fittest. Tigers slashing the deer. Lions gutting the wildebeest. It was sheer primal havoc where no one was safe.

So, shaking off my assailants and coming to my senses, I joined the fun by knocking over at least a dozen tender beauties, crawled over their heated bodies, and pulled myself to safe cover beneath one of the display tables.

I bumped into a pretty little worker girl who was also hiding under the enormous shoe bin. We chit-chatted a bit while the tornado above us roared on. Then just to kill time, we showed each other our superficial wounds. I got her phone number for later, so I could check on her and see how she was doing. Hee..hee..hee!

Just above us were the clashing sounds of excitement and anger as the ladies attacked the pile of shoes. I heard menacing cat fights over a pair of size-four pumps. I heard growling threats over a nice set of see-through spongy casual wear. I heard weeping and wheezing as the wrestling match exploded into its finale. I took my cell phone out of its zippered pocket to dial for help. Not familiar with the Thai numbers it was a hopeless effort in my attempt to be rescued.

As quickly as the blue-light special began, it ended. The crowd of zealous women had broken up and dissipated and headed in different directions in search of yet another sale. They were once again normal, everyday, pretty women and girls, as charming and dainty and happy as could be.

They were the spitting image of sugar and spice.

I got up from my safety zone and viewed the battlefield. There were left-over mangled shoes scattered in a fifty-meter circle. Torn leather straps and plastic heels and dislodged insoles peppered the sales tables and surrounding booths. The only footwear left on the tables was a mismatched pair of stiletto high heels, a couple pair of snow boots, and a size fourteen, extra-wide pair of sandals for one really big bitch who never showed up.

Several torn-off, blood stained blouses were strewn on the floor. Clumps of once beautiful long black hair were tangled in nearby clothes hangers. A platoon of tattered clerks were screaming for help to be transported from the massacre, all collateral damage from the daily shoe sale.

"Medic! We need a medic here!" I yelled in my valiant attempt to offer assistance.

The beaches of Normandy were not nearly as devastating as was this women's shoe department. I limped over to the men's sock section to gather my composure and make sure the coast was clear.

I am proud to say that I survived the onslaught of a full-fledge, genuine fifty-percent off all inventory shoe sale and will live to tell my grandchildren of it one day. I found my torn off sneakers, slipped them back on and headed far, far away from the women's clothing carousels.

I desperately needed a drink!

Chapter 33

I MEANDERED AWAY FROM the smoking disaster area in search of a quiet, men's-only bar. A cold beer right now would do wonders to calm me down and allow the pain from my multiple injuries to melt away. I rubbed the shoe prints off the side of my face, readjusted my boys, checked all the gear in my secret pockets, and cautiously moved forward. There were still lots of things to see.

Every time a pretty little Thai girl passed me at a quick pace I pulled back, still traumatized by the recent assault of the notorious shoe shoppers. My psyche, I'm certain, will be scarred for life from that violent event. I knew a hefty case of post-traumatic stress would be a part of my future whenever I saw more then two pair of women's shoe together.

A long line of teenie-boopers stood in front of a Mr. Donuts store that claimed to carry sixty-seven kinds of sweet treats. Yes, if you can believe it, they even had donuts on a stick. Why, I have no idea?

Right next door was a Swanson's Ice Cream shop packed with customers licking mango and kiwi double dipped cones. Further down I even saw a Dairy Qeen across the way. Yeah, yeah. I know what you're thinking. That's exactly what I thought too when I first saw the sign. Soft ice cream! What a great idea in such a hot climate.

I was actually surprised at the Thais' appetite for so many sugared sweets and fatty snacks. There was also an Eat Me Bakery—no bullshit, but great name, huh?— several candy stores, a Pizza Hut, Pizza House, Pizza World, and a Pisano's Pizza run by a transplanted Indian guy from New York City. He probably had Yankee posters tacked all over his walls. I swore never to eat in his place. A Kentucky Fried Chicken joint was busy selling their most popular item, vanilla ice cream topped with kernels of corn.

Don't even ask!

The Mall was filled with American franchising ingenuity and the locals were eating every calorie of it up. These Thai people were always eating something and not a one of them were overweight. Well, at least not yet. No doubt in twenty years or so this would be a great place to be a cardiologist or to own a Weight Watchers franchise.

I saw an absolutely gorgeous young lady in a light summer dress gracefully stream by me tossing her hair to the side in a flirtatious manner. Hey! You know I'm married, but I'm not dead yet.

Hooked me like a big-mouthed bass going for a tasty bait. Guys are so damn easy. I quickly overcame my fear of fast women on the move and approached the fresh, teasing thing.

"Excuse me," I said in my best Thai, as if she had dropped something, and me being the gentleman that I am, wanted to return it to her.

She stopped and gave me one of those big, pleasant smiles I like to see. "Yes?" she answered. I love when beautiful women say 'yes.'

"I couldn't help but notice you walking by me. You are a very attractive lady," I complimented her, laying the old B.S. charm on thick. They just love to hear that kind of shit. "I'm new here and was wondering if you were a model or a movie star."

Check.

The girl could understand some of what I was saying and giggled in response. "How flattering," she thought to her self. "He's a bit old for me and slightly overweight but he is kind of handsome for a tourist. I wonder if that wedding ring is for real. Wow! He thinks I'm a model or even a movie star. How great is that?"

Checkmate!

I moved in closer. "Well, I wonder if it would be possible for me to take your photograph? For my new movie, I mean. It's a romantic chick flick and I'm here looking for my leading lady."

The beautiful girl was giddy with excitement, though I suspected she comprehended only every other word. However, she apparently got the gist of my phony proposal and beamed with glee as she immediately began posing for me with a seductive lust for the camera. On lookers gave us no thought, most likely figuring the scene was just another one of those old retired white guys from America trying to pick up yet another beautiful Thai girl.

I started shooting her with my Sony and flaunted her to liven it up.

"Shake it baby! Show a little more skin."

Click, click.

She was taking it all in like a pro.

"Do that pouting thing you do so well. Look into the lens."

Click, click.

This girl knew how to show it off.

"Oh yeah! Who's your daddy?"

Click, click.

My new leading lady was making me hot, and she knew it.

"You're a natural."

Click, click.

She had a great body and a tantalizing smile. A true Asian beauty. I felt like a professional photographer on a shoot for the *Sports Illustrated* swimsuit issue, one of my favorite pieces of literature. The poor girl fell for the whole thing.

I started to feel guilty for fibbing about my new movie which would probably never be made, so I told her I was still in pre-production stage and would get back to her once the pictures were ready.

At least she had something exciting to tell her girlfriends and I had some super shots of my Ms. August.

Hank, you're gonna' love these!

After reviewing the pics in the camera with my new star the girl gave me her cell number and glided down the aisle dreaming of being the next super starlet of a slutty movie. I secured my camera and suddenly got a whiff of the best aroma in the world. I mean a strong cup of freshly brewed hot coffee. Uncharacteristically, I forgot about that cold beer.

Hell, I could catch up on my drinking later!

Before I took another step I saw a huge Starbucks sign beyond the row of make-up kiosks. It was mid-afternoon, a perfect time for a good cup of java since I was forgoing my daily nap. Back home I hardy ever took a nap, except for maybe Saturdays and Sundays after lunch or on the days I called in sick after watching the late, late, late show.

But ever since I've been in country, between two and three o'clock, at peak heat of the day, me and my women would drop like flies for a good hour or two. Our small bungalow looks like the aftermath of a Jonestown cool-aid party, bodies sprawled everywhere until supper time. It's like taking a friggin' Mexican siesta without the wicked heartburn. It's one of the three things I live for.

Snackie, nappie, nookie!

Then when I finally wake up I find myself in front of the boob tube, sans sub-titles, still dazed to the world, waiting for the old brainwaves to re-ignite. So this is a real treat for me to be up so late and have a cup of good coffee. Besides, this trip has been quite fun and adventurous, not to mention very memorable, and it's worth the risk of breaking away from the homestead and losing sleep.

The Starbucks store was a fantastic lounge-like shop with several cushy couches and comfortable looking armchairs like you see in airport VIP sections. The coffee bean smell was overwhelming and the grinding of oven-roasted beans from around the world was music to my ears. I swear they pumped the alluring aroma throughout The Mall to attract patrons.

Their prices were just like back home. Four bucks worth for a friggin' foo-foo drink. You know, one of those decaf lattes with non-fat skim milk, a shot of hazelnut flavoring, topped off with a generous head of whipped cream and a light sprinkling of cinnamon. What the fuck kind of coffee drink is that? Back in my Safeway's Starbucks I see the dandies ordering these queer drinks along with their girlfriends and I just have to shake my head at the feminization of men.

Fanny pack wearing, foo-foo drinking, ball-less bastards!

"Give me a coffee please, black," I ask the clerk who happened to look like the girl I met under the shoe table.

"What size sir?" she asked in very good English.

"Grande of course," I answered and raised my eyebrows so she knew size really did matter to me.

Two dollars for my coffee. I was getting dangerously low on cash and would have to find one of those exchange booths real soon if I ever planned on making it back to my bungalow.

I noticed a newspaper rack and picked up a complimentary English copy of the *Korat Times.* Then I sat down in a cushioned chair at a small table along the railing separating the shop from the rest of The Mall. From where I sat there was a terrific view of the shoppers walking to and fro, so in between sips of my coffee and reading a few articles I wouldn't miss anything.

You know what I'm referring to.

An article on the front page showed a horrific accident where a huge beer delivery truck ran over a tuk-tuk and flattened it into a two-inch piece of tin, which was perfect as an improvised roof for one of the nearby curious hotdog vendors. The one-eyed cabbie had barely escaped the wreckage with his life and was quoted as saying, "The goddamn truck came right up on me as I was trying to take a sharp curve in front of a group of tourists attempting to cross the street."

Well, that's not exactly what he said but I loosely translated it for you non-Thai speaking folks. The story went on to say that not a drop of the precious cargo was disturbed.

Thank god for small favors!

There was another article, along with a grainy photo, showing a squad of city cops suited in their riot gear and crash helmets arresting a bunch of ladies of the night after them causing a disturbance at a local bar called The Wet Spot.

Apparently some white guys, having discovered too late that they weren't receiving exactly what they had negotiated for, refused to pay the going rate. I thought I recognized my queer boy Ice in the picture, but he was wearing much more makeup than usual so I wasn't really certain if it was him.

The coffee was hot and strong. The surrounding atmosphere was cozy. The view from my chair was delightful. I was beginning to enjoy my visit more than I ever expected. The people were friendly for the most part, the level of service was excellent, the cost of living very reasonable, if not darn right cheap, except for faggy foo-foo coffee drinks. It was easy to get around, as safe as you could expect to be in a large city. And it was interestingly different. I was beginning to appreciate why most Thais were happy with their lives and smiled so damn much.

Before putting the newspaper down I flipped to the classified section just for shits and grins. Not that I was looking for employment. Hell, I was looking forward to permanent retirement.

Some of the help-wanted ads were unusual. There were things we would never see in American papers. Like this ad for a secretary: "Young, slender female for full time office administration position. Must be between 21 and 35 years old." Or, "Now hiring clothing store clerk, unmarried female preferred. Must be bi-lingual." Even, "Looking for attractive companions to entertain the retired tourist trade. Male or female okay. Apply in person at The Wet Spot."

Ah! The idiosyncrasies and lack of discriminatory controls in a crowded third world country. Tell it like it is. How refreshing!

I was about to get up and leave my tranquil corner when an older gentleman from two tables down came up to me. I was in a rather mellow mood and wondered who I should be next.

Chapter 34

"**Hello,**" **he said to** me in a mid-western accent that sounded as if he were from Chicago or some place like that. He was holding his coffee mug and had today's issue of *The Bangkok Times* folded under his arm. The Thai language version.

First thing I thought was, "Damn fucking literate showoff."

"I noticed you reading the local newspaper," he said matter-of-factly.

Well, no shit Sherlock. How friggin' observant.

"You must be an American," he added, extending his free hand and introducing himself. I'm Max Wilson."

I thought he was being pretty forward in assuming I wanted to meet the guy and have a conversation with a complete stranger. Hey man, I'm ready to hit the nearest beer joint and maybe shoot some snooker. I don't have that much time left on my furlough. Besides, this guy had no way of knowing whether or not if I was a mass murderer on a leave of absence from the postal service hiding out here at a Starbucks coffee shop in the middle of The Mall in Korat, Thailand.

You talk with me, you take your chances, bub!

I decided to let it play out, talk to the old man and find out what's up. He seemed harmless and almost normal, except for his bushy white eyebrows that fluttered over his tired eyes like hairy caterpillars. He reminded me of Andy Rooney, that ancient news guy on *60 Minutes* who always complained about the wad of cotton in the aspirin jars and stupid things like that.

"Nice to meet you Max," I said, not really meaning it. I wondered if that was his real first name. I wanted to ask him how he felt about the new sealed lids they put on ketchup bottles that are a real bitch to open. Then I debated whether I should pull another Blue Beard trick out of my hat or go with the real me.

"Have a seat," I offered him, wondering if my rich condo developer character would be a good fit for this encounter. That should blow him out of the water and send old gramps back to his corner a defeated man.

Jason Castlerock could brag to this Mr. Max how he has built thousands of high rise private apartments for the well-off emerging baby boomer-senior citizen clientele along the prestigious Florida Gold Coast.

He could tell tales of getting filthy rich by selling luxury residences to the wealthy and annoying snowbirds who flocked to the warm climate regions to enjoy the vast array of upscale amenities they demand as the chosen ones. He could boast how, through the rewards from his efforts, he had created a perpetual gold mine by charging exorbitant association fees to the condo owners by simply giving them a pool to look at and a doorman to open the friggin' front gates.

And with these riches, he could tell his coffee companion how he had purchased his very own island off the southern coast of Thailand near the resort town of Phuket. He could spoon on about how his private isle was complete with a mansion as huge as a regal hotel staffed by dozens of servants thrilled to be working for the famous Mr. Castlerock.

All these lies Jason Castlerock could rattle off to impress and intimidate, and to turn the boring, predictable, and good old boy Bob Swift into a more interesting and likable guy. He could rant on and on about his ingenious plans and schemes to sell decadent lifestyles to the rich and famous. He could make Max Wilson and anyone else envious of his unbelievable successes.

They would all wish they could be so lucky.

But I don't't really like that Castlerock fellow or his ways, so I took a big chance and went with the real me.

"I'm Bob Swift," I decided to tell him. Plain old, dull, just trying to get by Bob Swift, who in the whole realm of it all is nobody special.

"Where are you from?" I asked the well-dressed man who had to be at least eighty-five years old.

"I'm originally from Washington state. Retired a long time ago and discovered Thailand. Been living here in Korat for over twenty three years," he explained, a sense of pride coming over him.

"How in the hell did you end up here?" I wondered out loud.

Max settled in his seat. "After I got out of the Air Force I came here as a contractor for the government during the last phase of the war, then later as a translator for the State Department. Liked it so much I decided some day to move here."

He looked so old I didn't want to embarrass him and ask which war he was referring to. Maybe he rented trained elephants for President Lincoln's efforts against the South. The dumb ass rednecks would think they were being invaded by the biggest friggin' horses alive and promptly lay down their weapons and give that Lee guy hell for getting them in such a mess.

I really shouldn't be saying things like that. The man actually reminded me of my father who passed away too many years ago. Just like Max my dad was heavy-set, had a full head of gray-white hair, and a jolly face that made you want to like him. He was a tough old man with a suspicious nature but had a heart of gold. If you knew my dad you would immediately think of Ralph Kramden, the Jackie Gleeson character from *The Honeymooners* TV series, with a little touch of Archie Bunker in the old *All In The Family* series.

I told Max, "I'm just visiting right now, trying to see if we want to spend more time here. Maybe a few months out of the year."

"It's a fabulous place to live," his wrinkled face smiled, causing his rosy jowls to jiggle a bit. My Thai wife and I live well here on my pension and social security. I couldn't have it so good back in the States."

"It's pretty damn hot here, though."

"Well, no place is perfect. It's what you make of it," Max responded. He sipped his coffee and looked around. "Pretty here, isn't it?"

"Certainly is a great place to watch the girls," I answered without hesitation.

"Yes that too," the old guy grinned. "I meant here in general, anywhere in the country. The people, the way of life, the foods, the smells. There's always someone interesting to talk with or something interesting going on."

I guess he was right, all except for the smells. There're not too many dull moments here. That's for damn sure. Lots to see and do if one gets out there and mingles, becomes a part of the experience.

"I stay busy enough here, but not too busy. My wife and I do a little traveling, visit her family, and we have friends, a few Americans," Max rambled on.

"We have a small place near Chok Chai. I basically just hang around, go out to eat, you know, relax," I said, not having anything exciting to share and thought it really was none of his damn business to learn that my favorite past time was drinking the local beers.

"This is a wonderful country to do that," he assured me. "On occasion I'll go back to the States to see my son, but this is really my home now. I have a very nice life here. The way I figure, it's not a bad way to go out."

I sat there fiddling with my empty coffee cup. Maybe this guy was right. Maybe I was expecting too much. Maybe after all these years of living in such a rat race I had forgotten how to enjoy myself and the people around me.

Hell, there's no maybe about it. Every bit of it's true. Maybe simply being me was okay.

A beautiful young Thai girl stopped in front of our table. She looked very familiar but I couldn't place her face. The first thing that popped into my mind was that I was in some sort of trouble. I wondered if I did something that I couldn't remember. I haven't been drinking that much today so it couldn't be too serious, I thought.

"Excuse me," she said with a very friendly smile. "I was wondering if you have processed my photos yet?" she asked in broken Thai.

A surprised look formed on my face. I was completely clueless as to who in the world this lovely creature was asking about her photos. What? Do I look like the local One Hour Photo Mart?

"You know, the ones for your new movie," she said in fractured English, with a perky smile and a sexy glow in her eyes.

"Oh…!" I muttered. The fucking light bulb finally came on. "Ah… those pictures won't be ready for a few days my dear."

"Okay," she giggled, still excited about her new career. "I saw you here with your friend and thought I would ask."

"It's very nice to see you again. You'll hear from me soon." I told her leaving it at that, knowing deep down I was a pile of dog shit and on the surface I was worse than that.

"Thank you very much Mr. Spielberg," she said as she walked away swinging that tight little ass of hers.

I cringed a bit but still took about half a minute to say goodbye with my eyes.

Fucking dirty old man!

Max cleared his throat. His generous cheeks were showing a bit of blush color.

"Mr. Spielberg?" he said, knowing something was up, but understanding he probably shouldn't ask. He'd been around the block a few times himself.

"It's a long story," I told him, having no intention to explain.

"Nice to meet you Max." I stood up and once again shook his hand. "I must be going now. Perhaps some other day I'll run into you again."

"I look forward to it young man," he said, as I stepped out into The Mall.

"Take care of yourself Bob Swift."

Chapter 35

I was short on cash, having the equivalent of less than three bucks in baht. At this spending rate I wouldn't be able to walk through the rest of The Mall without becoming an indigent. Worse than that, I wouldn't have the money to pick up some beers when I got to the house, that is, if I even had enough bus fare. I decided on exchanging the twenty-dollar bill stashed in my wallet for Thai currency.

There were still a few more items I wanted to buy.

A few minutes after leaving Starbucks I found the escalator and went down to the lower street level. There was a huge inside roaring waterfall flowing into a shallow pond surrounded by a friggin' awesome food court. Several four-foot wide manta rays slowly floated through the pool next to outrageously large manatee-like fish, which resembled monstrous carp. I wondered if the cooks got their catch of the day there.

There must have been fifty, no hundred, food vendors working their narrow stalls, cooking up different concoctions of Asian fast foods. The place was in dire need of a humongous Glade air freshener. For being so late in the afternoon I was surprised at the number of diners crowding the order lines and tables.

I could tell the place was a pretty upscale joint because there were actual paper napkin holders instead of the kind on a roll I was used to.

I wasn't hungry after my McDonalds feast but I could use a little snack soon if I happened to see anything appealing.

There was a muffled rumbling noise coming from the far end of the complex. The columns holding the upper level swayed a bit and the big fish went hiding in the deep end of the pool.

A rumor was spreading through the place like wildfire that there was a two-for-one sale in the women's purse and wallet department. Most of the women, and quite a few feminine looking guys wearing stylish fanny packs, quickly dropped their chopsticks and rushed toward the accessories department.

The destruction in the shoe section was child's play compared to the devastation one could expect in The House of Leather. I could only imagine the widespread devastation lying ahead. No friggin' way was I going near that one, although it could be kind of fun watching the rampage from a distance.

I located a small money exchange booth at the tail end of the food court. It listed the daily currency exchange rate for 164 countries including U.S. dollars, Canadian fake dollars, Australian dollars, Euros, Yen, British pounds, a variety of Francs, and the Tonga Pa'anga, whatever the hell that is. Wouldn't you know they set the money stall right in front of a big ass cookie store. Now that's what I call creative merchandizing.

Tricky bastards!

Here I am trying to lose weight and everywhere I turn there's delicious temptations staring me in the face. Sweats and pastries, I mean. It just isn't fair. See Doc, I told you it wasn't my fault. I'm always put in these difficult situations. So I bought two pan-size oatmeal raisin cookies because they're easy to chew and give me my recommended daily fiber intake.

The petite girl sitting in the booth took my twenty-dollar note and marked the bill with one of those felt tip pens to make sure it's authentic. I have to tell you that always pisses me off.

Whenever I spend anything over a five-dollar bill, whether it's at the grocery store, the liquor package store, or even the fucking 7/11, the damn clerk takes out her trusty money-tester pen and checks to see if I'm trying to pass counterfeit money. She looks me square in the eyes as if I'm a seasoned thief with a super color copier in my basement where I print a gazillion bills then hang them to dry prior to my next spending spree at the Piggly Wiggly. I swear, every damn time the clerk looks disappointed that I'm not floating funny money.

Like that's how I've accumulated all my millions, by passing phony currency at the corner mini-mart.

Power hungry, domineering bitch!

I need to get me one of those markers. Next time I'm getting cash from the bank or change back from the convenience store I'll whip out my counterfeit detector and slowly swipe it across the bills. All the while staring into the bank teller's or store clerk's eyes as if she were attempting to pawn off some Monopoly money.

See how they like that!

The money girl handed me about seven hundred baht in exchange. In return I offered her one of my big cookies as a treat for her pleasant smile and quick service without trying to screw me out of the going rate. It bought me a great big smile too. Giving her the cookie, I mean. Girls love getting gifts from generous, good-looking gentlemen.

Flush with cash I felt great. With this kind of backup dough in my pockets I could splurge on a few little extras and maybe even buy something for my friends and definitely a special little surprise for my loving wife.

It was time for that beer I've been thinking about all afternoon.

I knew exactly where I wanted to sneak off to. In the basement floor of The Mall there was a pub called The Tiki Bar that looked like a beach shack with a thatched roof, fake palm trees, and not so fake young Thai waitresses wearing grass skirts and polished half coconut brassieres to complete the exotic motif. I went down to the bottom floor and sauntered into the bar.

The waitresses were shaking their grass things and pushing cocktails to the bleary eyed patrons. I was thinking of having a mai-tai in a real coconut but came to my senses and ordered a Singha, a cold one if they had it. A pretty little Tiki girl brought me my drink along with one of those famous radiant Thai smiles.

Ah! That first swig is wonderfully refreshing. "Where have you been all day?" I said to the frosty bottle of battery acid tainted brew.

I was minding my own business, watching the waitresses, and enjoying my drink when I heard, "Hey Joe!" Someone yelled out from the back of the bar where a group of Thai gangsters were playing billiards. I didn't pay attention to the thugs since my name wasn't Joe.

"Hey you. GI Joe!" one of the pool players called out, nodding his head my way. I was confused because I wasn't Joe and I wasn't a GI, so I knew the fool was mistaken. The last person who called me Joe was a fucking commie VC bastard who infiltrated our hooch area back in Korat in a failed attempt to blow up our latrine while our NCO-in-charge was doing his business.

Just for the record I called the fucking infiltrator 'Charlie' right before I knocked his friggin' head off with a thick bamboo stick. There we were on an Air Force base, thinking we were safe, and it just wasn't right trying to blast the hell out of our only bathroom. Oh yeah, and it was up to our guys and no one else, to bust the NCO's balls. The real point here is I don't like being called Joe.

End of story!

I looked at Spike from my table near the bar. "You talkin' to me?" I said, doing the DiNero thing to intimidate the scrawny bastard. I moved closer toward him and said it again just for the fucking effect. "Are you talkin' to me?"

The guy was a punk with spiked black hair, dragon tattoos on his skinny arms, and a T-shirt silk-screened with a picture of Rocky Balboa, my most favorite actor. I wanted to ask him where he got the shirt but decided not to. The bitch had a pool stick in his hand and nodded at me to play.

Okay punk. You want to play?

"Do you feel lucky?" I said loud enough for him to hear.

"Well, do you? Punk!" That's from Clint Eastwood if you weren't sure.

He had no idea what he was getting himself into. Hope he brought lots of baht. Years ago back home I had a barroom size slate pool table that took quarters, but I rigged it so I could play for free. Hell, it was in my house, so why not? Playing eight ball I'd clear the table in a matter of minutes and cream my opponents. The kids would always go crying to their mother and claim I cheated them out of their allowance. When it came to shooting pool their father had pure talent, so they just had to deal with it.

"I'll play you, Charlie," I said in a challenging tone. I walked over to the table with the bottle of beer in my hand and stared him down like those clerks do me when I'm cashing a ten-dollar bill.

"We play eight ball, Joe," he said, a wise ass grin on his ugly face.

I pointed at him with a threatening finger to correct his mistake of addressing me by someone else's name. I remembered how much they hated that. The poor slob didn't realize how close he had come to meeting his Oriental maker.

Instead of beating the shit out of him I wanted to take his money and humiliate the bastard in front of his gang of friends and the cute coconut girls.

"The name's Swift," I said. "Bob Swift."

Chapter 36

"Okay Joe."

This jerk was a lost cause. I asked him, "How much?"

"One hundred baht a game for you Joe." The guy didn't know when to quit fucking with me.

I was actually thinking about playing for only twenty baht a game. A hundred was a bit rich, but what the hell. I had plenty of money in the cargo holds and belligerently answered, "I have time for one game, so you're on, pal."

One of his buds racked up the balls and Charlie let me break since I was the guest. There was only one cue stick left leaning against the corner and of course it had a whopping curve like JLo's ass. The plastic tip was also very fucked up. No problem, I thought. I'll take this joker down in seven shots.

I positioned myself in front of the scuffed white cue ball and aimed just off center of the head ball. Rearing back my stick I gave it a powerful thrust in a dazzling attempt to pocket two or three balls. I wanted to scare the shit out of this dude with one swift stroke. To my surprise my crooked stick completely missed the cue ball.

The group of wannabe pool sharks laughed at my errant stroke.

"That's enough practice," I said. "Haven't played since early this morning over at that other place down the street. I'm ready now." The snickering in the background died down.

My break knocked two low numbered balls in the corner pockets just as I planned. I took a long drink of beer and threw the empty to the side for effect. "Don't fuck with the Swiftman," I mumbled through my gritted teeth. Most of the group's eyes were wide open in disbelief as if they were being hustled by the Great One. Paul Newman couldn't have done much better in *The Hustler*.

In the next few minutes I put three more solid colored balls in their called pockets. One was a gimme and two were shear luck, but I'll take luck any day. I played it up like a champ. My opponent's spiked hair began to droop. He kept combing his cheesy Fu Manchu goatee with his fingers. The boys were getting nervous. They must have been thinking, "Who in the fuck is this guy?"

As if I've been playing this way my entire life, in rapid succession I dropped the last two low balls into their leather pockets. The lonely eight ball was all I had left. It was knocked behind a cluster-fuck of striped balls and would most certainly take a miraculous shot to end the game.

I slowly walked around the table eyeballing my possible shots like a professional reading the greens in those sudden death tournaments. I took my ever-loving sweet fucking time so Charlie boy could simmer in the agony of defeat.

"Show me your money, Charlie. It's about to get ugly," I told him with all the confidence in the world.

I found my shot. If I banked the cue ball off the side and back off the far railing it would hit the black and nudge it between my man's nine and fourteen balls just enough to kiss the side pocket edge and drop in. I called the shot so there would be no mistake as to where I was aiming.

The coconut girls were behind me all the way, backing me up like a squadron of sweet little brown cheerleaders.

"Go Joe! Go Joe! Go Joe!"

I was in my element, on my game, invincible. Then I pulled back my stick, took a deep slow breath, and gently let loose. It was going to be the shot of a lifetime. That's when the fucking tip fell off the stick as I barely nicked the cue ball.

"Motherfucker!"

My opponent and his crew chuckled like idiots. My cheerleading squad stopped sharply at my unfortunate mishap.

It was the punk's turn to play. He had an uphill battle to contend with. By now everyone in the bar was watching the battle. There was a sense of edginess in the joint and the asshole's buddies were rooting for him.

"Beat he ass!"

"You da man!"

"Joe not good!"

I wasn't rattled a bit by the peanut gallery. I was up seven zip and there was no friggin' way in hell the puke could beat me. I sat down on a stool to relax and enjoy the blood fest.

"Don't choke Charlie. Here comes some easy money," I tried to stifle my laughter.

He quickly slammed two balls in. Then, with an outrageous spin on the cue he knocked in another. It was no big deal. I was still four up on him. He had a freebie shot on the fifteen ball in the corner that a light breeze would have knocked in. Hell, this kid even jumped the cue over the eight ball to pocket yet another.

"Fuck me!" I mumbled under my breath so he couldn't hear my distress.

"Hey Joe," he turned to me. "Watch this!"

The bastard had one of those Thai smiles I could hate. He bent over to view his two remaining balls in the middle of the pool table. With amazing execution he rammed his stick so the cue ball tapped both balls at a precise geometric angle. The balls split with just enough momentum to force each one into their respective side pockets.

A fucking lucky, never-happen-again trick shot is all I could think of.

I wiped the smug grin from my face. It was now down to the wire and the wise ass tattoo boy was still up. The final point on the felt was the eight ball, which thankfully was way the hell down on the far side resting against the bank. It was an almost impossible shot. A hundred to one bet, if I had to bet.

"Joe, you want double or no win on this one shot?" the arrogant little twit asked me in broken English. He was beginning to annoy me.

"Damn straight!" I said without hesitation. I wasn't going to be bullied by this half-pint. There was no way in hell he could make this fucking shot.

"Sure. Double or nothing. Two hundred baht." I stood up, leaned on my fucked up stick, and hoped to hell the guy would have a heart attack or seizure or something within the next thirty seconds.

Against every law of physics that I've ever heard of the son-of-a-bitch's cue ball lightly touched the black eight ball causing it to slowly and painfully drift along the hard bank toward the back corner and drop in like a dead weight.

I couldn't believe what just happened. The bastard beat me. "Lucky ass shot!" is all I could say. I lost the game. Holy shit, I lost two hundred baht!

Fuck me to tears!

That was a lot of money. He and his compadres were laughing, high-fiving, and savoring the thrill of victory with the come back of the century. All because I had a defective pool stick.

The fucking, cheating bastard!

"Okay Joe. Pay up," the ungrateful winner said with his hand shoved in my face.

"Good game Joe, you lose."

"No shit, Charlie Brown." The fix was in. I didn't want to pay the thieving bastard.

"My wallet's in my car," I told him like a poker player bluffing for the pot with a wicked shitty hand. I shook his hand so he would know I was good for it.

"I'm parked right out front," I assured him. I called one of the coconut girls over and ordered another beer so he knew for certain that I would return with the cash.

"It will only take me a minute, two tops," I smiled.

Charlie wasn't too happy about me not having the money on me. I guess he wasn't as dumb as he looked. "No! You not go anywhere. I want my money now," he said, a bit aggravated and somewhat suspicious.

As well he should be because there was no way in hell I was going to pay him.

"Hey man. What? You don't trust me? You think I'm a piker? Listen pal, I pay my debts. Like I just told you. My fucking wallet is in the car. It'll take me one fucking minute out of your friggin' life for me to go get it. That's the way it is bub," I rebuffed him for even having the audacity to think I would skip out on a bet.

He just stood there realizing it would not be in his best interest to mess with this wild old white man who, in such an agitated state, could do some serious damage if pushed over the edge.

"Don't touch my beer!" I yelled at him, pointing to it sitting on the table near my seat. "I'll be right back. Oh…I'm going to put my bag in the car too so I won't have to carry it around all day."

I walked out of the bar toward the up escalator, all the while hoping I wasn't going to be shot in the back. I could feel leering eyes boring into me. When I reached the top level I turned and gave a reassuring nod to the guys below that I'd be back in a flash. From where they were standing they couldn't see the front doors leading out of The Mall.

Of course my car wasn't there. It was parked twelve thousand miles due west.

"You dumbshits!"

I back tracked and headed into the building wearing one of my Red Sock baseball caps low over my ears like a friggin' retard lost in the store looking for his mommy.

The dipshits would never recognize me!

Chapter 37

Just to be safe I walked quickly to the far, far side of the building and took the escalator up to the main level, then continued all the way to the fifth floor. I kept looking back over my shoulder to make sure the pool room punks weren't following me. I peered over the railing down the open atrium to see if there were any crazies with spiked hair and dragon tattoos running around.

The dumb asses were probably out in the front parking area searching for me and wondering which car was mine. "It's the Hummer with the decal that says, 'Screw you suckers!'" I snickered to myself. I'd bet two hundred baht they were really pissed off when they figured out they had been duped by GI Joe.

Fuck 'em!

I headed toward the back of The Mall, which had to be a quarter mile or more away.

Passing through the sporting goods department I noticed a bin filled with florescent colored Frisbees. I haven't played with one of those things in ages, ever since that time in the park when I was flipping back and forth with my friend Grover whose Labrador retriever kept trying to, well…retrieve the Frisbee. I gave the plastic disc a wicked hard throw and lazy Grover couldn't get close enough to it because he didn't want to spill his beer. His poor dog chased the thing into the busy street and that was the end of old Sparky.

So guess who got blamed?

Hey, Grover should have caught the damn thing!

Putting old playtime memories aside, I bought two, an orange one and a bright green one. The kids around the house could have some good old fashion American fun and learn how to spin with the best of us.

I could teach them how to toss a bitching floating flip that would hover above their heads until the sun went down. Keep the Frisbees away from the dogs, kids. I'm sure I'll get blamed if someone gets hurt. And watch out for that old bitch next door.

Heaven forbid the Frisbee goes into her yard.

There was an expensive display of professional golf clubs, competition balls, high-end golf bags, and all the tools of the gentlemen's game. They even had a small artificial-turf putting green, like a putt-putt miniature golf course without the castles and clowns, so serious golfers could practice their short strokes and then maybe buy something.

I tried to play golf once with a group of other working stiffs from the Elks Lodge. It was a weekend mini-tournament put on by the local service clubs with proceeds going toward some charities like Alcoholics Anonymous or Marriage Counseling Classes, or some foolish group like those.

Anyway, we all pretty much sucked at trying to hit that little fucker straight down the fairway. How in the hell are you supposed to aim that small ball all the way down there with a friggin' stick? We kept score by subtracting the number of balls found from the number lost. It was easier that way and I ended up with four extra balls from some guy named Wilson. The fun part was actually driving those electric go-carts and seeing who could down the most beers between each hole.

I'm proud to say I won the first six holes and tied the next two with No Neck Bubba.

No brag, just fact!

It was a joyous day spent outside in the fresh air with a bunch of my buddies whose most common form of exercise was getting up to look for more potato chips in the pantry during the Sunday afternoon baseball game. Hell, just the walk from the cart to the tee off thingie wore me out. Guess I'm more of a spectator player.

It's a good thing most of the luxury homes along the course have plexi-glass windows and closed-in back patios, otherwise we'd still be paying for the damages. Also, I'm glad we were smart enough to buy insurance on the golf carts and rental clubs. After wrapping my five-iron around a pine tree they planted right in my way and driving my golf cart into the friggin' duck pond, I came to realize that golf is really not for me. It's too slow, too frustrating, and too damn dangerous.

Not to mention we were asked by the management not to ever play there again.

Besides, I'm still not fat enough to play with the regular club members.

I remembered where the grocery store was located from the last trip with my fabulous wife when we were "browsing these delightful stores looking for table clothes and cabinet drawer linings." How fucking thrilling, I thought. The food market was five floors below the bowling alley, which I just passed, so I took the moving stairs down, hoping the bar thugs had accepted their losses and forgot about me.

They would never think to look for GI Joe so far from their cave.

The food store was massive, even larger than any Super Wal-Mart I've ever been in. The one thing I really like about it is all the free samples they give out. In just about every aisle there's a cute Thai girl dressed in her store uniform doling out small cups of juices, and nuts, and slices of pizzas, or pieces of fruit. If a guy wanted to he could enjoy a filling lunch just by making the full rounds, which in my case took me no more than twenty minutes flat.

Entering the store I gracefully declined the offer of a pushcart by the people-greeter out front. You know me and shopping don't mix very well. I despise pushing one of those baskets with the fucked up wheels around a bunch of blue-haired bitties who insist on catching up on old times in the middle of the row, sharing the latest gossip right in my fucking way.

I try to be nice.

I really do, but a man can be pushed only so far.

"Excuse me ladies, I need to get through your friggin' knitting circle before my fucking ice cream melts, thank you very much. Hey, go to the friggin' coffee shop if you want to reminisce. I'm in a damn hurry."

So instead I grab one of those hand baskets to load my shit into.

Another thing that's absolutely great here is the service. I may have mentioned it before but for some reason the attention to the shoppers' needs over here, particularly in this store, is nothing less than fantastic. It's like the workers really care for the people paying their wages. At the front of each aisle there's not one, but two lovely girls just waiting to help you. Their job is to service the customer.

Wow! What a friggin' concept.

"Hello my dear. Could you please tell me where the pancake syrup is?" You might ask. The hottie who works the breakfast cereal and pancake aisle doesn't simply point to aisle thirty-two and then run like hell to the break room knowing full well there's not even an aisle thirty-two. I've fallen for that trick too many times at Home Depot and Wal-Mart.

It's not like back home when you wait for help until your dick falls off. Oops! Sorry ladies! Instead, your personal shopping attendant takes you by your hand and leads you to the item you asked for. Then she'll even ask if you need any further assistance.

Weird, huh?

So the breakfast aisle cutie shows me where my pancake mix and syrup are. At least once a week I cook breakfast.

Yeah, really! Pancakes are my thing. That and toast are about the only foods I can cook. I hate to brag but I'm actually kind of famous for my specialty shaped hot cakes. Silver dollar size, huge full pan flapjacks, and heart-shaped pancakes for my darling wife. I've even experimented with different forms of animals and letters. I once cooked up a batch of alphabet pancakes that read E-A-T M-E and U S-U-C-K.

They were a huge breakfast hit with the guys before the early Sunday game.

My best pancake invention to date, though, is the one I cooked specially for my single sister-in-law, the one who needs some help in the dating department. It took a lot of hard work and a little ingenuity but the Big Prick pancake with two silver dollar balls attached to its base, was, I must say, my proudest achievement on the stove. My sister-in-law must have loved it too because she ate the whole friggin' thing, then with a smile on her drowsy face went to take a nap.

Then I went to the meat department. I was looking for some hot Italian sausages, which are great grilled on the hibachi we have on the back stoop. The closest thing I could find was a package of Himie Jun's smokehouse sausages, so I got one.

Next I went in search of the bean aisle. There's nothing like beans and sausages with a cold beer. In fact, that's probably my favorite meal. I think, if ever I was a condemned man and had the choice, that would be my final supper.

I heard some footsteps pounding in the background over near the fruits and vegetables. Kids, I figured, or maybe there was a hot special on avocados. Who cares? I thought. All I wanted were beans.

"Excuse me dear." I found a lovely attendant. "Where are the beans located?" I asked. Surprisingly she partly understood me and escorted this charming man to the health and beauty aids section where she promptly pointed at a display of family size Bean-O bottles.

"Thank you sweetie," I volunteered, not wanting to embarrass the little girl. Oh, the stories I could tell her if I only had the time. Since I was already there I picked up a smaller container of gas relief pills and decided to find the damn beans myself.

I saw a trio of young Thai men running back and forth through the grocery aisles. Why don't they just ask one of the girls for help? I naturally thought. Then I recognized one of them, the wiry one with the greasy spiked black hair and his tattooed dragons breathing fire out of their nostrils.

"Oh shit!" I quickly yelped.

The pool hustler fuckers were still looking for me. I had to get out of there before I was two hundred baht lighter and one step closer to the intensive care unit. I hid behind a tall stack of Chung beer cases. Hey, that's a damn good price, I reasoned. But a whole case would be too heavy to lug all the way home. Especially if Charlie and his crew caught up with me. So I picked up two single serving sizes of Mrs. Bushna's beans and dropped them in my hand held basket.

Trying to stay ahead of the punks I snuck around the corner and went two rows down back to the cereal aisle. I peeked around the edge and saw them sampling some trail mix being offered by one of the girls. Then I walked toward the end of the row looking for a fast escape route.

Well, what do you know. They had some of my favorite cereals. Frootie Loopies, Rice Crinkles, and Choco-Bits with pieces of dried mangos. I wish I had more time and room to pick up a couple boxes, but at the moment my life was more important than a few heavenly bowls of breakfast sugar delights. Maybe just one box of Loopies, just in case.

I ran like hell through the feminine protection aisle trying to avoid being detected. What in the hell is all this stuff? I mentally inquired after browsing through at least a thousand different female products. I didn't know what half the things were for or where they went but there sure was a ton of this shit. These women have some serious issues if you ask me.

It's so much easier being a man. No creams, no lotions, no things with wings. Hell, us rugged ones don't even have to wear under drawers.

I was ready to head toward the check out when I heard a high shrieking sound.

"There he is. That's the man!"

A beautiful young lady was yelling in Thai, but I instinctively knew what she was screaming by the way she was pointing at me. My Miss August photo playmate was with two very large bodyguards who looked as if they were ready to jump into the World Wrestling Federation ring and tear somebody's head off. Like mine. Even though I knew damn well that all that shit they do on television is fake, these two guys scared the hell out of me.

I didn't want to get slam dunked, and needed to disappear, but quick!

Chapter 38

Now I had two groups of Asian banditos after me. Holy shit, Batman! I was in deep trouble, and I still hadn't finished my shopping.

I ducked behind a large Pepsi display then joined a family pushing their overloaded cart toward the exit. They probably wondered who in the hell this white guy was tagging along with them and carrying two of their little ones in an attempt to blend in, as if I was their long lost Uncle Lin. Unfortunately, I blended in with this frail Chinese couple like a big white sore thumb, and was quickly spotted by my Miss August photo girl and her muscle.

I sprinted down the spaghetti lane to get out of the line of fire from my persuers. The aisle girl looked very friendly so I decided to take a short breather and chat with her until I could catch my wind. She was giving out freshly made garlic bread samples, so I eat a few.

"This is very delicious rice bread slathered with coagulated garlicky flavored oil based imitation butter, my dear," I complimented her after taking my first bite.

The sweet kid smiled as if she had just seen Santa Claus and giggled herself silly with the prospect that she was actually going to sell some of this crap.

I asked her where I could find a bag of this horrible bread and she was kind enough to show me. I thanked her profusely for the help and her gracious concern shown to me. When she returned to her station to lay some of this shit on other unsuspecting clients I spit out the wet glob of doughy, tasteless paste and looked for something to clean out my mouth, like Extra Strength Drano.

I hadn't forgotten about Charlie, who I'm sure was still somewhere in the store, but I was most concerned about Miss August's boys. Checking out the pasta sauces I came up with a brilliant idea. I needed to create a diversion, which would allow me to slip through the check-out register and get the hell out of there.

Right across from my crouched position behind an Italian spice rack was a big crowd of shoppers milling around a bunch of cookie shelves and digging through the mountain of packaged minty thins, peanut butter crunches, apple crisps, and sugar sprinkled butternut cookies. I remembered I wanted to buy a box of special cookies my very particular wife enjoyed since she's been so nice to me during our vacation.

Charlie and his hit men eyed me checking out the cookie counter and split up as they ran my way. I had to act fast. I grabbed a one-liter jar of spaghetti sauce with meat and mushrooms and was ready to execute my getaway plan.

"Hey! Rago. They have Rago sauce here," I almost yelled out. "Cool man. We can have a nice spaghetti dinner with good sauce, sans the buttery garlic bread."

I tossed the bottle of red sauce into the cookie crowd. I figured it would smash into a million pieces and splash meaty tomato sauce all over the middle aisle. The giant mess would clog up the shopping traffic and make it impossible for my killers to reach me. The patrons would be splattered to hell, but it was a small price to save a man's life.

The jar of Rago's Supreme dropped solidly in the center of my fellow shoppers.

"Sorry guys," I muttered my apology.

The bottle hit squarely where I aimed. I was ready to scoot out of my hiding place and head home. But to my surprise the jar didn't break. It didn't shatter, nor disperse the mob. It didn't flood the tiled floor with a terrible mess or even cause a single bit of commotion. My cover was blown and I slithered back to my hole.

"Fucking plastic bottle!" I cursed.

I clutched another bottle of sauce, this time a store brand, and made damn sure it was made of glass. Then I thought it wouldn't be safe to have exploding shards of glass penetrate the innocent shoppers, or myself. So instead I picked up another plastic jar, a great big family size this time. In order to make this work I unscrewed the lid just enough and quickly flung the missile like a ripe hand grenade where I had thrown the practice shot.

"Incoming!" I roared, to warn the twenty or so people standing around.

For a brief moment I was back in the war trying to evade the commie VC who was determined on blowing up my toilet. I readied myself in a crouched position to sprint forward once the explosion hit.

Bam!

The sauce bomb bounced on the floor between two women gossiping about their neighbor, who apparently had too much free time on her hands and was fooling around with the mailman while her husband was at work fooling around with his secretary. I wanted to stick around and hear more but the clock was ticking.

The loose lid popped off that sucker like a champagne cork, causing the plastic jar to spin like a gyroscope and bounce around like a Mexican jumping bean. Tomato sauce sprayed everything and everybody within a ten-meter radius. It was absolutely beautiful, almost better than watching the Fourth of July fireworks back home. My plan worked and no one was injured.

The welcomed chaos was exactly what I needed and I quickly pounced to my feet.

The screaming was instantaneous and all eyes in the place turned toward ground zero. "Come on guys. It's only spaghetti sauce."

I grabbed my shit and ran to the nearest register. That's when I saw Charlie and his Pips charge closer toward me. There was no way they could get through the blockade of stained and angry patrons. Then they ran down the cooking oil aisle, detouring around the sloppy mess figuring they could go around and get me from the right flank.

Anyway, that's what they thought.

"Who the hell do you think you're dealing with, pal?" I laughed out loud at their predictable manuever.

Knowing full well the back aisle was a possible gap in my defense, while browsing through the corn oil and safflower oil shelves I opened several two liter jugs of the slippery substance and made sure the floor was thickly coated to prevent any passage. I've seen enough Bond movies and *Mission Impossible* shows to stay way ahead of the bad guys.

"Kiss my furry white ass dudes. I'm outa here."

A high-pitched voice came over the store's loud speaker. "Crean up in aisles sewen, eight, nine, ten, eighteen and nineteen. Prease hurry!"

I got in the check out line for fifteen items or less which was fine with me to help with my speedy exit. Except, the lady in front of me was taking her sweet friggin' time fumbling through her massive suitcase sized purse.

"Hey lady. Don't you know you're supposed to have your money ready?" I told her with a teeth-grinning smile so as not to upset her and slow down her progress even further. She finally paid the cashier, then absentmindedly recalled that she had a discount coupon for some facial cream she just bought.

Coupons in Thailand! Can you believe that?

I didn't have the heart to tell her no amount of beauty cream would help as she painstakingly searched through her purse. The heat was after me and I knew the road-blocks weren't going to hold back my adversaries too much longer. Hurry the fuck up, I wanted to scream.

"Here," I said instead to the excruciatingly slow broad. "Take this two baht in place of your friggin' coupon."

She apparently understood some of my offer but with her old lady pride and stubbornness refused the more than generous gift. I wanted to knock her on her bony ass and jump ahead of her but finally she found the damn two baht off coupon and presented it to the girl.

At last it was my turn. I gave a weary smile to the clerk as I loaded my basket onto the moving conveyor belt. "Hurry, hurry, hurry!" I kept saying under my breath as I looked around nervously.

I was almost done checking out when I heard from my photo pin up girl.

"There he is, Bull!"

Bull? Fuck me! I was spotted again.

Holy shit, her friend was a bull, more like a water buffalo, and his glaring eyes caught mine from several rows back. She must have told her bulky friends about the movie thing and discovered it was nothing but a scam for me to take her half naked pictures and maybe hook up with her later.

Mr. Spielberg, you no good son-of-a-bitch!

"Please God. Get me out of this jam and I promise not to drink as much," I began pleading with my estranged Maker. "Father Donnelly is a friend on mine," I name dropped my old priest for good measure.

"Hurry, hurry, hurry!" I insisted to the cashier girl.

She was ringing up my last item. "Oh, oh," she said.

I hate when people say "Oh, oh." It's never a good thing.

"No pwice on this sywup. I call for pwice check."

"No, no. That's okay. Forget it. I don't really want it anyway," I said in a very urgent tone. There's ten thousand things in this fucking store and how come I get the one friggin' item without a price on it?

She picked up the intercom mike, "Pwice check on Aunt Jarepun's maple sywup."

OMG!

If there is a hell I was standing in it at the express lane waiting for a friggin' price check on a bottle of fake maple syrup while several killers were honing in on me. After what seemed like a lifetime a stock boy came over and told the girl the price.

She rang up my tally then asked me, "Yo have VIP card sir?" I couldn't believe what was happening. I might as well have been in Safeway being checked out by the one-armed cashier, getting grilled for my ID and home phone number so I could save half off on beef burritos.

I took a deep breath and told the sweet girl, "I no have VIP card." I was so flustered I was beginning to talk like a native.

"So sowwy sir, you no have card I have to charge full pwice."

"Yeah, whatever," I said, done with the whole mess.

And you wonder why I hate shopping!

I picked up my bags and rapidly moved toward the front of The Mall. I was one minute outside the grocery store when it dawned on me that I forgot my check-in bag. So I quietly snuck back to the bag drop-off booth.

Not surprising the same old coupon lady was in front of me waiting to pick up her checked bag. The baggage clerk handed her a flimsy tote bag and, wouldn't you know it, the clumsy old broad spilled its contents all over the counter and onto my feet. What the hell did she need a tube of K-Y jelly for? On second thought I really didn't want to know.

I shoved the irritating woman aside and quickly handed my tickie to the kid behind the counter and scurried away to safety with my shit. Then I ditched the Red Sock cap and put on my black and purple Dimondbacks hat to throw the bad guys off my trail.

I began zigging and zagging through the rows of clothing and household goods, moving in and out of small storefronts to lose my opponents. I swung by the Eat Me Bakery and stood in line to buy a dozen of those bean-filled Chinese pastry cookies my adorable wife likes so much.

Out of the corner of my eye I noticed a gorgeous Thai woman walking an aisle away from me. She had on that blue dress I've come to like so much. Her luscious long hair danced with her every step. Her rounded hips swayed with her gracious strides. Even from the back I had no doubt it was my new girlfriend from the bus ride to town.

All my worries about me being sliced and diced by my armies of enemies fell by the wayside.

This was love, not war!

Still dragging along my bags I ran to catch up with her. This time I had my camera ready to shoot a portrait of my living angel.

"Sawadee. Excuse me," I said to her as I edged up next to the girl of my dreams. They were three more words than I had the courage to say before. This time I wasn't going to make the same wimpy mistake. She stopped in mid stride, her perfectly shaped feminine legs taut in her high heels.

I looked straight into her face and was surprised, confused, almost horrified. She had a heavy five o'clock shadow on her cheeks and chin and very noticeable sideburns. It wasn't even four- thirty yet and I could tell that she was a he. No fucking way was this person my girlfriend, especially not under the harsh lights of The Mall.

She, or he, must have been going to work in one of those dark places with the really dim mood lighting. I'll bet she was one of Ice's drag queen friends. I took a quick picture of her/him anyway so my buddy Hank wouldn't doubt me. Who knows, he may even like it.

Thank god she wasn't my girlfriend or I'd really have an unbelievable story to live down.

I passed the food court and saw the pool area through the large front windows. I was almost at the entrance. Then I noticed a guy who looked familiar. He had an ugly, bent over old women clinging to his leg like a kid who didn't want to go home holding onto his mother.

He saw me, and even in my baseball cap disguise recognized who I was. It was the bus rider who had kept giving me the evil eye. The one I gave the used up whore to in the eight baht bus. He looked extremely pissed off but couldn't move too quickly with Suzy Q latched onto him for dear life. Apparently this time the octogenarian had found her man and had no intention on giving him up.

What a nightmare I found myself in.

It was the perfect fucking storm!

I had everyone and their brother trying to get me. Miss August and her thugs, Charlie and his crew, and now this dude from the bus with my old squeeze in tow.

I prayed once more, promising to cut back on greasy foods if I could somehow get home. I even vowed to be nice to everyone I met from here on in. If I had to.

I hit the exit doors with a cry for freedom, like a convict does when he gets released from his five to ten years in the joint without conjugal visits. I was weighed down with all these bags, tired from running for my life, frustrated as hell with my shopping experience, and was being chased by half of Korat.

And it was still fucking hot and sticky.

"Yo, Taxi!"

Chapter 39

In Thailand you don't have to call for a taxi because once you exit a building at least twenty cabbies are in your face. "Where to sir?" "Wery clean ride, sir." "Take you anywhere for little baht, sir." "You need woman, mister?" "Maybe young boy?"

I just can't get over the terrific personal service in this great city. But you have to be careful since it's common practice to negotiate the price of the fare. There are no meters on the tuk-tuks. So in order not to get ripped off you absolutely have to set the rate with the driver before you ever step a foot in his back seat, otherwise the sky's the limit.

Trust me!

I was in a big rush but still didn't want to pay more than the going rate. I told the first hack I wanted to go to the bus stop on the other side of town. From there the bus would take me on a leisurely ride straight to my home. After the previous ride with my negotiating wife I knew the trip from The Mall should cost no more than sixty baht, seventy tops.

The cabbie could tell I needed the first coach out of Dodge, with my bags all amiss and my worried-white-guy-all-by-myself look. "One hundred baht, mister. I take you now. Get there wery fast."

"One hundred? No fucking way pal," I let him know in no uncertain terms that I wasn't the usual foreign tourist pushover who could be so easily gouged for basic three-wheeled transportation.

It was clear this guy couldn't be trusted so I interviewed the next tuk-tuk pilot. This type of street negotiation was quite expected. In fact, if you didn't attempt to haggle over the price you were considered a real dork and deserved to be taken advantage of.

"Eighty baht to bus stop," the alternate driver said, trying to read my steadfast poker face. "I get you there in ten minutes fast," the guy tried to make a case for his still inflated fare.

It was a twist on the old bait and switch con job, which I refused to bite. I knew it was only a matter of seconds before the triad of pissed off killers would crash through the front doors of The Mall.

In no time they'd be running down the stairs to the tuk-tuk parking lot, anxious to chop the head off GI Joe, the dick off Mr. Spielberg, and the balls off Boob the bastard man.

I didn't want to stick around for that!

The third taxi man saw the way I handled myself with his associates and stepped up with his reasonable offer. "Only sixty baht for you Joe. We go now."

I let the reference to Joe go without comment since he was giving me a damn good price to hit the road. The afternoon rush hour traffic was picking up and I needed to get going. I loaded my plastic bags onto the floor of his taxi and squeezed into the small back seat.

Just as my driver pulled the rope to start up his rig I looked back and saw all three main mall doors blow open. There they stood. Images of evil. Visions of death. Legends of torture. Savages of destruction. And directly behind these groups of school children leaving the pool area I saw the true avengers.

And in unison they saw me.

"Hurry man, hurry!" I yelled at my driver. Without looking both ways he pulled his motor-trike into the flow of traffic barely missing becoming the hood ornament of a huge Mitsubishi truck speeding down the boulevard. My groceries and stuff scattered around the floor and I lost my treasured baseball cap in the traffic wind. My hunters, screaming their damn lungs out, were yelling rude remarks at me and making obscene gestures, some of which I really didn't think Thai people knew.

Fortunately for me my hostile opponents were blocked off from my escape by the exiting class of kids in their swimsuits and oversized flippers.

Charlie the billiards hustler threw his bag of iced tea my way and missed by a mile. "I find you, I kill you GI," he screamed as loud as he could. He was very upset and was turning a bright red from all the excitement. If he didn't calm down he would most assuredly burst a blood vessel in his neck and there'd be one less idiot for me to worry about.

The almost-movie-star-photo girl was yelling hysterically too. She never would have been a good leading lady but maybe she could handle one of those crying bits in a horror flick. Sorry kid, that's how the business is. Her hired help were flexing their steroid enhanced bi-ceps and breaking my imaginary bones with their bare hands.

I bent over my open tuk-tuk seat and mooned the bastards just to let them know I had muscles too.

Finally, Suzi Q's new boyfriend was rigid with hatred. He appeared to be violently deranged and kept swatting at his love bunny who was still wrapped around his calf like a piece of Canadian bacon tooth-picked around an aged rib eye steak.

Um…I should have picked up a few steaks.

"I don't want this expired old wrinkled up bag hanging on me forever. I can't get this bloodsucking leech off me. You get back here and take her, you no good son-of-a-bitching contemptible whore monger," his piercing voice got lost in the street noise.

Well, I don't think those were his exact words but that was the gist of his outrageous tirade. Poor sucker, I thought. He'll never be right again.

From a few hundred meters down the road, in what I considered pretty safe territory, I flipped my new friends the bird with both hands. And then, to really piss them off, I turned my upright middle fingers and pointed at them. My final salute made them go berserk. From where I was sitting it was fun to watch.

Most likely I wasn't going back to The Mall for some time.

My daring and resourceful tuk-tuk driver, who I just named Tonto, put it in high gear and pulled a wheelie as we raced toward the bus station. We were riding a 'fiery horse with the speed of light, a cloud of dust and a hearty Hi Ho Silver, away!' Bob Swift rides again to live yet another day.

Suck on that!

We stayed abreast of the heavy traffic with the best of them as Tonto whipped around the big rigs, the clusters of hundreds of motorcycles, and the rest of his crazy three-wheeling cousins.

He was no Pirate Eddie but could move like a son of a gun around busy corners, through narrow alleys, and along pedestrian congested right-of-ways. He didn't even try to hit anyone, which actually made the ride kind of boring. He was a serious tuk-tuk pilot, took pride in his job, and knew how urgent it was to get me as far away from The Mall as quickly as possible.

I decided his diligence would earn him a generous tip.

At first, not recognizing any stores or landmarks I thought my driver was taking me on one of those rides where the tourist never returns and his ravaged body ends up in a trash heap behind one of the Happee-Happee bars. But then I realized old Tonto was taking a short cut through people's back yards and front bar-be-cue areas to make sure we weren't being followed.

I waved at the citizens as we roared through their front yard dining mats laid out on the ground where I couldn't resist lifting a small sample of shrimp on a stick from the hot coals. We maneuvered around piles of laundry being scrubbed with rocks the old fashion way. "Looks like you could use a new rock," I commented to one of the ladies, in my friendly manner. Most of the city dwellers just looked at me and my taxi and waved like we were someone they knew who only had a second to swing by and say hello.

Everyone of them smiled.

I was beginning to really like this guy Tonto, and felt I was in competent hands. Before I knew it we were back on the main drag chasing some mopeds with young girls in their short skirts riding side-saddle on the back. I started to recognize some familiar places and felt a bit relieved that we were indeed going in the right direction, retracing the steps of my morning's adventurous trip.

Tonto knew his shit!

We drove past the beautiful Thai temples I admired so much in the middle of the city. We slowed down in front of my massage parlor as I stretched my neck to see if I could recognize anyone I knew inside.

Memories were good enough for the moment and I vowed, "I shall return." Tonto even attempted a looksie, as if he too had a good friend inside. He gave out a wild, drunken laugh and stepped on the gas as the wheelbarrow-like tires peeled out.

He was all right!

A few minutes later my cab took a sharp corner and nearly wiped out a huge white tent covering some sort of small building off the walkway. There was a long strip of that yellow crime scene tape wrapped around the tent and tied off between a tree and a fence post.

I saw several men in what appeared to be haz-mat suits with the red warning labels on the back of their gear. They were all wearing heavy-duty oxygen masks and shaking their heads, as if they were too frightened to clean up an atomic waste site or plutonium spill.

There was a white van parked in the roped off street with a huge flexible vent-like hose running from an exhaust suction fan inside. An ambulance crew was rolling out one of the workers still in his safety suit on a stretched out gurney a safe distance from the public toilet. Apparently there was some kind of accident or overflow or something which required immediate attention from the city's public waste team.

Who in the world would cause such a horrible disaster? I thought to myself.

There were four cops with rifles guarding the premises and directing traffic away from the restroom, which obviously would have to be torn down. Tonto pulled his bandana over his nose as we weaved around the treacherous scene. I quickly looked into the police car parked in the middle of the road and saw my bathroom attendant locked in the rear seat with Chinese handcuffs secured on his index fingers.

It looked as if the fucking toll thief got caught ripping off innocent, baht paying tourists. Perhaps he was also being accused with the unnatural and inhumane use of public facilities. Good for him, the no good, fifty-baht-a-shit, sorry-no-toilet-paper, fucking thief. Serves him right.

Sometimes justice prevails!

We quickly stopped at the traffic light near my favorite restaurant, the old white man hang out. The supper crowd was streaming in.

"I want to check on something," I told my driver. I was feeling bad after what I had gone through and wanted to help someone, if I could. After all, I did make a promise to the big guy upstairs that I would try to be nice if he helped me escape from The Mall.

Yeah, yeah. I also said I'd cut back on the beer and greasy food too. But one thing at a time.

"I'll be right back. Okay?" I said to Tonto. "Don't take my stuff." We were friends, but not that good of friends.

I ran into the restaurant and guess who I saw? The sun tanned Australian crock full of shit Jamie Crock. He was yapping away at another foreigner, no doubt telling tall tales again. The lying, thieving bastard. Be careful my man, I wanted to warn the new guy. This friggin' convict probably has his eyes on your watch or cell phone. Or maybe he wants another pair of sunglasses. By critchy.

I went into the bathroom hoping not to see what I saw.

The poor son-of-a-bitch Brit, Bradley, was still there, squatting over the ceramic bowl fast asleep, waiting for someone, anyone, to bring him a roll of napkins. It was a pitiful sight. I felt sorry for the dip shit, but nobody should be left like that.

He looked pretty damn relaxed though, and I didn't want to wake him. So I gently pulled out my paperback book from my cargo pants pocket, opened it up past the missing pages to chapter four and softly placed it in his lap.

"So long Brad and Billy," I said, bidding farewell to both the British gentleman and Mr. Clinton.

I hated that book anyway!

Chapter 40

I RETURNED TO MY waiting tuk-tuk and was glad to see all my bags were still in place. Tonto was leaning against his funny looking taxi, smoking a hand rolled cigarette and ogling the parade of beautiful young ladies walking by. He shook his head as if he knew life wasn't fair, and jumped into the driver's seat. Then he threw me a toothy what-the-hell smile, the way men communicate with each other about women without uttering a word.

He must have been a married guy too.

Before my driver pulled away from the curb he lightly tapped his horn as a humble gesture of respect for the honorable statue in the courtyard across the street. I kicked up my feet in the back seat of my sixty baht limousine. "Home James," I instructed the guy in front who was fast becoming my good buddy.

We continued past a long line of tourist buses parked near the heroic monument and entered the more seedy side of old Korat. Sidewalk bars and sleazy nightclubs peppered both sides of the street. More massage parlors, beer vendors, and short time hotels dominated the red light district. The sidewalk merchants were out in force preparing their foods and wares for the night shift. Scantily clad women strutted around warming up the crowd of prospective clients.

It was like riding in a pimp mobile, checking out all the options in front of me.

We tuk-tukked along the same route I had taken earlier coming into town. The girls in the corner jewelry shop were still behind the glittery counter helping their customers pick out the perfect gold rings and bracelets. I waved at the cuties as if they should remember me for not buying anything from them. A minute later me and Tonto drove by my baseball cap guy. I had extra money and wanted to buy some more hats but was afraid I might miss the bus back home.

I watched the many people walking around, shopping, eating, haggling over prices, doing what they do everyday. Dumb ass foreigners were still falling into open sidewalk gaps. Tall fuckers continued to bash the hell out of their heads on low hanging clothes poles. Eye patch vendors were still doing a bang up business with the banged up pedestrians.

I hadn't heard much from Big Slick in awhile.

Thank god!

For once he was being a good boy by staying out of my business. I sprawled out in the open-air back seat to take advantage of the street breeze since it was still pretty damn hot and muggy. Fresh air flowed up my pants legs giving Slick and the twins a cool break from being cooped up all day. The big guy down there muttered a thankful, "Oh yeah." It was like a scene straight out of a country western movie where the dog sticks his head out the window of the pick-up truck enjoying the wind hitting his face.

This had actually been a nice trip with Slick and his little brothers.

Except for that one time on the bus, and oh yeah, back at the massage parlor, but I could understand what he was after since I was there too. We've known each other our entire lives, but for some odd reason today's journey together has afforded us the private time to get to know one another even better. I think we understand each other more. Not that we'll always be in agreement on certain issues, but at least now there's a true sense of respect between us.

My man Slick.

A funny thought popped into my head how most guys, the ones that I know anyway, tend to name their private members. They christen them with simple street names like Willie or Big John. There's other names right out of the wrestler's handbook, like Chester the Molester, or Peter the Penetrator, or Hungry Hombre. A few are more graphic as in Doctor Bucky's Famous Painless Meat Injector, or Tuna's Delight. Pretty stupid if you want my opinion.

Me, I go for the simple ones. Hey, when you have it there's no need to brag about it. Am I right? The point here is that all that bullshit about a dog being man's best friend doesn't hold a drop of water. Every man knows his best friend is always within hands reach.

We were coming up on a large open produce and meat market, which I remembered from before. It was getting close to five thirty but I knew the buses never leave on time so I told Tonto to stop for a minute. I wanted to pick up a few ripe mangos to bring home.

Mangos, my friends, are the most underrated, under appreciated fruit on the planet. Their sweet juices and tender fibers hold the secrets of youth discovered through eons of science and generations of old men looking for a little loving.

It's a fact, Jack!

There's something in mangos that rejuvenates men's worn out, ah...egos. Every time I eat a sliced up delicious mango I want to get laid. I thought it was a fluke the first time so I tried it again. Yep, had the same results. That's when my wife stopped buying them. Here in Thailand mangos are plentiful, fresh, and ripe. My tired wife is always hiding them from me for some reason.

Hey, this is great health food. I need my damn mangos!

Anyway, back to the fruit lesson.

About a year ago my loving wife and I were spending a quiet Saturday evening at home watching CSI on the tube. I opened the screw off top of a bottle of good wine. We were getting a little frisky after finishing off the liter of Boone's Farm Strawberry Hill. My tipsy wife was turning silly and I was getting horny. I knew the fun would begin at the next commercial break.

I got up from the loveseat and looked for some mangos. I wanted to make sure this old stud muffin had some stamina and longevity. Either my wife had thrown them away or she was hiding the passion fruit from me. I knew I'd need some help in the erectile department so, unable to chomp on a few pieces of sex fruit, which really work like a charm, I went to the bathroom and popped one of my blue buddies.

Months earlier my fat doctor had given me a few samples of that stud saving pill, Viagra. He then gave me a prescription for a month's supply. Nine pills at eleven bucks a hit. Holy shit! I've never paid that much to get laid.

Hell, only nine pills? I thought at first. What a rip off! Then I remembered that nine love pills were most likely enough for almost a year. Who am I kidding. Maybe longer than that. Old man sex was getting expensive and at that price I had to conserve them. Mangos were much cheaper.

If I could have found the fucking things!

CSI was over at ten, which gave my blue pill plenty of time to locate the blood in my dick. I wondered how in the hell does a little pill know where it's supposed to go. The miracle of science I guess. What would happen if the pill took a wrong turn and ended up some place else in my body? Like in the hemorrhoids hanging out my ass or the middle finger on my writing hand. Worse yet, what if, for some reason, the friggin' pill couldn't find Big Slick?

That would be darn right disappointing and a damn waste of eleven hard earned dollars.

So my tipsy wife and I enjoyed our quality time together with Mister Woody. And it wasn't even my birthday! I promptly fell asleep, and after dreaming of a menage a trois (you thought I forgot my French, didn't you?) with Bo Derek and JLo, I woke up in a sweat. Slick was in heaven waiting for more action, but my dear wife wasn't in bed. I rolled over wondering about tomorrow's baseball game but I had to get up.

It was nearly two thirty in the morning and I couldn't go back to sleep, I didn't know where my adorable wife was, and I had a stiffy that was harder than a wedding prick. I suddenly got worried. The prescription instructions read, "If you experience an erection for more than four hours, call your doctor." I remember seeing that exact same warning on a TV commercial and thought it was ridiculous. Why the hell would you want to call your doctor?

Instead you'd be looking around to poke somebody.

I was concerned for Big Slick in his condition, however. If he stayed like that forever how would I ever go pee again? I'd have to lean against the toilet wall and hold a Big Gulp cup over it. I wouldn't be able to go out in public. I remembered the time I was a kid at the beach running around with my little pecker towel rack.

So I did what I was instructed to do. I called my doctor.

"Hello..."

"Hey, Doc. It's me, Bob Swift."

"Who...?"

"Your patient. You gave me some Viagra samples. Remember me?"

"Mr. Swift. Why are you calling? It's...it's the middle of the night."

"Yeah, I know Doc. But this is important. Could be a matter of life and death. I had to call you."

The doctor was awake by then. "What do you want?" My doctor sounded a bit ticked off.

"Well Doc, I took one of those blue Viagra pills you gave me since I couldn't find any mangos in the house."

"Huh?"

"Never mind. But it's been more than four hours and I still have a wicked hard on. What should I do?"

"You what?" my doctor said with surprise. "Just try to go to sleep, Mr. Swift. It will go away in a while. Trust me."

"You heard me," I told my doctor. "I haven't had one this stiff since my second junior prom." Then I figured this was not a good time to go into that wonderful, carefree, spontaneous time of my life, when I was actually somewhat happy.

"Mr. Swift. I don't know what to tell you. Try sleeping on your stomach."

"I did," I said. "But I can't, this damn thing keeps pole vaulting me out of bed. I almost landed in the hallway."

I could hear that my doctor was getting frustrated. "Then sleep on your damn back," he yelled at me.

"Tried that too," I said, completely exacerbated. "But I can't see the TV."

I could tell my doctor was done with me. What ever happened to that Hippocratic oath these guys take?

"Then ask your wife to massage your back. That should put you at ease and help you sleep."

"She's gone," I said. "She must have left when my thingie still wanted to play. I don't know where she is." I was desperate for assistance.

Maybe my insomniac wife was afraid and went to the twenty-four hour Wal-Mart.

"Mr. Swift, I'm going to hang up now. Just take a cold shower and you'll be fine," my doctor said and then hung up on me.

That's a good idea, I thought. I'll have to thank my doctor, next time I see him. I'm staying away from those blue buddies and sticking to the mangos. They're a lot safer. Cheaper too.

So Tonto my tuk-tuk driver pulled over and I jumped out to buy a half dozen mangos from this cute little market girl selling all kinds of fruit. She handed me my bag of mangos and I raised my eyebrows at her like Groucho Marx does when he means trouble. She smiled back at me and gave me the thumbs up signal.

The word about mangos is on the street.

Mangos rule!

We drove just a couple more blocks to the bus station where Tonto came to a screeching halt. I gave him his fare plus a twenty baht tip for saving my life. We shook hands like old pals and I tossed him a mango just in case he got lucky enough to use it after work.

There was a row of city buses parked along the curb in front of vendors selling cold drinks in baggies and snacks on sticks. A bunch of bus drivers, tuk-tuk pilots, and samlor pedalers where sitting around concrete tables and playing some sort of checkers-like board game with bottle caps as their play pieces.

Several people where standing by with their groceries and children waiting to get on the sun-baked bus. The driver climbed into the front seat and revved up the engine. "All aboard," he said, or something like that.

I stepped onto my bus home.

Chapter 41

It was a new bus. At least it appeared to have been built in this century.

The seats had tall headrests and weren't worn up. The floor was made of corrugated steel and every fan hanging from the ceiling was whirling at full speed. The driver's dash had a stock stereo system, which was cranked all the way up. There was even a television screen built into the upper console for the passenger's video pleasure.

This was uptown all the way!

I recognized a few old patrons from this morning's trip. The mother with the young boy must have been returning home too. Several plastic shopping bags were stuffed under her seat. The boy remembered the strange white man and smiled. I flared my nostrils just to let him know I remembered him too. The poor guy who injured his arm with that fat bitch was also on the bus. Apparently he had learned his lesson and was sitting next to the window so there would be no more aisle assaults.

I couldn't believe it but that skinny, ancient women with the shitty smelling fish was on the return trip too. This time, thank god, there were no fish. She must have sold out to a bunch of smelly fish eating fools. I hunkered down in my seat hoping she wouldn't see me. The chicken cage was empty also, its contents probably being served this very minute with a pot of steaming rice.

I sat near the front, opened my window, and let the curtain flap in the light breeze. Most of the seats were empty, there were no animals on my bus, and the Thai music playing throughout sounded pretty good.

It promised to be a comfortable, quiet ride.

The driver worked his coach through a series of narrow roads barely scraping by parked cars, pushcart vendors, and oncoming vehicles. Slowing down around sharp corners he picked up a few stragglers without actually stopping and in a couple of minutes hit the main drag leading out of town. A young boy carried a cloth satchel and began collecting the fares.

Wow! A two-man operation. When it was my turn to pay I told him in my best Thai where I wanted to get off. I hoped he got what I was saying but would keep an eye ahead to make sure the bus would stop at my neighborhood.

It was getting late in the day and a lot of buses were on the road. My bus made its first stop at a little corner store. An older, thin gentleman waited to board. He attempted to climb the steep stairs but his crutch got in the way and his one good leg wasn't strong enough to lift him up. The bus driver put his rig in park and got up to help the man. Nice touch, I thought. It was obvious they knew one another. The older man was most likely a regular passenger.

The crippled man thanked his friend and sat next to me allowing himself plenty of leg room. "Sawadee," I said. He nodded and offered a smile filled with missing teeth.

"Army?" he asked me in broken English.

"No, I'm visiting Korat with my Thai wife," I told him in my broken Thai.

"Ah," he said, understanding what I was trying to say. "Good GI. You good GI."

"Yes, thank you," I said.

"Me GI too," he said, then pointed to his useless leg. "VC." And he made an explosion sound. "VC no good."

The best I could figure is he was an old Thai soldier who was wounded by the VC bastards during the war. He continued to smile and looked at me with his tired, yellowed eyes. They were trying to tell me something. They had a history to them, stories of good and bad, that only the eyes can relay. I felt as if I was a youngster sitting with my grandfather and listening to his tales of a hard, but honest life.

The man put his rough, leather-skinned hand on mine in a gesture of friendship, or maybe it was gratitude. All I could do was smile back at him, understanding what he had been through and how his country had been saved by the American military when he was a much younger man.

"Thailand good, VC no good. VC suck," I agreed with him.

There's a specialness about these Thai people. Not that I get along with everyone of them, or even like all of them, but there seems to be an innate goodness that comes across. There's something inexplicable that I really like about this place and its inhabitants.

Maybe the smiles are just a small part of it all.

By now the bus kept stopping and it was quickly filling up. A group of young and middle age women in white smocks boarded from their job at the entrance of a huge bread bakery. They talked amongst themselves glad to be done with work for today and in a hurry to get to their homes and families. One lady waved at a friend in the back of the bus. I sensed an air of giddiness coming from most of the women happy to be among friends.

School kids, all in tidy uniforms, hopped on the late afternoon bus and paid their half fares, since most regions had no school buses. They carried their books and backpacks. Some sipped a soft drink from a plastic baggie, others chewed on sugar candy or fried snacks. They were generally quiet and very well behaved. They shyly looked at me, the stranger in the crowd. A cloud of respectfulness hung over them.

I was fortunate to be seated on the shady side of the bus, the ceiling fans and opened windows giving only a little relief from the late sun. I was almost half way home. I was looking forward to seeing my loving wife and sharing some of the goodies I was toting. Maybe we could have her brothers over and I could grill the sausages and heat up some beans. Over cold beers I could show the guys what a good meal really was. Tomorrow I could show the kids how to play Frisbee.

But later tonight I wanted to see how well the local mangos really worked.

Right, honey bunny?

We were coming up on the bus stop where my gorgeous girlfriend in her seductive blue dress had gotten off. Wouldn't it be wonderful if she just happened to board my bus again, sit next to me, and rekindle our lost relationship? I'd have to kick the old man with the crutch out of my seat but I'm sure he'd understand. He'd do the same to me if the opportunity arose. After all, he was young once too.

But the bus continued down the highway without stopping for my girl. I looked out the window in futile hope, realizing the whole thing was probably not even real. Never meant to be. A figment of my imagination. An encounter of impossible possibilities. A mere fantasy of something that could have been right in my life.

Too damn bad!

However, at home I had a terrific wife waiting for me, her man forever. She was a women who really loved me, for whatever reason I could never figure out. I had family who cared for me and liked me, even the way I am. I had friends too, both here and at home. They were real, no matter how much they might deny it. Ha ha!

Maybe tomorrow morning I would make some pancakes. The special shaped ones with lots of genuine imitation maple syrup. I could watch my new movies, have a nice fried rice and beer lunch, and catch a nap in my private hammock out front. Then later in the day I could take a leisurely walk with my great wife and have coffee together up at Mike's store.

I could simply enjoy the day and the great people around me.

Simple and uncomplicated.

Maybe that's how life is supposed to be.

The bus was packed now with standing room only. Factory workers, school children, shoppers, returning vendors, and one old white dude who didn't feel so out of place any more. The kids exited in groups, saying good bye to their school mates and leaving in an unusually orderly fashion.

Workers stepped off and headed by foot down long roadways toward their homes set in small villages off the beaten path. Vendors picked up their folded bags and empty woven cages to be filled and readied for yet another day. And every one of them laughed and grinned and bid farewell and smiled as their day was coming to an end.

This simple, easy lifestyle was somehow contagious.

The passengers were thinning out as we moved further from Korat. The old veteran sat still beside me and occasionally looked at me with his kind and weathered face. People smiled at me as they departed and went home. The bus driver nodded his head at me through the reflection of his rearview mirror as if to indicate he would get me home soon too. The little boy collecting fares put his small hand on my shoulder to let me know he didn't forget where I wanted to get off.

I was liking being here!

It was certainly one heck of a day, my trip to the city. The excitement of being on my own, the danger of exploring the unknown, the exhilarating sense of being part of this great and welcoming place.

I sure did run into a mixed bag of people. I met some plain common folk, like the kid bus driver taking us to town and enjoying the trip no matter how many times he drove it. And the children and young people who laughed at my silly facial expressions and thought I was one weird foreigner. There were the lovely girls in the jewelry store and the hat and tee shirt merchants. Even the eye patch vendor. There was the sweet coffee girl in Starbucks and the cookie girl exchanging money. And the attendants at the shoe sale bin.

All good people!

Who could not like the tuk-tuk drivers? Tonto was the best and kind of fun to have around, though I will miss Pirate Eddie and his daredevil pranks. I'll also miss my masseuse girl and the special massage she gave me. You can rest assured I will go back there one day soon. If my jealous wife lets me. Oh yeah, I can't forget the mango girl who was nice too.

I also ran into some odd balls today.

ICE the drag queen has to top the list. He was cute in his own way but if I never run into him again it's all right by me. And how about the blob of a female who almost flipped over my bus and eventually got stuck in the seats. That woman definitely needs to go on a veggie diet and burn her pizza take out numbers. And there was the bug man selling deep fried protein by the kilo who almost had me with the crunchy crickets.

There were a few people I never want to see again.

Like Charlie the troublemaker from the bar who wanted to do me harm. Get over it pal. It's only two hundred baht. And of course there's the sexy Miss August and her hulky cohorts. At least I have her pictures. And who in the world could forget about that Mad Dog character with his love-starved Suzy Q? That poor bastard has no idea how much loving he's about to get for the price of a mere apple. I kind of hope I don't run into him again either.

Not to mention the variety of strange foreigners visiting Korat.

The fucking Russian who can't see straight and everyone disliked. And Jamie Crock from Down Under who couldn't tell a straight story if he had a ruler. Of course the two queers from Switzerland wouldn't even think of meeting up with me again for fear of being branded. And I'd bet neither would Uncle Bradley, who, god bless his soul, has by now woken up and used the rest of my history book.

They're all a bunch of no good, lying, thieving, phoney son-of-a-bitches anyway and not a one of them could be trusted for a far as I could throw them. But in their own way they were a fun group.

Then of course there were my own Blue Beard characters straight out of the funny farm. Each one of them was an unconscious take-off of someone I knew back home. Crazy Jack was based on an old farmer-cowboy I ran into back in Arizona. He was indeed a crazy son-of-a-bitch and always spoke his peace until he died drunk out of his mind in a cattle stampede.

Chicken Eddie was the character from one of my Air Force buddies who was stationed in Las Vegas and had a sweet deal answering the phone for a lady of the night friend. I'm not sure if I believed him when he told me he had first dibs with the professional entertainer as payment, but he sure was living it up and always had a shit eating grin on his mug.

Rich Diamond reminded me of this guy I know who actually wanted to legally change his name to that and make a million dollars by scamming little old ladies from their pensions and starting his own Ponzi scheme. Last I heard he was doing fifteen to twenty up state with a bunch of truly mean bastards who like tender young white guys.

And last, but certainly not least, there were the Thai women, who in my estimation will always be worth the trip. I definitely got plenty of pictures and when I get back to the States my buddy Hank and me are going to finish our Asian Lovelies calendar and sell them as Christmas gifts.

Of course, there was my fantastic girlfriend who I could never forget and never want to.

I guess my solo trip taught me a few things about the people living here and the wonderful surroundings in this tropical paradise. Maybe I learned a couple things about myself too. Like perhaps I should just try to work on me and not worry so much about anyone else. That would be a good start. Though, in all honesty, I won't be able to change that much.

Hey, this is the one and only Bob Swift, warts and all.

I think I may have figured out why the Thai people tend to smile all the time. They're a patient, quiet people who live with an overwhelming sense of gratitude for what they have, whether large or small. They also live every day with a halo of humility hanging over them. They like what they do. They like the people around them. I think they just like life.

Not a bad way of looking at things.

Its no wonder they smile!

I didn't forget my promise to the Big Guy either. I will try to cut down on my beer consumption, maybe knock it down to only a six-pack a day. I also will do my best to limit my intake of greasy foods. Maybe do Macs only twice a week.

Hey, nobody said it would be easy!

The bus driver came to another stop near a cluster of small stores and cooking stalls along the road. The veteran Thai soldier next to me put his wrinkled hand out to mine. He was getting off here and wanted to say goodbye. I helped him with his crutch and eased him down the stairs to the pavement. Then I waved so long to a great gentleman.

Up the hill ahead of us was my stop. The boy said something to the driver and motioned to me. I gathered my bags of goodies and worked my way to the open doorway as we came to my stop.

"Sawadee," I said to the driver as I left my journey of great memories behind.

Chapter 42

I EXITED THE BUS as it came to a California stop at the giant water fountain in front of my neighborhood.

My hands were loaded with bags of Chinese cookies and other sweets, three American movies, all of which I've seen on TV numerous times, a Willie Nelson CD, hopefully not dubbed in Thai, and my souvenir baseball caps. These were the treasures of my successful solo excursion.

I also had a box of pancake mix for my special breakfast along with a bottle of Aunt Punjub's maple-like syrup, a package of what I hoped were hot Italian sausages and some cans of beans, not Boston baked beans for sure, but they would do. A few other items filled out the bags. And for health reasons I had a bunch of ripe mangos that I swear worked ten times better than a handful of my Viagra blue buddies.

Just ask my amorous wife.

It was much later than I thought and I wondered if my darling wife had returned from her shopping trip. I was looking forward to a nice relaxing evening, a good meal, a quiet time to watch one of my Steven Seigal movies, and maybe, if the cookies worked, I'd get lucky around bedtime. I was glad to be home, though I had enjoyed my day on the road and learned much from my adventurous journey to the big city.

I had just enough Thai money left over to buy four cans of Singha or six bottles of Pepsi from the mini-mart. I walked over to the store, my dry throat thirsty as hell for a tall cold one. My good friend Mike, the Thai manager of the small store, was about to lock up when he saw his best customer fall off the bus.

"You go shopping by yourself?" he asked me with a big smirk on his face. Mike had spent several years in California, doing what, I never asked, and his English was almost as good as mine.

"Yeah," I said. "I took the bus to Korat to see the sites, pick up a few necessities. You know, just get out of the house to check things out."

Mike's eyebrows raised and he closed his eyes in a disappointed way. Like when your grade school teacher looked at you as if it's about time to give up on the little guy. "That not a good thing my friend. You in big shit trouble when you go home."

I had no idea what he was talking about. Hey, I come bearing gifts. I'm in the pink. "What the hell do you mean?"

The store manager simply shook his round head as if I was some kind of retard who had just fallen off the bus.

I was totally clueless.

"You not know? Women no like when man go to town by his self. Bad things happen. Very bad things."

"Hey Mike. Nothing bad happened to me. See, I'm safe and sound." I turned around in the middle of the small store. "No harm, no foul. I'm okay pal. Good as new. In fact, better."

"I not mean get hurt. I mean find women. They everywhere in Korat, and they looking wery nice," he said. A strange smile emerged on his brown face. Only the devil knows what was bouncing around in his brain.

I stared at him with a how-in-the-hell-do-you-know-that look. How in the hell did he know that?

"You in big shit trouble Bob. You show too much fun on your face," Mike warned me with a serious frown on his face.

At first I had to laugh. Then all of a sudden I did feel like a big load of shit. Guilt must have been written all over my face, as the saying goes. Then I realized I really was showing too much fun on my face. It was a dead giveaway that I had a good time on my own. I had to revert back to the old, bored, uninteresting, semi-depressed, never-did-nothing-wrong Bob Swift.

"Hey pal, I just want to buy a few beers. That's all."

Mike left it at that, still slightly shaking his head, hoping he wasn't going to lose his best customer tonight.

I got my beers, picked up my loaded bags, and walked past the guard shack. I saw my poor buddy George holding down his post with still a couple of hours left on his shift of pure boredom and drudgery. I waved at him and he eagerly saluted me, as was his typical custom. Damn good attitude that guy had.

Fuck it, I thought!

I tossed him a cold can of beer. He deserved a break. Leave the friggin' gate open tonight, Georgie. Who gives a damn? What's the worse that can happen?

"Sawadee, my friend," I hollered as he caught and cradled the life saving beer.

He said something like 'Thank you' and took a long, hard swig of the best damn Singha he had ever drunk. I saw him shaking his capped head at me as if he knew I needed a case full of luck when I arrived home.

I dragged my tired ass to our cute little house. The friggin' bags were getting heavier. I was glad to be here. I mean not just at my house, but here in Thailand, with so many good people around me. The Thai fam. My new friends. People who always had a big smile for me. People who were concerned for me and my welfare.

I removed my smelly sneakers in Thai tradition and left them on the front porch. I opened the door to my small castle. The girls were in, my beautiful wife and her two sisters. I had had a pretty damn good day and was in a great mood, appreciating everything I had always taken for granted. I forgot everything Mike had just told me. What the hell did he know anyway?

"Hi honey, I'm home!"

My wife stood in the middle of the living room to greet me. I was prepared for a big sloppy kiss, a long warm loving hug, an I-missed-you-so-bad smile, but she didn't look very happy to see her muffin man. I've seen that look before. Her face wasn't showing too much fun.

My safety shield automatically went up.

It does that instinctively whenever my subconscious senses pending trouble. Just like when I have the urgent need to sleep on my stomach to protect what's left of my manhood. You never know what an angry woman might resort to in the middle of the night while you're snoring away with a stupid, telling smile on your face. Natural primal instincts take over when they're needed for survival of the species. That's a proven fact invented by the legendary Charlie Darwin.

The burning fire in my wife's most beautiful eyes was also a clue that for some reason she was really pissed off at me. Plus, her lovely tanned arms adorned with sparkling gold bracelets where welded to her hips. Definitely a sure sign not to cross the woman, any women for that fact.

When the hands are holding the hips, you are in deep shit.

That's another one of those man laws.

The woman before me, my typically dear and docile wife, had that dragon glare that warned me something was drastically wrong. I felt like shrinking down to an invisible atomic particle and hiding behind a flowerpot or something so she couldn't see me. My mind was traveling a hundred miles a minute.

I had to get my story straight.

Fucking Mike! How come he didn't warn me this morning before I got on the bus? Sometimes, I swear, I get in trouble for doing absolutely nothing wrong.

But I don't make the calls!

"Hi honey. I brought you some cookies. The kind you like," I said, making an offering to the gods for whatever it was I had done. Maybe I left the toilet seat up when I left this morning. Maybe the top of the toothpaste tube wasn't screwed on tight enough. I might have put the toilet paper roll on backwards. Perhaps I forgot to take out the trash. I could have gotten the wrong fucking cookies.

Who the hell knows?

"I must say dear, you're looking exceptionally beautiful this evening," I said, complimenting her gorgeous looks with my big loving smile. Women love that sort of stuff. They live for flattery. It soothes the savage beast. I had to come up with some more killer lines to seal the deal and save my life.

She didn't appear to be very soothed. She stood ramrod straight, as stern as the wicked Catholic nun teachers who enjoyed smacking me on my knuckles and young ass for any tiny infractions. I swear, I was always getting whacked for something. Hey, it wasn't me who set off the fire alarms. I don't know who booby trapped the girl's restroom either. Makes me want to renounce my religion and become a Seventh Day Adventurist.

Both my wife's arms rested on her slender and sweet inviting hips that carried our two wonderful children into this world, which, again, any man worth his salt knows it means there's trouble a brewing in the homeland.

Body language tells all.

Oh, oh! I saw the sign. It read, 'You're dead meat, mister.' Was it a mere coincidence or an omen of my forthcoming demise. I was too young and innocent to die before I could explain away my indiscretions or before my vacation was even over.

My adorable wife was wearing a lovely blue dress with lace trim and one of those cloth belts snugged tightly under her full but aging breasts. I inadvertently remembered my bus trip. The one going into town. The one where my new girlfriend wearing the exact same dress sat down beside me and just about thrust herself upon me. She wanted me to embrace her in my arms, take her right there on the bus, to be with her forever.

Since I had recently come to believe there is no such thing as a coincidence I knew my ass was grass. How in the world could the two women I love in this crazy world be wearing the same dress on the very same day? It was a Rod Serling's *Twilight Zone* moment where I entered another dimension of twisted reality. Maybe I could at least keep the cookies. I suspected there wasn't going to be any loving tonight.

"I really love that blue dress you have on, sweetie pie. It makes you look very sexy," I tried to swoon her.

Her red demon-like eyes burnt a hole through my face. For some reason I felt my extremely kind comments weren't working like they were supposed to. My loving remarks were as effective as shooting blank bullets at Superman's impenetrable steel chest. They merely ricocheted into outer space and made her even angrier.

She was one pissed off woman!

Over the many years of my married life I've discovered one true fact of husbandly survival. Whenever you encounter an adversarial woman in a full frontal assault, which doesn't seem to be going your way, it's time to change strategies. It's time to search for your opponent's weak spot, their underbelly, their Achilles' heal.

It's time for Plan B!

"Ah, sweetheart," I said to her in my transparent attempt of sucking up. "I got you these cookies." I reached into one of my bags. "The kind you really like," I stumbled in my pathetic pleading for mercy.

Deep down in the dark hidden recesses of my rotting soul I knew I was caught. Women know when their men stray and fall to temptation no matter how violently and persistently we resist. It is widely acknowledged that we are not nearly as insightful as they are. Women have that ESPN thing, a feminine intuition that somehow tells them they have been betrayed. There's no natural explanation to this awesome power of theirs, but as sure as the sun rises every morning before noon, it is a force to be reckoned with.

How else could she know?

When all else fails and you know the battle is lost, in order to save your no-good lying ass you must resort to the final, and I have to admit, disgraceful behavior of a man about to be halved. Which, as every guy who has ever been put on the spot knows, is Plan C.

It's very simple. You turn around, forsake every bit of dignity you once possessed and give up all of your worldly belongings, and run like hell.

Run Bob! Run!

But I was no coward. Not this time anyway. I stood my ground and let my upset wife of thirty-seven fun-filled years have her way with this hollow core of a man I had become. My miserable life was over.

Take me oh Lord!

I was dead meat. Caught with my hands in the cookie jar as it were, or in this case, the nookie jar, if you really want to make light of the situation.

Sorry!

This is serious shit and it is definitely no time for bad jokes, although that was a pretty good one if I do say so myself. My fetching smile and flaring nostrils did nothing to dispel my wife's anger.

Hey, what did I do?

I had a fun, exciting, educational, innocent trip to the city. I mixed well with the locals, improved my conversational Thai, had a few laughs with some new friends, and spent some quality time by myself absorbing the culture of a strange and unusual land, a country, I must say, that I've come to like even more than I ever expected. I learned a few things about living in peace with myself and striving to be stress free.

But this wasn't really the time to talk about the esoteric qualities of life.

Even Big Slick and his little brothers enjoyed their walk and brief taste of freedom. Sure, we've had our disagreements, but the events of the day have brought us closer than we've ever been. We're a real family again.

But I guess I was asking for too much. I was nothing but a selfish bastard only concerned about my own superficial, fragile male needs, my shallow desires, and juvenile behavior.

I'm not such a bad guy, though. I really didn't do anything wrong. So how come I feel like a condemned man waiting for the guillotine to fall and cut off something vital? Where's my final cigarette, a last meal for a doomed man?

Bad karma had finally caught up with me.

It was a moral conflict I could only blame on my Catholic upbringing. Maybe I shouldn't have spent the dimes my mother gave me for the offering basket on penny candy. In Sunday School I told Father Donnelly I couldn't make it. I pleaded with him in the confessional to give me some slack. Instead of going all the way to heaven maybe I could just float above the earth like a patrolling angel. The worldly temptations were too overpowering, even at only ten years old.

Three hail Mary's? Hell, that wasn't enough. I needed direction. I needed discipline!

This time I couldn't be saved.

It had to be about my girlfriend!

Chapter 43

THE BEAUTIFUL PRINCESS IN the tight blue dress had twisted me like the mythical and unrelenting sirens calling me to my amoral death through the turbulent straits of a violent sea.

How could a man like me ever resist such sweet seduction? It was just a minor fling. A quickie love affair. An intoxicating moment where fantasy had met true love. An innocent bus ride that had gone further than was ever intended. A mere few moments of disgusting bodily pleasure and ecstasy of the mind.

It was great!

I ask you, should a man be thrown into the pit of endless eternal burning hell, or have half his shit taken away, for mere fantasy, simple happenstance? I think not! Don't blame me, the all-powerful gods had put us together.

It didn't mean anything, honey.

Honest to god!

In my tumultuous state I tried to recall the sage advice I had read in a book my buddy Hank had given me. It was entitled, "Deny, Delay, Avoid, and Divert," written by some crazy bastard whose name escapes me. It was a man's complete guide to understanding women. The fabulous study was filled with interesting and proven ways to deny, delay, avoid, and divert anything a man was accused of by a woman. Kind of a 'How-To' survival guide for the weaker sex.

This guy was a fucking prophet!

If I had to rank the book I would most definitely put it at the top of my reading list, even above *MAXIM.*

But right now, I was standing in a pool of sweat, in the line of fire with a big red bulls-eye stamped on my forehead, or maybe a bit lower where Big Slick and his little brothers live. I couldn't for the sake of me remember a single rule or gem of manly advice to save my sorry ass. In my hands I once had the words of a published genius and at that very moment I cursed myself for failing to finish the twenty-two page self-help booklet.

I had to face the truth:

I was shit!

I was dog shit!

A big dog turd!

How could I have so blatantly disregarded all that my understanding wife and I have had over those years and casually indulge myself in the base pleasures of flesh and fancy? I was a hedonistic pig and truly deserved to be punished for my errant sins.

At that point I knew for certain I was going straight to hell. Take me Satan, angel of deception and death, for I have sold my miserable soul for a quick piece of ass.

I was about to throw in the towel. I was ready to kneel and admit my selfish transgressions, promise to change my misguided ways, ask for absolution and forgiveness. If I were worthy of it. I was willing to work on repairing the torn trust that had once flourished between us in a loving union of husband and wife.

The first step was to acknowledge my errors and be prepared for a long and arduous path toward healing the wounds I unintentionally inflicted. I was ready to admit my guilt as a mortal human being, and to accept my prescribed penance. For no man is perfect but our Maker. So I squirmed and tossed and turned and laid myself at the mercy of the highly pissed off woman standing boldly before me.

I also had to go pee really, really bad!

My dear wife turned away and retreated into our bedroom. There was obvious hurt in her eyes and a sad sense of disappointment in her quivering face. I expected her to slam the door, lock me out of her life forever, and fall onto our bed crying away the tears, a clouded mixture of love and hatred uncontrollably flowing in such a lost moment.

In my sad mind I saw her weep for our failed marriage, a farce of a sacred union between two people who once so loved one another, and I hated what I had done. I hated when she cried too. For when a scorned woman begins to cry in tearful memory of her loss and suffers for her misery, the man had best just get the hell out of her way or he shall indeed get his ass kicked.

Only a few moments later my distressed wife re-entered the living room. Her gentle face was red as a pink rose, but there were no tears. There was no crying. Maybe she was willing to accept me as the simple man that I am with all my despicable faults and flaws. Forgiveness is truly a god given trait, I wanted to remind her, but thought it best to just shut the hell up.

She held something in her hand!

I looked at the stack of clothes, though it was difficult to see through my misty and sorrowful eyes. I instantly realized she was throwing me out, leaving me with nothing but a paltry bundle of old vacation clothing, some of which I never liked anyway. Where were my new shoes? I stupidly thought, and realized that my passport was more important.

"Why, Bob? Why?" she asked, a scowl of egregious disappointment in her still beautiful dry eyes.

I thought to myself, "Hey, why the hell not! I just took a damn bus ride into town."

But I knew that wasn't the answer she had sought. I knew at that moment that even if I were banned from her existence I would forever love her.

Except for at moments like this!

If the truth be told I had no answer for her. I was weak. I was sorry.

Oh, so sorry!

I looked up at her with a heavy heart and a remorseful soul. I even flashed my big wet puppy eyes asking for a second chance, but to no avail.

"How could you do this?" she asked, knowing I could not explain it away.

"After all these years," she said, in a voice that convinced me she was ready to end it all right here and now.

There was nothing I could say.

She peered down at her pitiful excuse of a husband and thrust her hands toward me filled with piles of my fresh, laundered, un-used underpants.

"Why aren't you wearing these?"

Busted!

No!

I suddenly felt a joyous smile deep within me as the heavens above opened up the evening skies, spreading the clouds apart and sending a welcomed blessing down to me on the vibrant golden rays of the setting sun, the miserable retch that I was. I was saved and once again worthy of my being.

Hallelujah! There really is a god!

"I'm sorry honey," I said with forced sincerity.

I moved closer toward her and gave her my Hollywood smile. I slowly wrapped my arms around her gorgeous body in that fantastic blue dress with the lace trim. I was a young man again, and she a younger woman still, as passionate as two mortal beings could be.

I was Cary Grant with his leading lady.

I gently pulled her tighter against my taut body and kissed her on her sweet porcelain cheeks, then once again tenderly on her perfectly moist pink lips, hungry for her love. I then embraced her as if I hadn't seen her in a hundred years and would not see her for a thousand more.

I guess a solo trip to Bangkok next week was out of the question.

"I'll never do that again, honey. I promise."

My loving wife hugged my trembling body, accepting me as I am.

"Never again," I said one last time, my fingers crossed behind her back.

Just in case!

THE
N
D

In order of appearance each character in the book was allowed to give a short comment about the story. Author's note: Do not believe everything they say.

Landscape crew: "Sawadee Boob. Ha…ha! You wery funny."

George the guard: "One beer and I get fired!"

Cute girls in mini-mart: "You our favorite white man."

Music loving bus driver: "Hey dude, stop harassing my passengers."

James Blunt: "You're BEAU..ti..FUL!"

Chuck Norris: "You best be careful bub."

Ms. Antoinee, the French teacher: "I wear no undies too. Tres bien, n'est pas?"

Lady with smelly fish: "You can have me if you can catch me, big boy."

Old friend Hank: "Don't believe a word he writes."

Hank's brother Darrell: "1..2..3..4..5..ah….6?"

Girlfriend in the blue dress: "What white guy?"

Big Slick: "You fucking pussy!"

The twins: "We're with him."

Queer boy Ice: "Haro Bobby. I miss yo."

Barry White: "Don't you be messing with the Love Master."

Pitts from the latrine: "You were looking at my dick?"

Chucky Baby the NCO: "I caught the clap because of you pricks."

Barry Manilow: "I have soft skin, want to feel it?"

Father Donnelly: "We need to talk, son."

Jabba the fat bitch: "Who took my pizza?"

Uncle Joe: "I'm proud of you boy."

Insect vendor: "Yummm! Grasshopper wery tasty."

Russian tourist: "Fuckin' American tourist!"

Gold store attendants: "Stop wasting our friggin' time."

Swiss beer drinkers: "That man is sooo rude."

Crazy Jack: "Fucking queers!"

Chicken Eddie: "Here's a better name for your book, *Looking for Nookie*."

Bradley the Brit: "You're quite okay for an uncivilized barbarian."

Hairy Bulgarian guy: "What'd you do with my girlfriend?"

Bulgarian guy's girl: "I married now with English man. No hair!"

Jamie Crock: "Friggin' lying Yanks, by critchy."

Rich Diamond: "What's this fool's gold stuff?"

Thieving beggar outside restaurant: "Nice sunglasses, dude."

Street cook: "Who in the world doesn't like cow's heart soup?"

Public toilet toll collector: "Ha, almost had you at a hundred baht a roll."

Thai masseuse: "Mister man, my suitcase is ready!"

Mister Rogers: "I love this place....where am I?"

Leggy co-eds in 8-baht bus: "I'll take him if you don't want him." "No, no. I want him!"

Mad Dog hombre in 8-baht bus: "Now I'm stuck with this old bag, you son-of-a-bitch!"

Suzie Q: "I remember now. You one bastard man!"

Poor woman at The Mall: "Thank you so we can eat today, kind sir."

Ronald McDonald: "No comment."

Cute girl under the shoe table: "Swifty, why haven't you called me?"

Exchange booth girl: "Thanks for the big cookie, cutie."

Photo girl: "So is the movie still on?"

Max Wilson: "Wait a minute. You remind me of one of my recruits back in '69."

Mr. Spielberg: "You'll be hearing from my attorneys."

Charlie the pool hustler: "I find you Joe, you dead!"

Tonto the tuk-tuk driver: "You one cool crazy bastard foreigner."

Mango sales girl: "You need mango, just whistle. You know how to whistle, don't you?"

Old Thai veteran on bus: "You damn good GI."

Mike, the mini-market manager: “You tell everything. Now you really have big shit problem, friend.”

Mrs. Swift: “You’ve done it now, buster!”

Bob Swift: “Next time I’m telling nobody nothing.”

LaVergne, TN USA
14 April 2010
179269LV00004B/198/P